Tinker Bell

GREAT FAIRY RESCUE

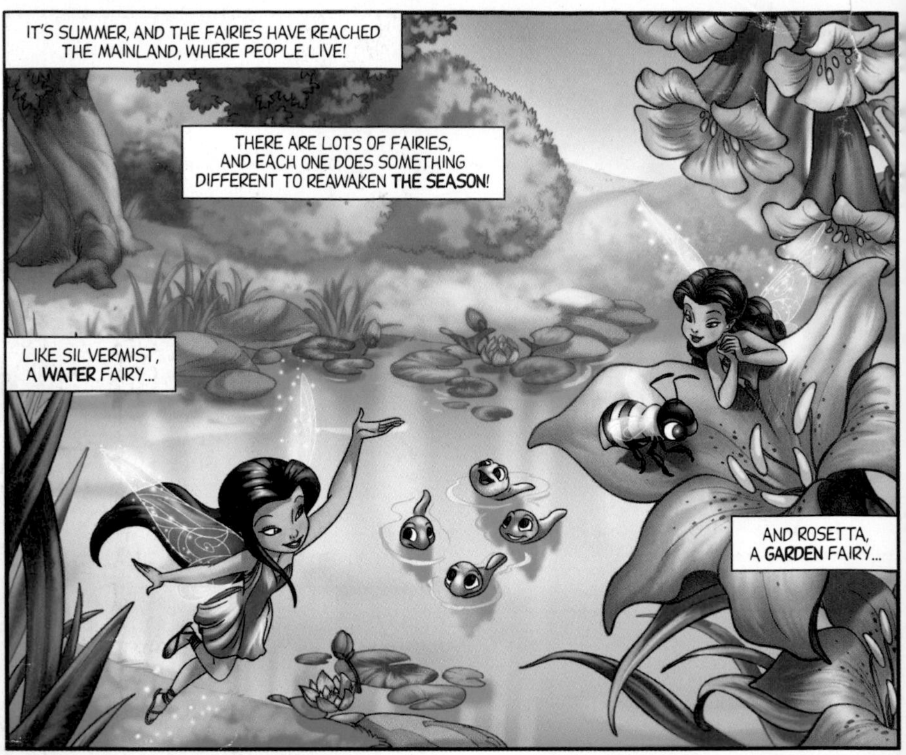
IT'S SUMMER, AND THE FAIRIES HAVE REACHED THE MAINLAND, WHERE PEOPLE LIVE!
THERE ARE LOTS OF FAIRIES, AND EACH ONE DOES SOMETHING DIFFERENT TO REAWAKEN **THE SEASON**!
LIKE SILVERMIST, A **WATER** FAIRY...
AND ROSETTA, A **GARDEN** FAIRY...

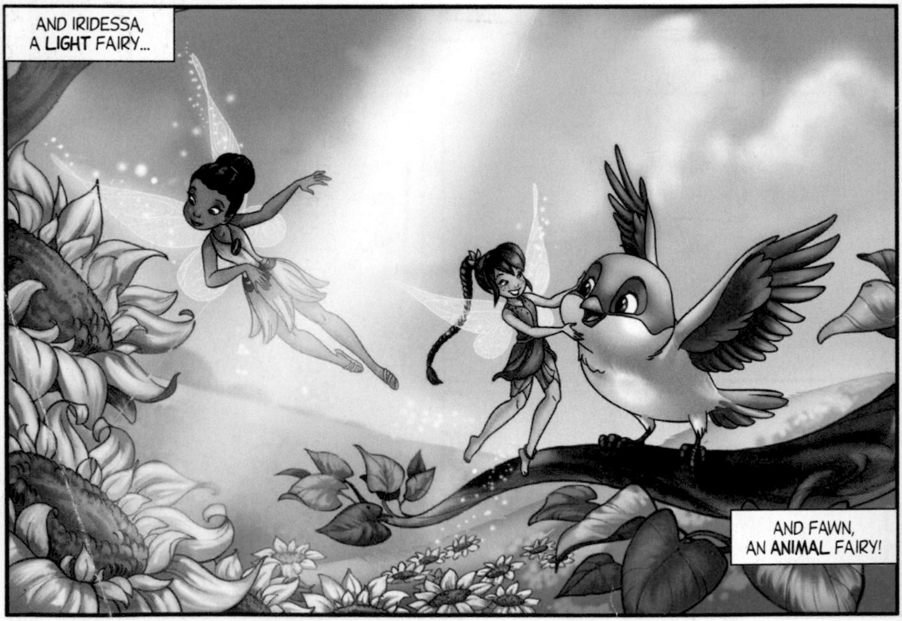
AND IRIDESSA, A **LIGHT** FAIRY...
AND FAWN, AN **ANIMAL** FAIRY!

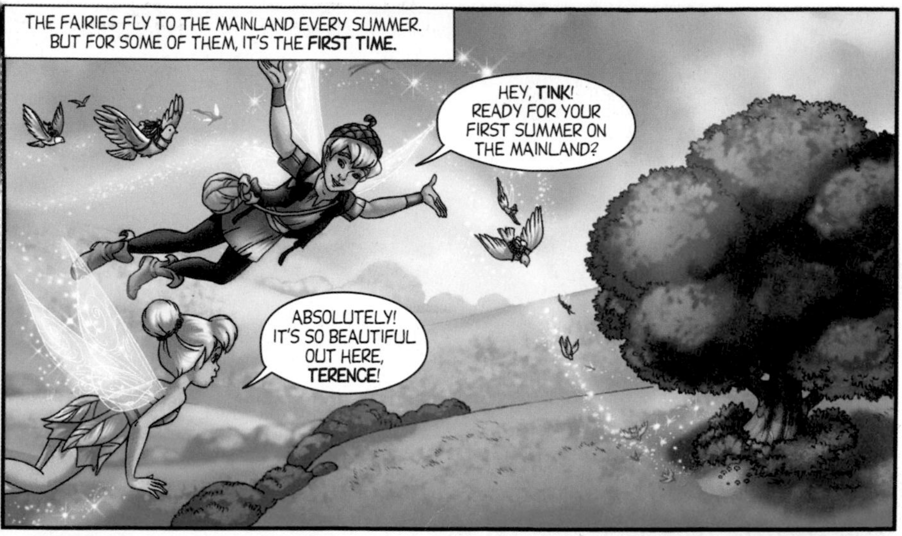
THE FAIRIES FLY TO THE MAINLAND EVERY SUMMER. BUT FOR SOME OF THEM, IT'S THE **FIRST TIME.**
HEY, **TINK**! READY FOR YOUR FIRST SUMMER ON THE MAINLAND?
ABSOLUTELY! IT'S SO BEAUTIFUL OUT HERE, **TERENCE**!

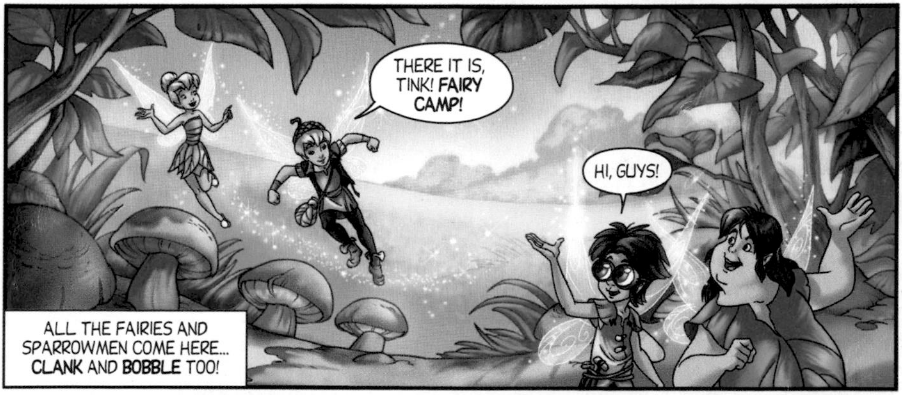
THERE IT IS, TINK! **FAIRY CAMP!**
HI, GUYS!
ALL THE FAIRIES AND SPARROWMEN COME HERE... **CLANK** AND **BOBBLE** TOO!

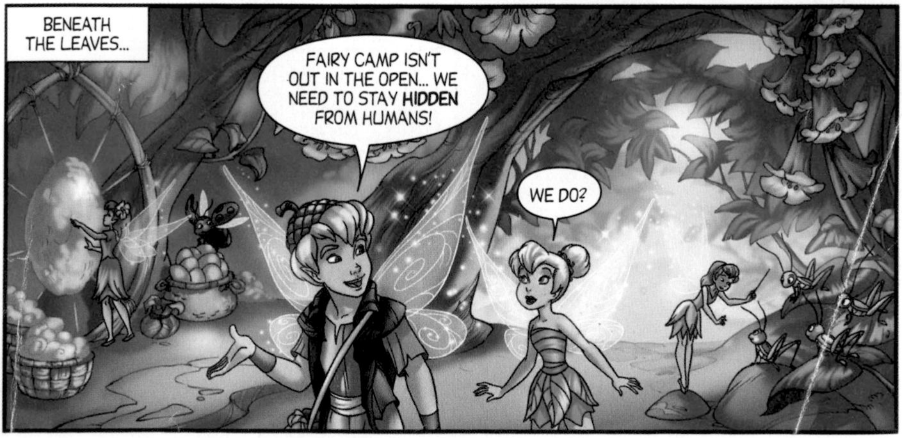
BENEATH THE LEAVES...
FAIRY CAMP ISN'T OUT IN THE OPEN... WE NEED TO STAY **HIDDEN** FROM HUMANS!
WE DO?

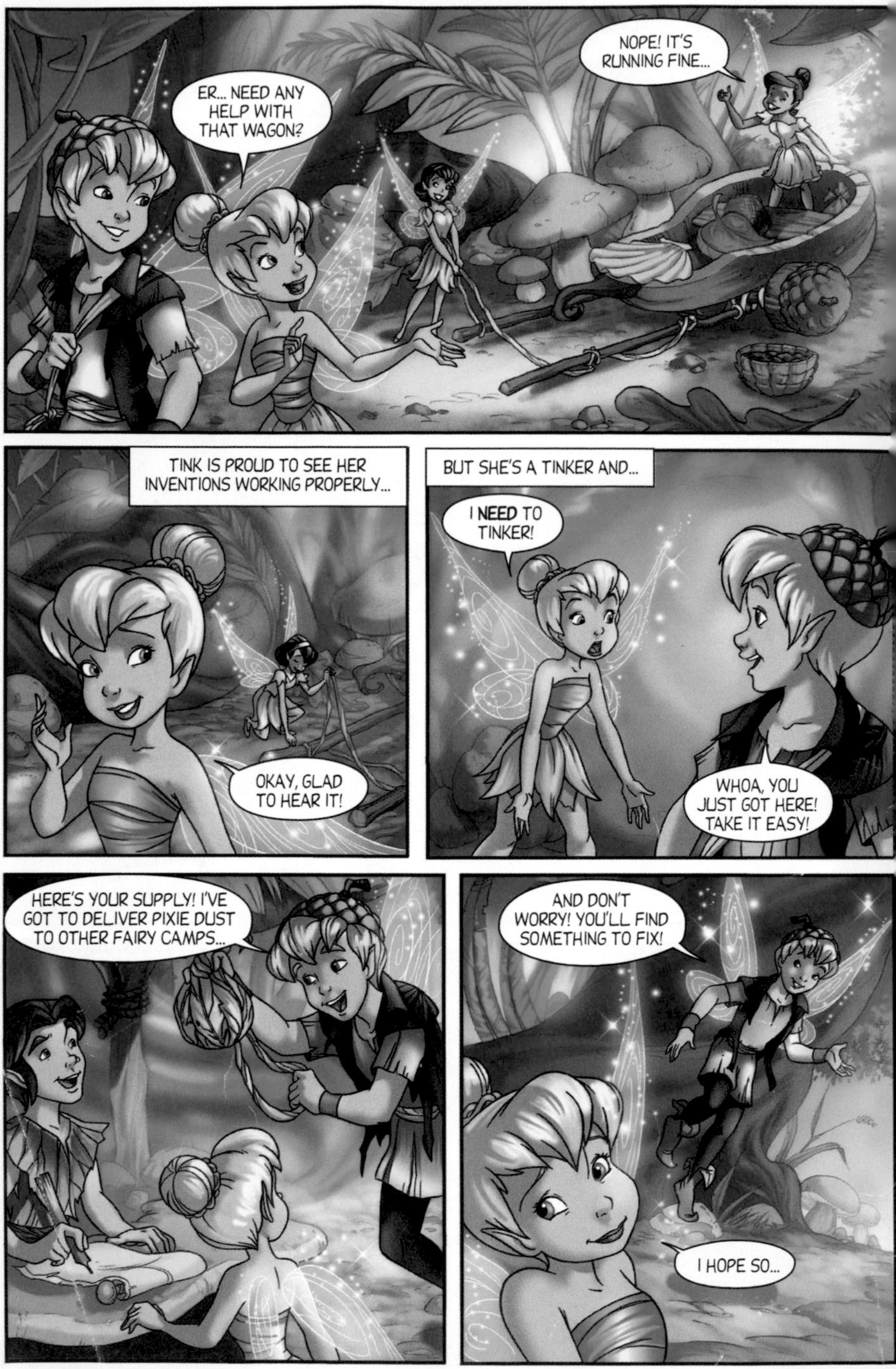

ER... NEED ANY HELP WITH THAT WAGON?
NOPE! IT'S RUNNING FINE...
TINK IS PROUD TO SEE HER INVENTIONS WORKING PROPERLY...
OKAY, GLAD TO HEAR IT!
BUT SHE'S A TINKER AND...
I **NEED** TO TINKER!
WHOA, YOU JUST GOT HERE! TAKE IT EASY!
HERE'S YOUR SUPPLY! I'VE GOT TO DELIVER PIXIE DUST TO OTHER FAIRY CAMPS...
AND DON'T WORRY! YOU'LL FIND SOMETHING TO FIX!
I HOPE SO...

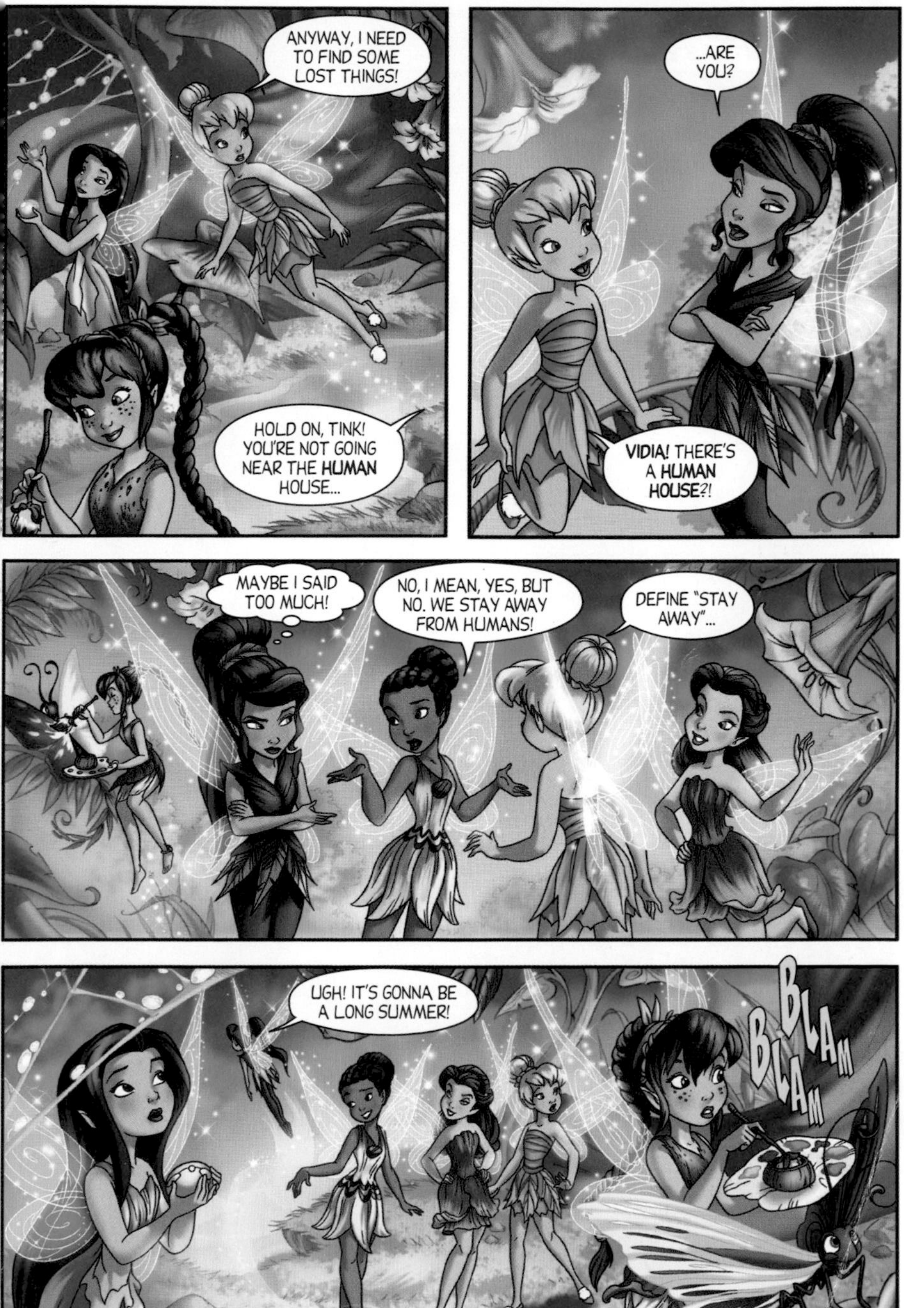
ANYWAY, I NEED TO FIND SOME LOST THINGS!
HOLD ON, TINK! YOU'RE NOT GOING NEAR THE **HUMAN** HOUSE...
...ARE YOU?
VIDIA! THERE'S A **HUMAN HOUSE**?!
MAYBE I SAID TOO MUCH!
NO, I MEAN, YES, BUT NO. WE STAY AWAY FROM HUMANS!
DEFINE "STAY AWAY"...
UGH! IT'S GONNA BE A LONG SUMMER!
BLAM BLAM
SUDDENLY, A STRANGE NOISE IS HEARD!

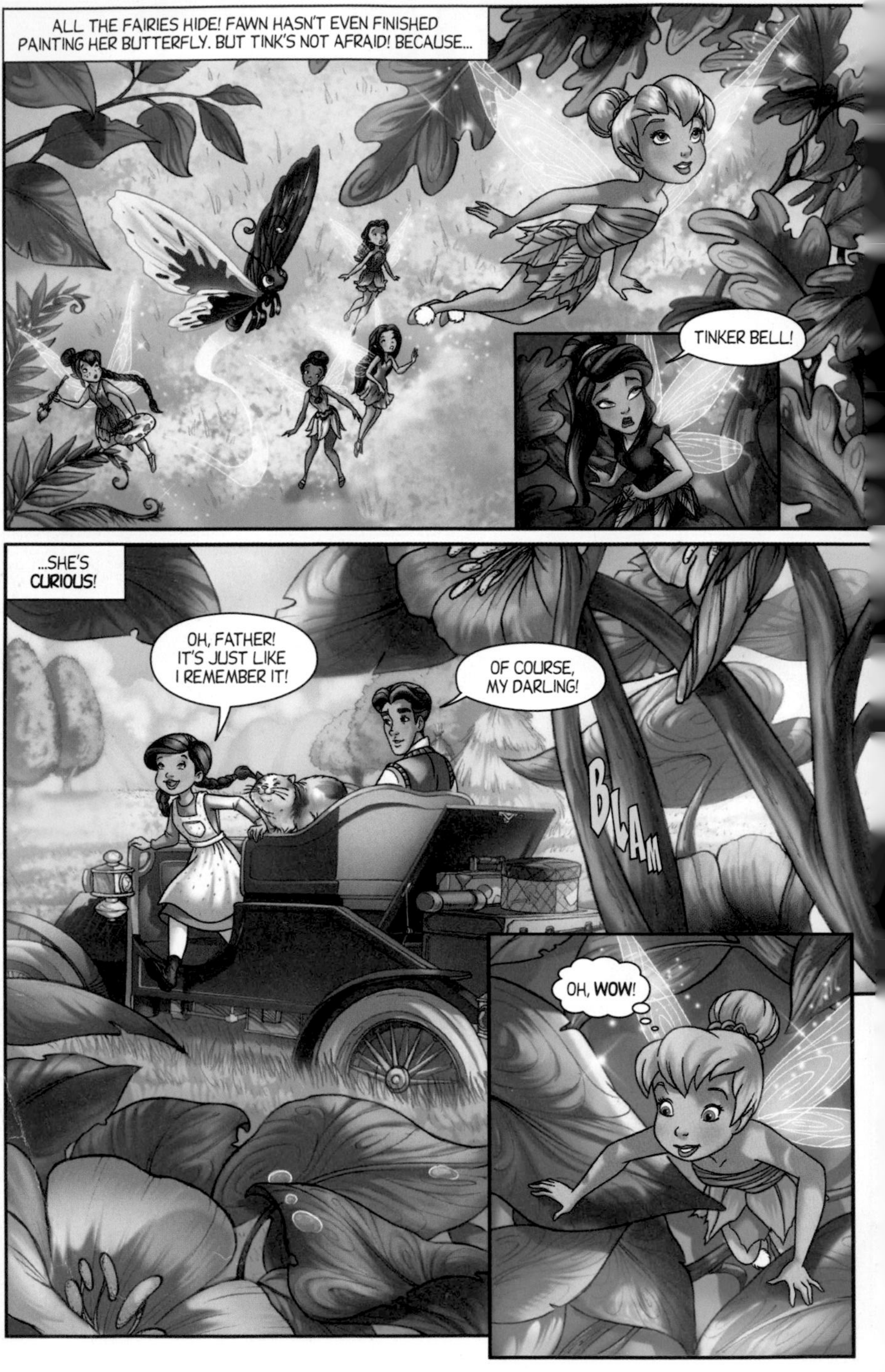
ALL THE FAIRIES HIDE! FAWN HASN'T EVEN FINISHED PAINTING HER BUTTERFLY. BUT TINK'S NOT AFRAID! BECAUSE...
TINKER BELL!
...SHE'S **CURIOUS**!
OH, FATHER! IT'S JUST LIKE I REMEMBER IT!
OF COURSE, MY DARLING!
BLAM
OH, **WOW**!

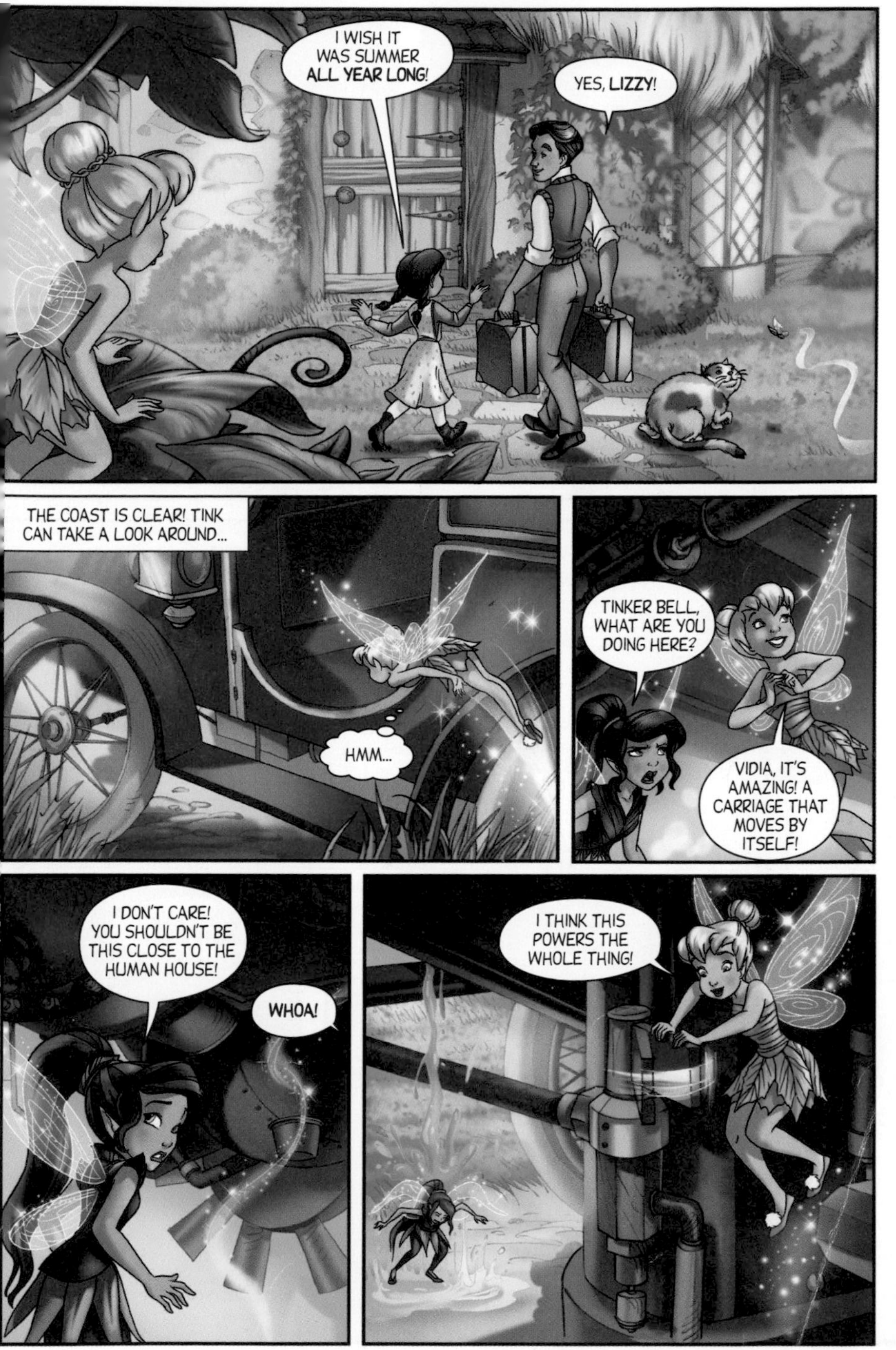
I WISH IT WAS SUMMER **ALL YEAR LONG**!
YES, **LIZZY**!
THE COAST IS CLEAR! TINK CAN TAKE A LOOK AROUND...
HMM...
TINKER BELL, WHAT ARE YOU DOING HERE?
VIDIA, IT'S AMAZING! A CARRIAGE THAT MOVES BY ITSELF!
I DON'T CARE! YOU SHOULDN'T BE THIS CLOSE TO THE HUMAN HOUSE!
WHOA!
I THINK THIS POWERS THE WHOLE THING!

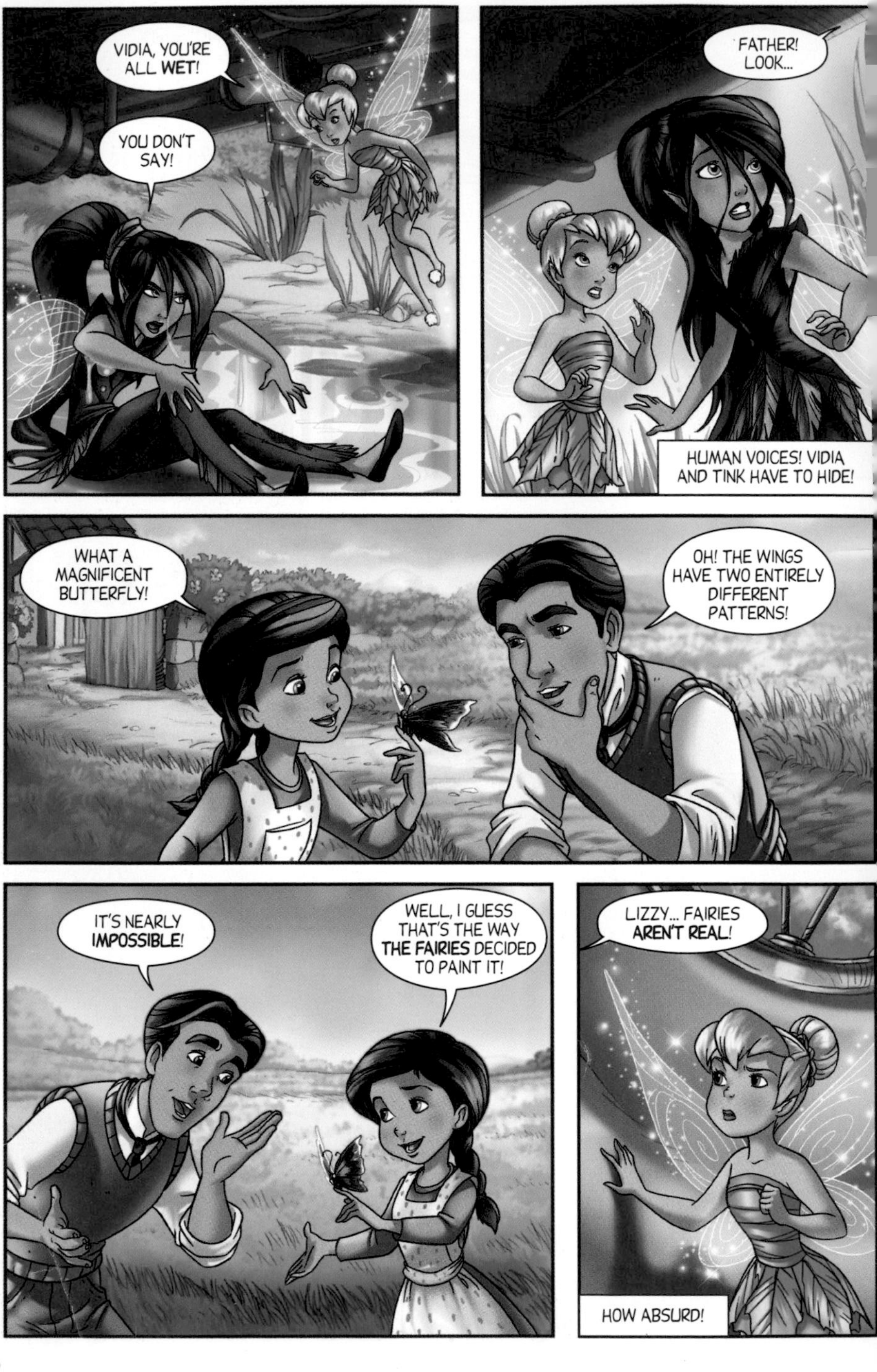
VIDIA, YOU'RE ALL **WET**!
YOU DON'T SAY!
FATHER! LOOK...
HUMAN VOICES! VIDIA AND TINK HAVE TO HIDE!
WHAT A MAGNIFICENT BUTTERFLY!
OH! THE WINGS HAVE TWO ENTIRELY DIFFERENT PATTERNS!
IT'S NEARLY **IMPOSSIBLE**!
WELL, I GUESS THAT'S THE WAY **THE FAIRIES** DECIDED TO PAINT IT!
LIZZY... FAIRIES **AREN'T REAL**!
HOW ABSURD!

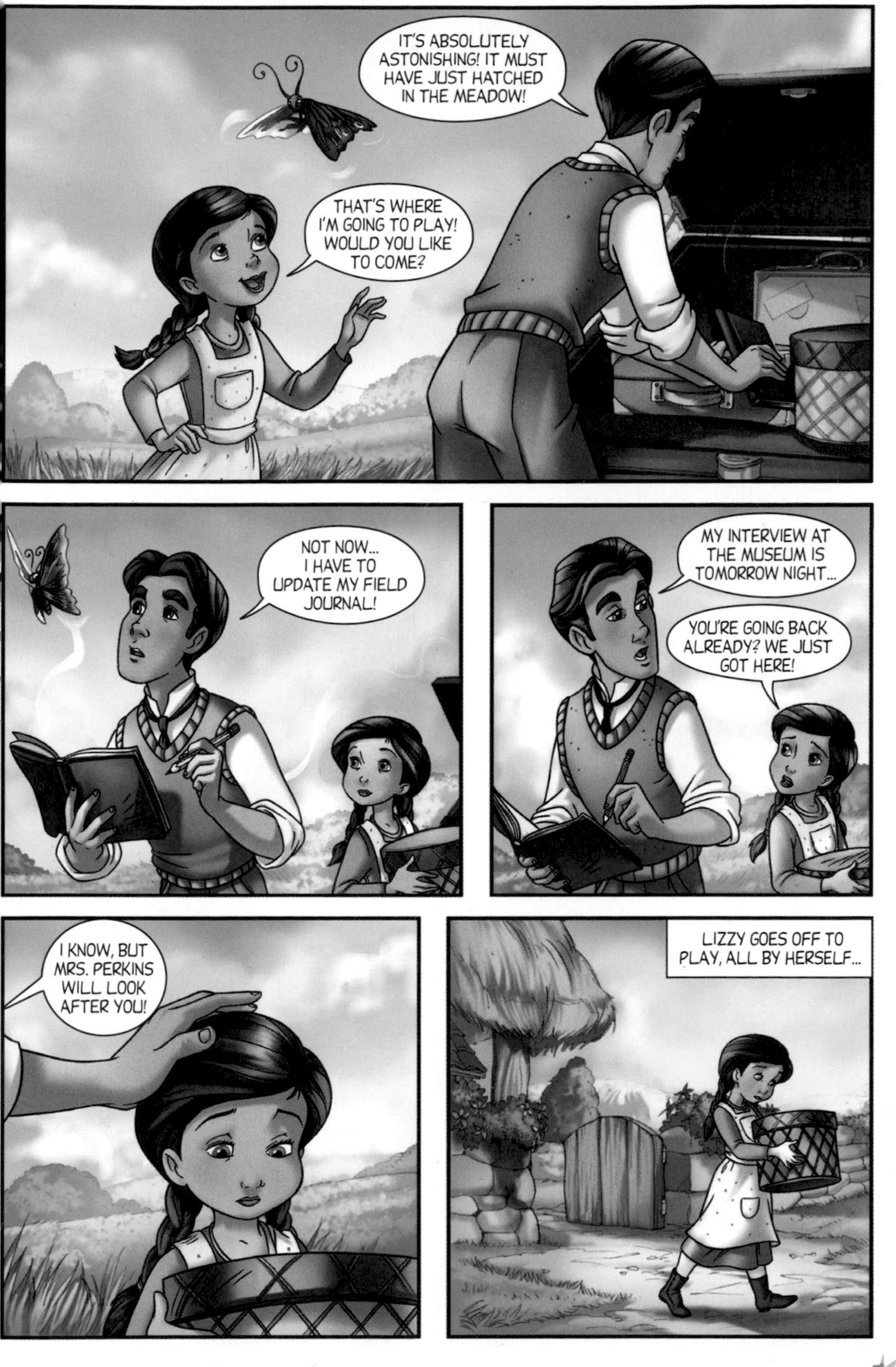
IT'S ABSOLUTELY ASTONISHING! IT MUST HAVE JUST HATCHED IN THE MEADOW!
THAT'S WHERE I'M GOING TO PLAY! WOULD YOU LIKE TO COME?
NOT NOW... I HAVE TO UPDATE MY FIELD JOURNAL!
MY INTERVIEW AT THE MUSEUM IS TOMORROW NIGHT...
YOU'RE GOING BACK ALREADY? WE JUST GOT HERE!
I KNOW, BUT MRS. PERKINS WILL LOOK AFTER YOU!
LIZZY GOES OFF TO PLAY, ALL BY HERSELF...

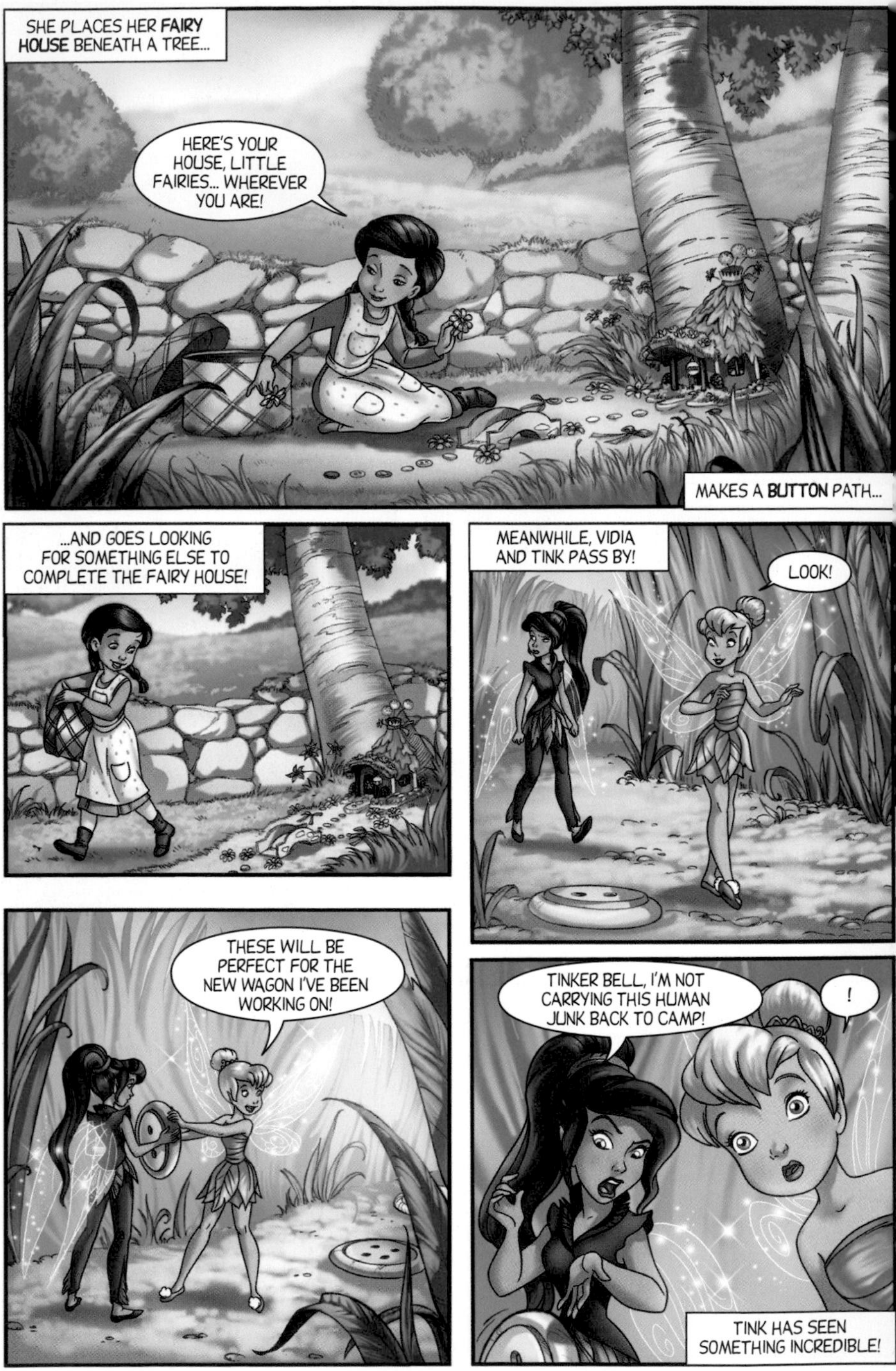

SHE PLACES HER **FAIRY HOUSE** BENEATH A TREE...
HERE'S YOUR HOUSE, LITTLE FAIRIES... WHEREVER YOU ARE!
MAKES A **BUTTON** PATH...
...AND GOES LOOKING FOR SOMETHING ELSE TO COMPLETE THE FAIRY HOUSE!
MEANWHILE, VIDIA AND TINK PASS BY!
LOOK!
THESE WILL BE PERFECT FOR THE NEW WAGON I'VE BEEN WORKING ON!
TINKER BELL, I'M NOT CARRYING THIS HUMAN JUNK BACK TO CAMP!
!
TINK HAS SEEN SOMETHING INCREDIBLE!

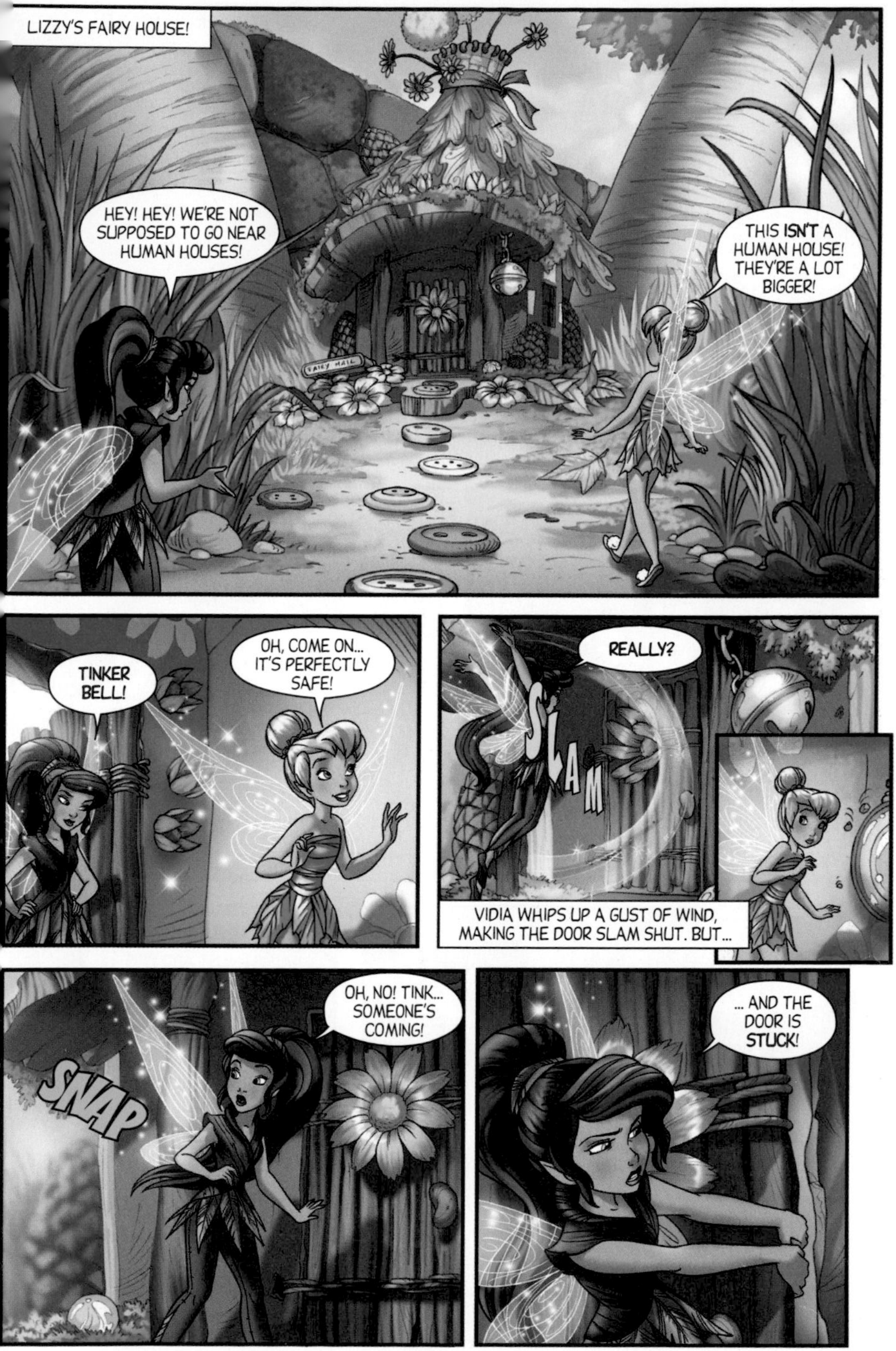
LIZZY'S FAIRY HOUSE!
HEY! HEY! WE'RE NOT SUPPOSED TO GO NEAR HUMAN HOUSES!
THIS **ISN'T** A HUMAN HOUSE! THEY'RE A LOT BIGGER!
FAIRY MAIL
TINKER BELL!
OH, COME ON... IT'S PERFECTLY SAFE!
REALLY?
SLAM
VIDIA WHIPS UP A GUST OF WIND, MAKING THE DOOR SLAM SHUT. BUT...
SNAP
OH, NO! TINK... SOMEONE'S COMING!
... AND THE DOOR IS **STUCK**!

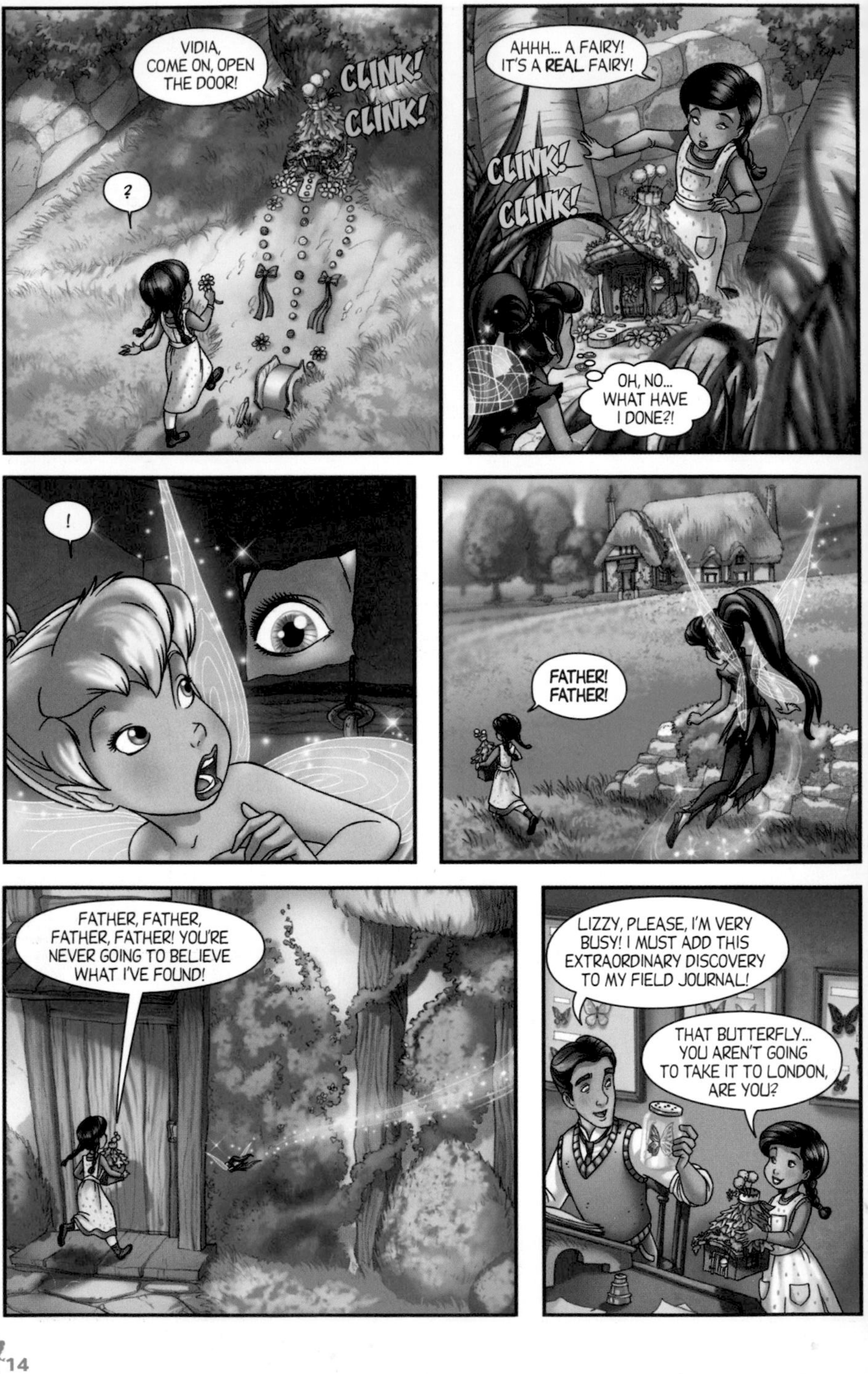
VIDIA, COME ON, OPEN THE DOOR!
CLINK!
CLINK!
?
AHHH... A FAIRY! IT'S A **REAL** FAIRY!
CLINK!
CLINK!
OH, NO... WHAT HAVE I DONE?!
!
FATHER! FATHER!
FATHER, FATHER, FATHER, FATHER! YOU'RE NEVER GOING TO BELIEVE WHAT I'VE FOUND!
LIZZY, PLEASE, I'M VERY BUSY! I MUST ADD THIS EXTRAORDINARY DISCOVERY TO MY FIELD JOURNAL!
THAT BUTTERFLY... YOU AREN'T GOING TO TAKE IT TO LONDON, ARE YOU?

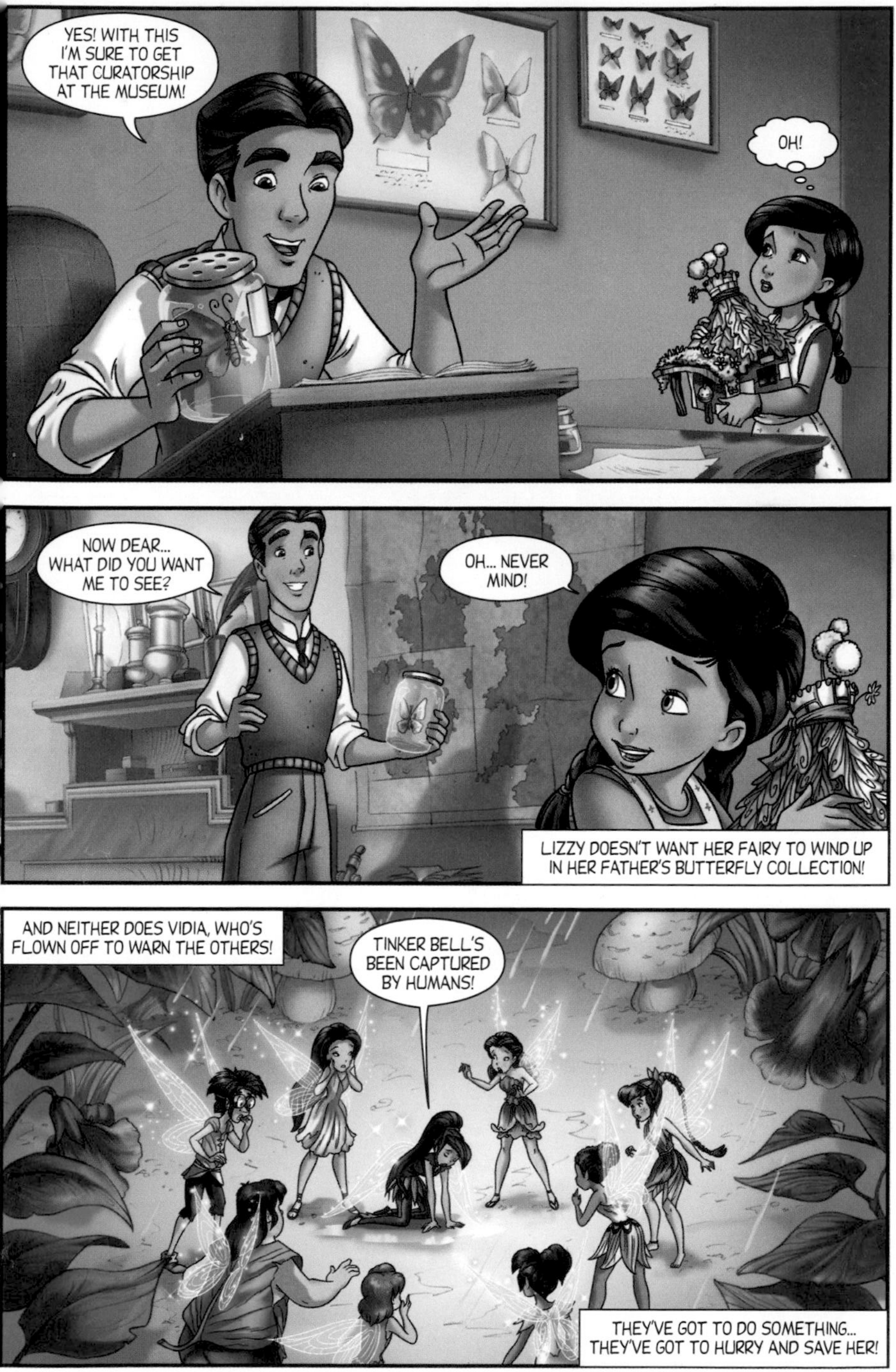
YES! WITH THIS I'M SURE TO GET THAT CURATORSHIP AT THE MUSEUM!
OH!
NOW DEAR... WHAT DID YOU WANT ME TO SEE?
OH... NEVER MIND!
LIZZY DOESN'T WANT HER FAIRY TO WIND UP IN HER FATHER'S BUTTERFLY COLLECTION!
AND NEITHER DOES VIDIA, WHO'S FLOWN OFF TO WARN THE OTHERS!
TINKER BELL'S BEEN CAPTURED BY HUMANS!
THEY'VE GOT TO DO SOMETHING... THEY'VE GOT TO HURRY AND SAVE HER!

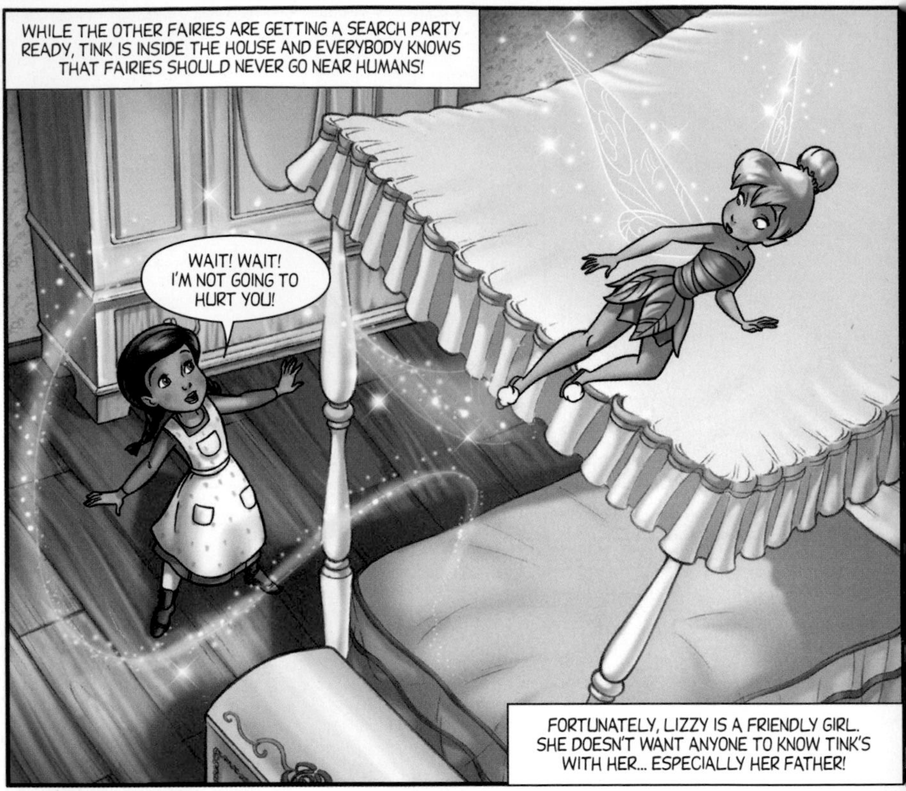
WHILE THE OTHER FAIRIES ARE GETTING A SEARCH PARTY READY, TINK IS INSIDE THE HOUSE AND EVERYBODY KNOWS THAT FAIRIES SHOULD NEVER GO NEAR HUMANS!
WAIT! WAIT! I'M NOT GOING TO HURT YOU!
FORTUNATELY, LIZZY IS A FRIENDLY GIRL. SHE DOESN'T WANT ANYONE TO KNOW TINK'S WITH HER... ESPECIALLY HER FATHER!

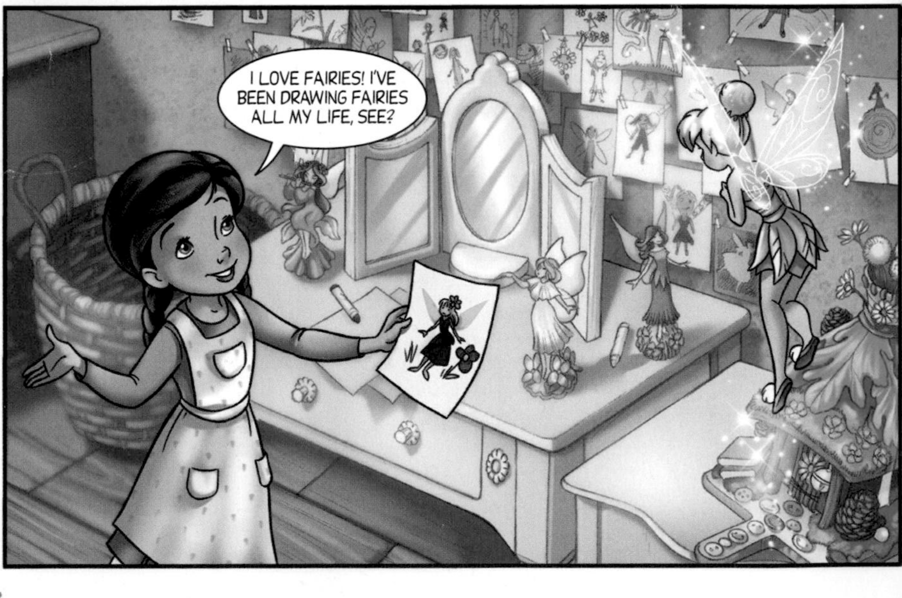
I LOVE FAIRIES! I'VE BEEN DRAWING FAIRIES ALL MY LIFE, SEE?

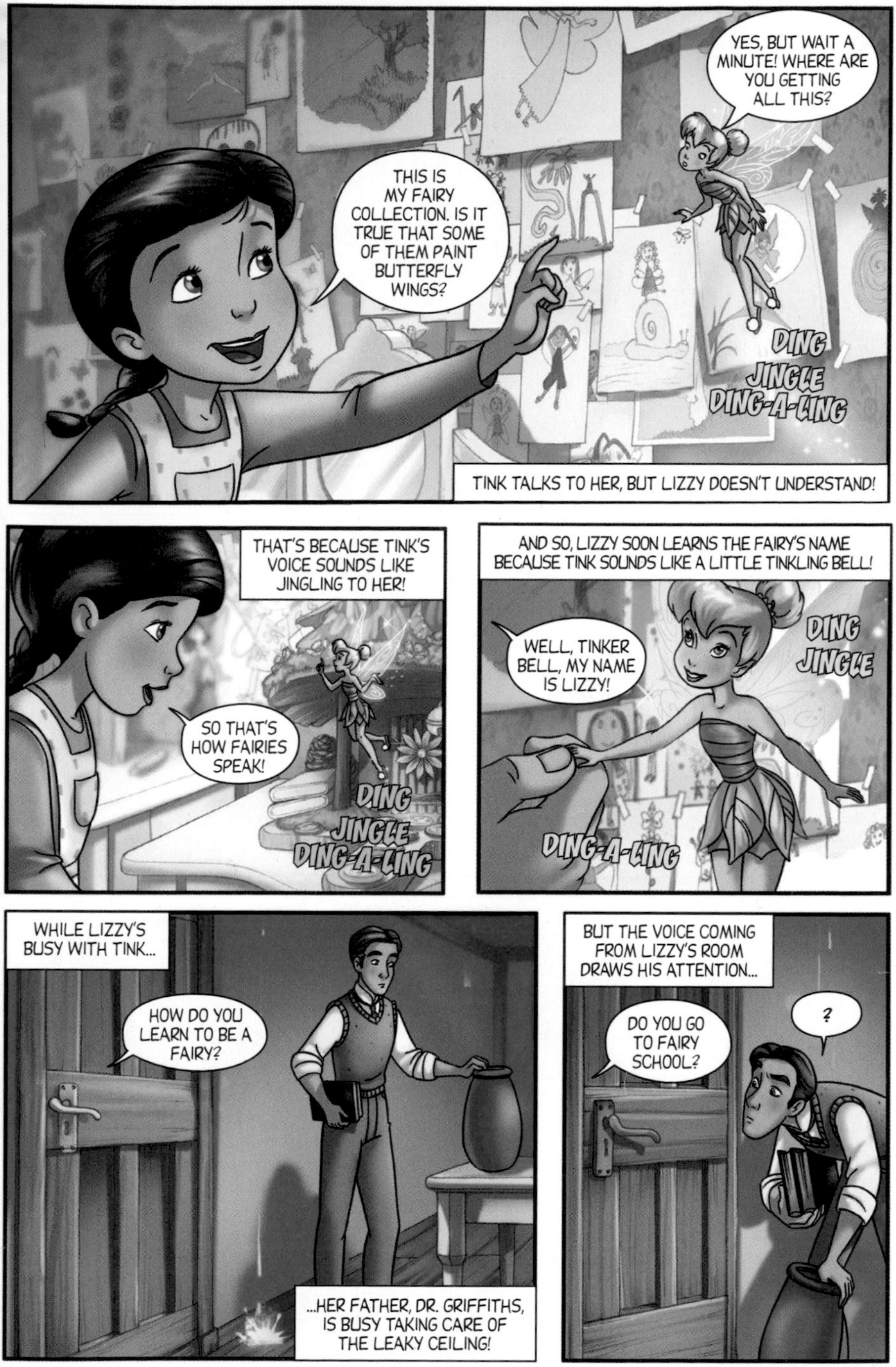
THIS IS MY FAIRY COLLECTION. IS IT TRUE THAT SOME OF THEM PAINT BUTTERFLY WINGS?
YES, BUT WAIT A MINUTE! WHERE ARE YOU GETTING ALL THIS?
DING
JINGLE
DING-A-LING
TINK TALKS TO HER, BUT LIZZY DOESN'T UNDERSTAND!
THAT'S BECAUSE TINK'S VOICE SOUNDS LIKE JINGLING TO HER!
SO THAT'S HOW FAIRIES SPEAK!
DING
JINGLE
DING-A-LING
AND SO, LIZZY SOON LEARNS THE FAIRY'S NAME BECAUSE TINK SOUNDS LIKE A LITTLE TINKLING BELL!
WELL, TINKER BELL, MY NAME IS LIZZY!
DING
JINGLE
DING-A-LING
WHILE LIZZY'S BUSY WITH TINK...
HOW DO YOU LEARN TO BE A FAIRY?
...HER FATHER, DR. GRIFFITHS, IS BUSY TAKING CARE OF THE LEAKY CEILING!
BUT THE VOICE COMING FROM LIZZY'S ROOM DRAWS HIS ATTENTION...
DO YOU GO TO FAIRY SCHOOL?
?

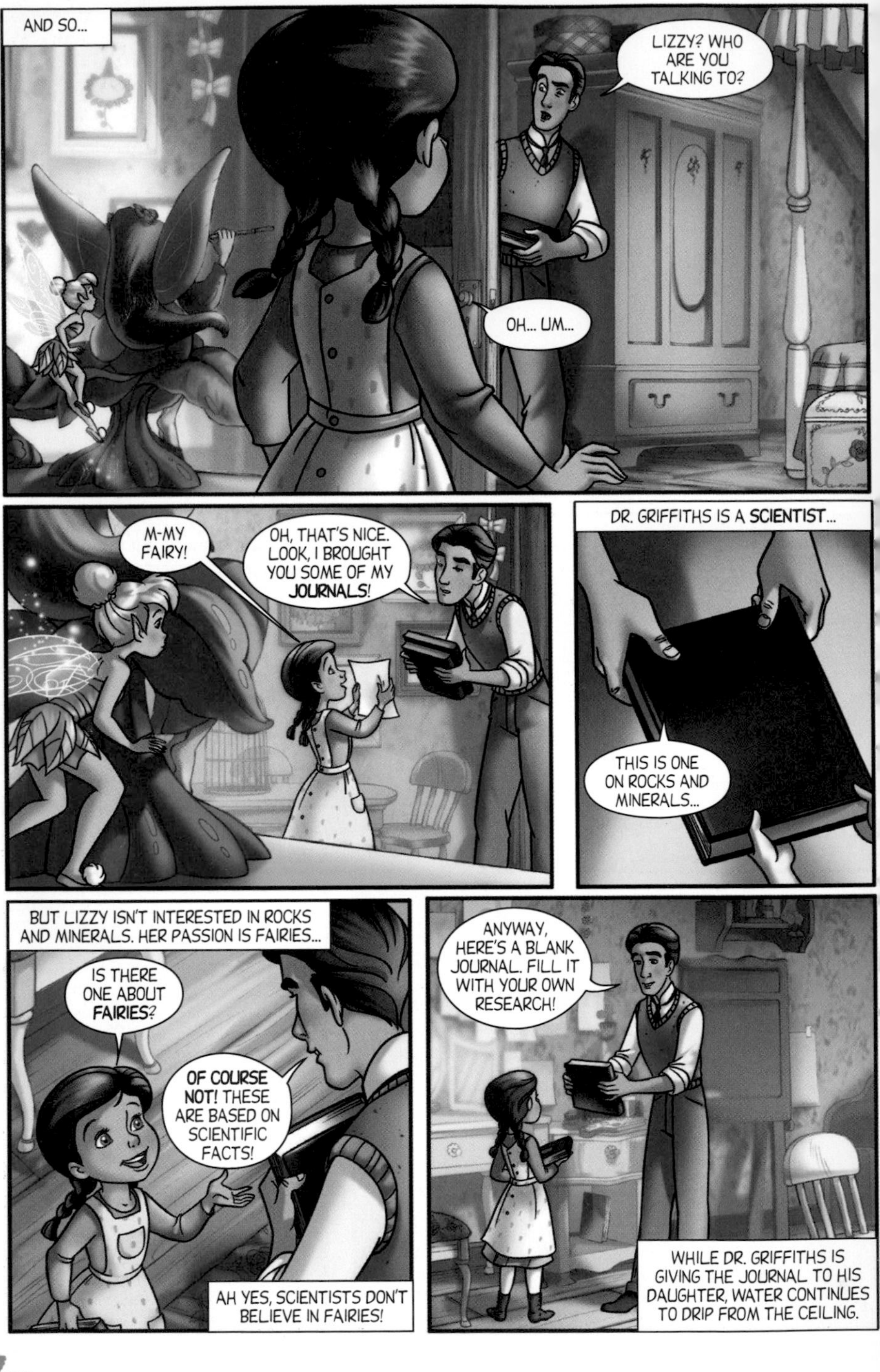

AND SO...
LIZZY? WHO ARE YOU TALKING TO?
OH... UM...
M-MY FAIRY!
OH, THAT'S NICE. LOOK, I BROUGHT YOU SOME OF MY **JOURNALS**!
DR. GRIFFITHS IS A **SCIENTIST**...
THIS IS ONE ON ROCKS AND MINERALS...
BUT LIZZY ISN'T INTERESTED IN ROCKS AND MINERALS. HER PASSION IS FAIRIES...
IS THERE ONE ABOUT **FAIRIES**?
OF COURSE NOT! THESE ARE BASED ON SCIENTIFIC FACTS!
AH YES, SCIENTISTS DON'T BELIEVE IN FAIRIES!
ANYWAY, HERE'S A BLANK JOURNAL. FILL IT WITH YOUR OWN RESEARCH!
WHILE DR. GRIFFITHS IS GIVING THE JOURNAL TO HIS DAUGHTER, WATER CONTINUES TO DRIP FROM THE CEILING.

SIGH! IF ONLY THESE LEAKS WERE JUST PRETEND...

DR. GRIFFITHS IS GONE. THE COAST IS CLEAR FOR TINK!

YOU CAN COME OUT NOW!

LOOK, LIZZY, THANKS FOR SHOWING ME YOUR COLLECTION, BUT I REALLY SHOULD BE...

DING JINGLE DING-A-LING

YOU WANT TO GO?

DING JINGLE DING-A-LING

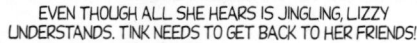

EVEN THOUGH ALL SHE HEARS IS JINGLING, LIZZY UNDERSTANDS. TINK NEEDS TO GET BACK TO HER FRIENDS!

OH, I REALLY WISH YOU'D STAY... BUT I UNDERSTAND! SO, I GUESS THIS IS GOODBYE...

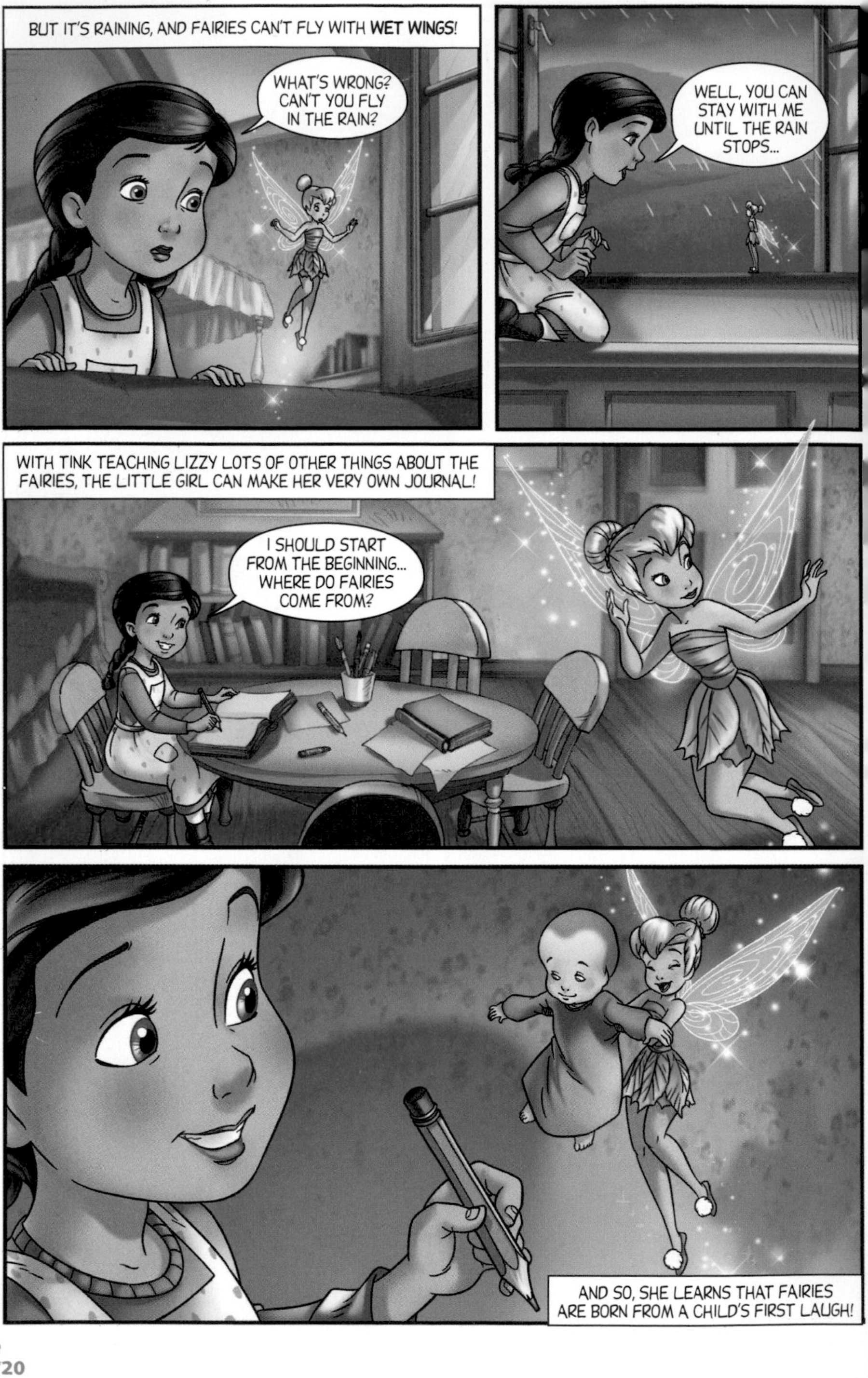
BUT IT'S RAINING, AND FAIRIES CAN'T FLY WITH **WET WINGS**!
WHAT'S WRONG? CAN'T YOU FLY IN THE RAIN?
WELL, YOU CAN STAY WITH ME UNTIL THE RAIN STOPS...
WITH TINK TEACHING LIZZY LOTS OF OTHER THINGS ABOUT THE FAIRIES, THE LITTLE GIRL CAN MAKE HER VERY OWN JOURNAL!
I SHOULD START FROM THE BEGINNING... WHERE DO FAIRIES COME FROM?
AND SO, SHE LEARNS THAT FAIRIES ARE BORN FROM A CHILD'S FIRST LAUGH!

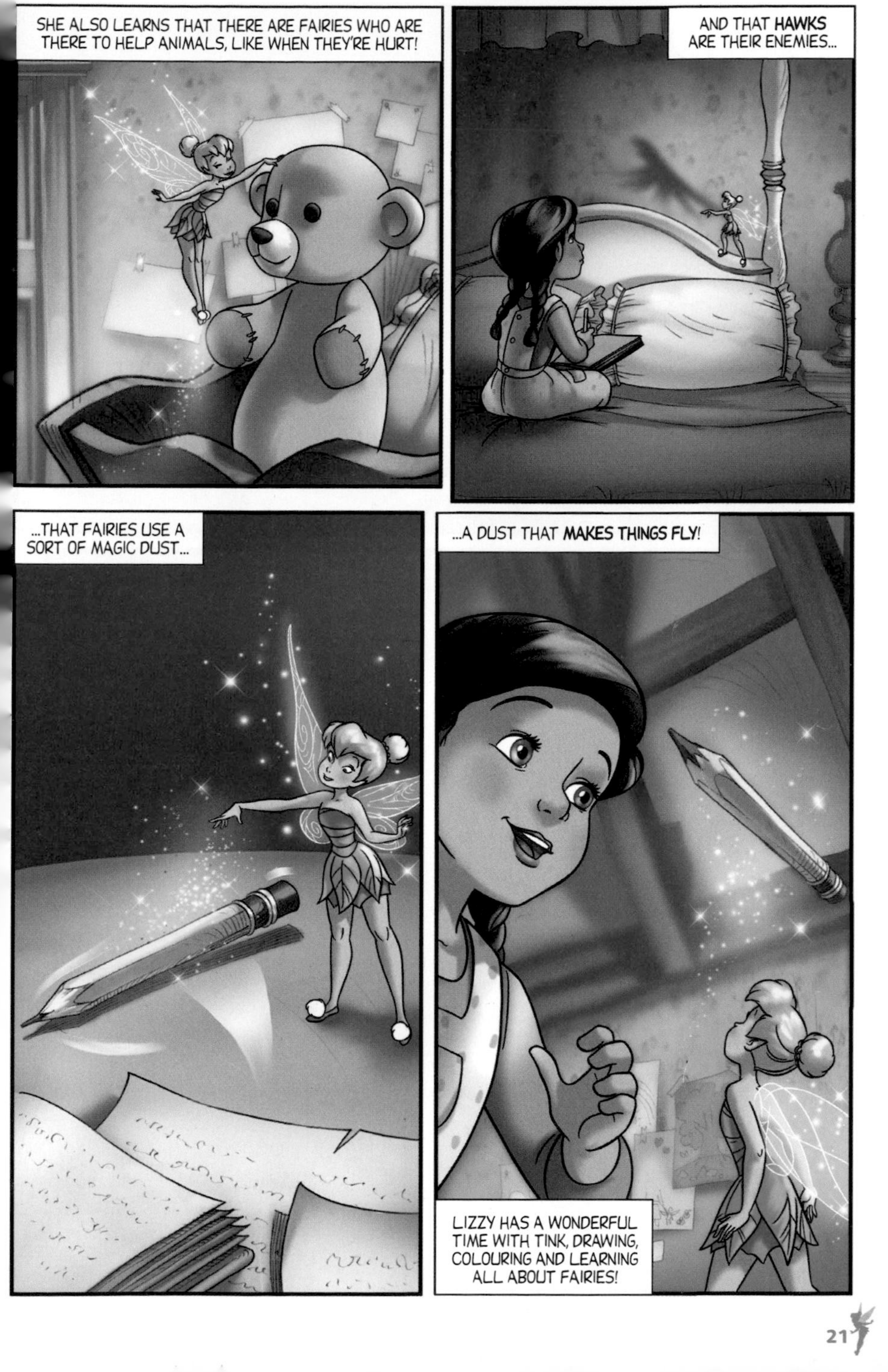
SHE ALSO LEARNS THAT THERE ARE FAIRIES WHO ARE THERE TO HELP ANIMALS, LIKE WHEN THEY'RE HURT!
AND THAT **HAWKS** ARE THEIR ENEMIES...
...THAT FAIRIES USE A SORT OF MAGIC DUST...
...A DUST THAT **MAKES THINGS FLY**!
LIZZY HAS A WONDERFUL TIME WITH TINK, DRAWING, COLOURING AND LEARNING ALL ABOUT FAIRIES!

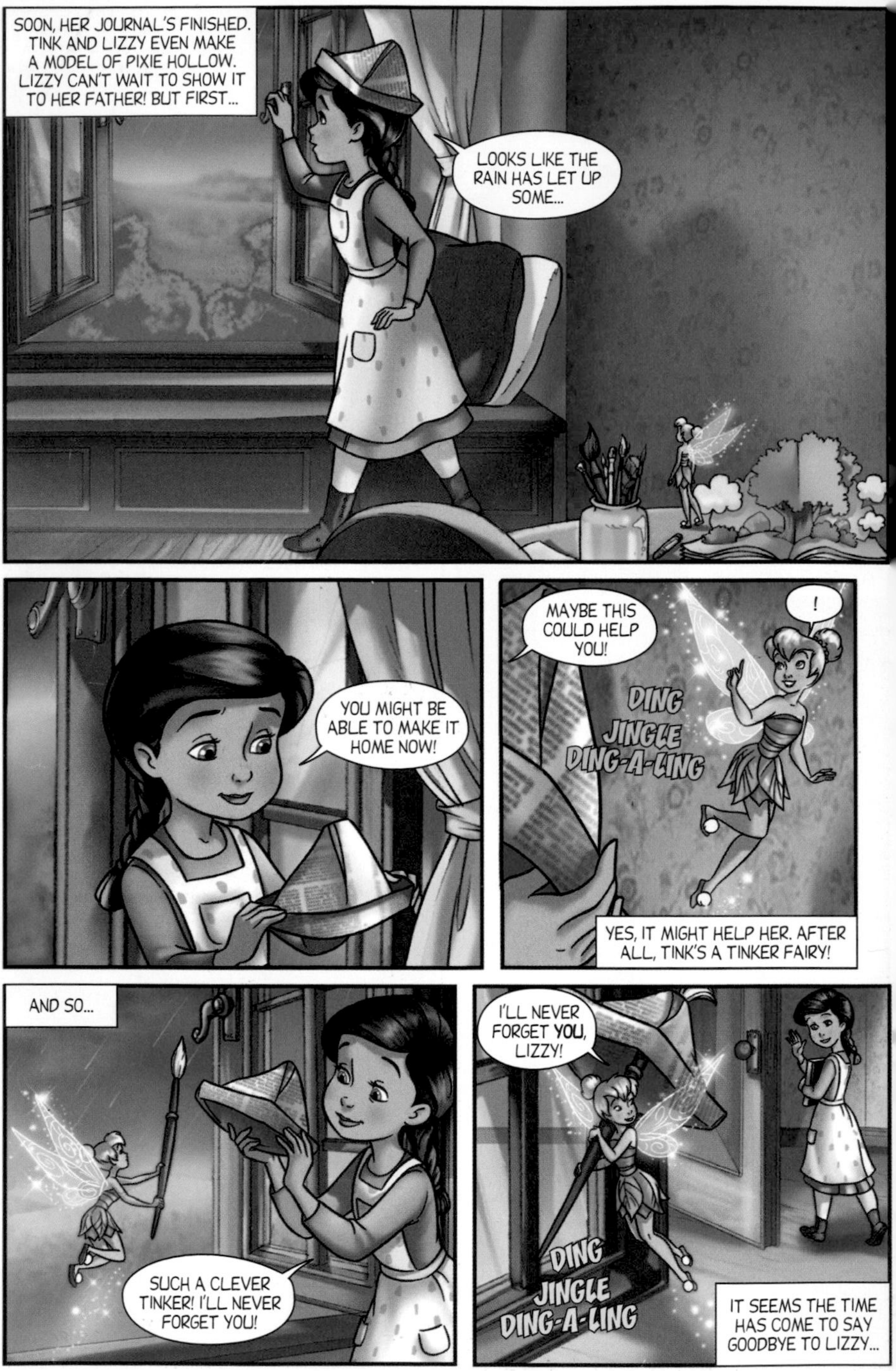
SOON, HER JOURNAL'S FINISHED. TINK AND LIZZY EVEN MAKE A MODEL OF PIXIE HOLLOW. LIZZY CAN'T WAIT TO SHOW IT TO HER FATHER! BUT FIRST...
LOOKS LIKE THE RAIN HAS LET UP SOME...
YOU MIGHT BE ABLE TO MAKE IT HOME NOW!
MAYBE THIS COULD HELP YOU!
!
DING JINGLE DING-A-LING
YES, IT MIGHT HELP HER. AFTER ALL, TINK'S A TINKER FAIRY!
AND SO...
SUCH A CLEVER TINKER! I'LL NEVER FORGET YOU!
I'LL NEVER FORGET **YOU**, LIZZY!
DING JINGLE DING-A-LING
IT SEEMS THE TIME HAS COME TO SAY GOODBYE TO LIZZY...

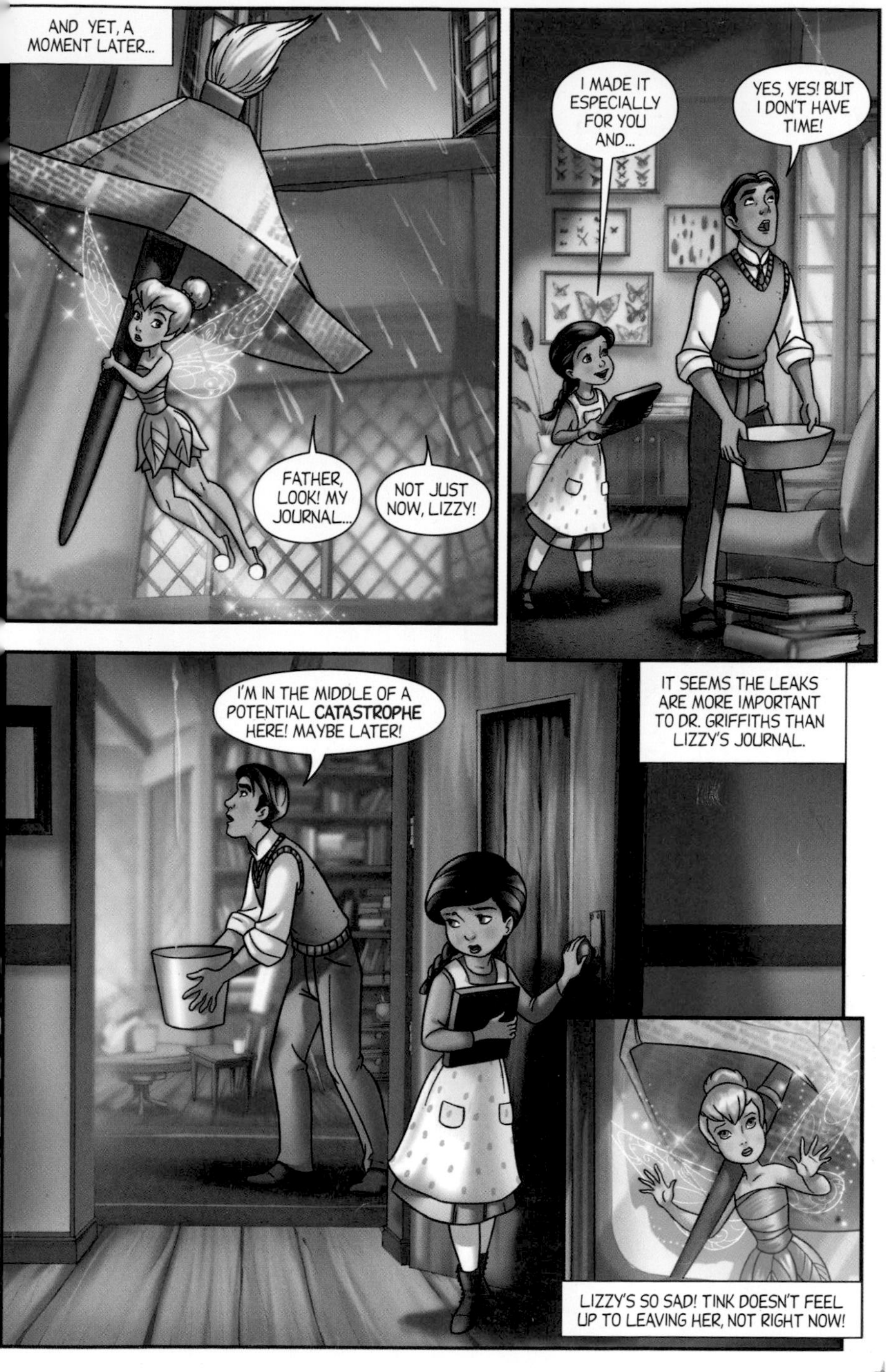
AND YET, A MOMENT LATER...
FATHER, LOOK! MY JOURNAL...
NOT JUST NOW, LIZZY!
I MADE IT ESPECIALLY FOR YOU AND...
YES, YES! BUT I DON'T HAVE TIME!
I'M IN THE MIDDLE OF A POTENTIAL CATASTROPHE HERE! MAYBE LATER!
IT SEEMS THE LEAKS ARE MORE IMPORTANT TO DR. GRIFFITHS THAN LIZZY'S JOURNAL.
LIZZY'S SO SAD! TINK DOESN'T FEEL UP TO LEAVING HER, NOT RIGHT NOW!

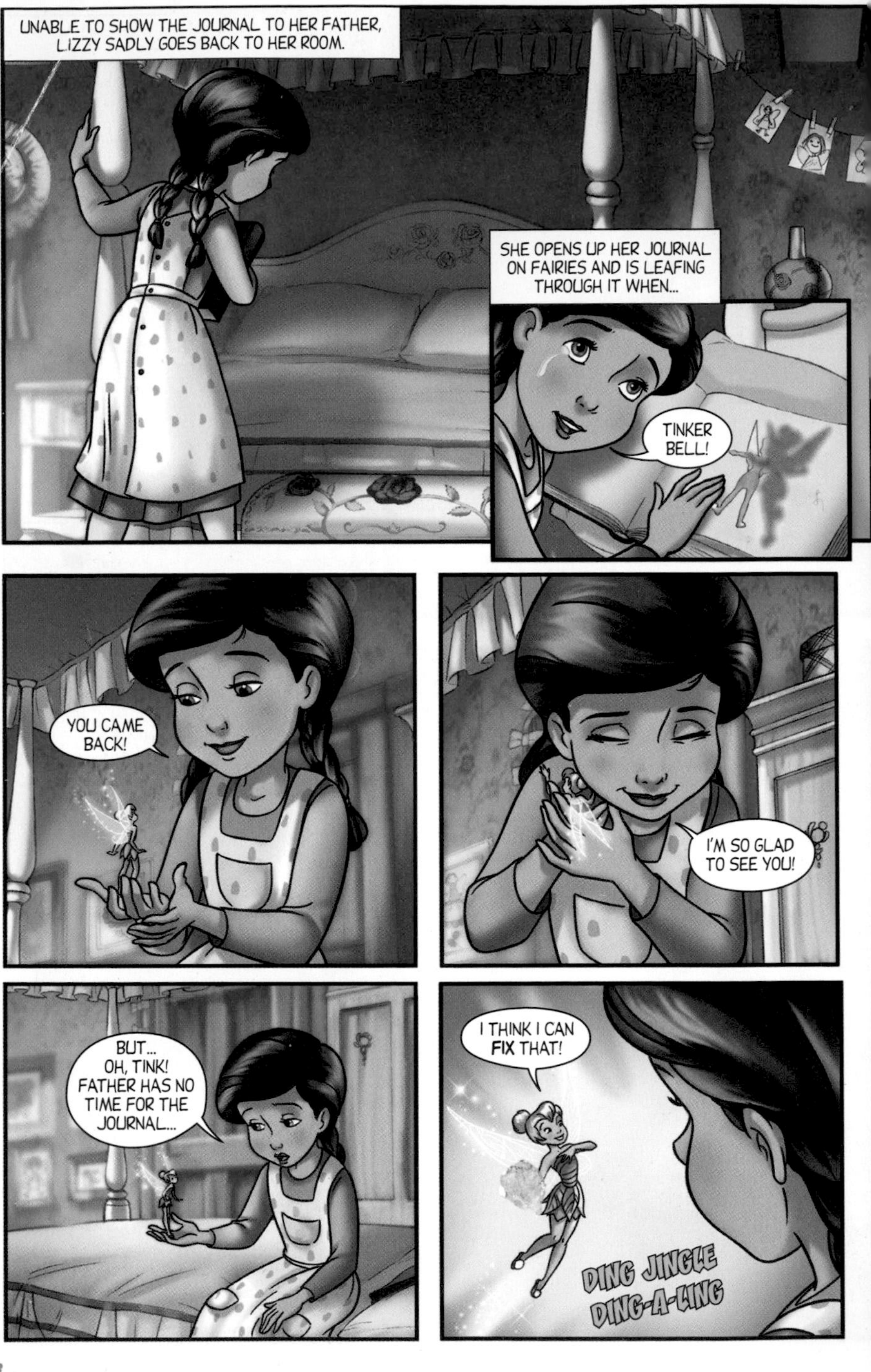
UNABLE TO SHOW THE JOURNAL TO HER FATHER, LIZZY SADLY GOES BACK TO HER ROOM.
SHE OPENS UP HER JOURNAL ON FAIRIES AND IS LEAFING THROUGH IT WHEN...
TINKER BELL!
YOU CAME BACK!
I'M SO GLAD TO SEE YOU!
BUT... OH, TINK! FATHER HAS NO TIME FOR THE JOURNAL...
I THINK I CAN **FIX** THAT!
DING JINGLE DING-A-LING

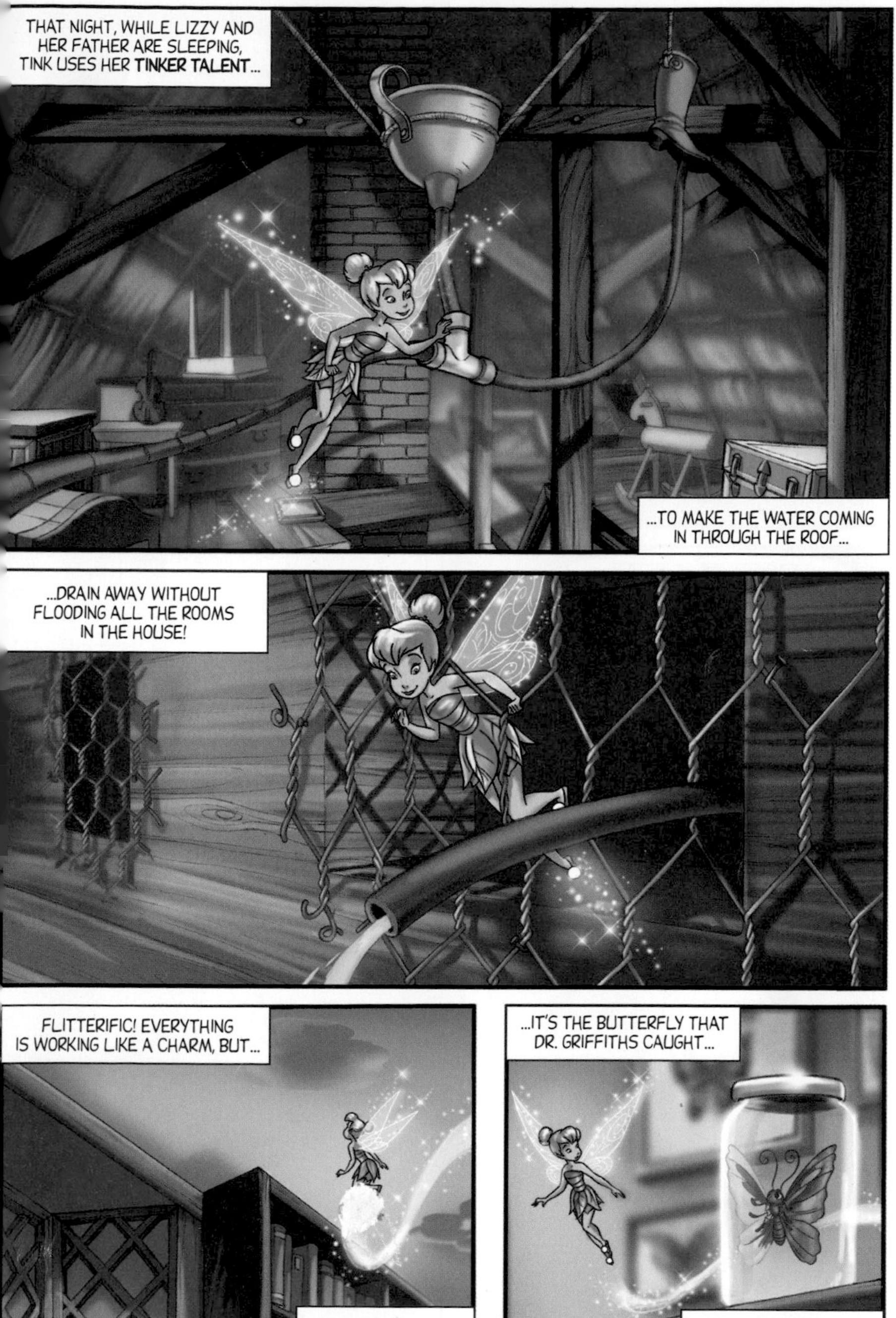
THAT NIGHT, WHILE LIZZY AND HER FATHER ARE SLEEPING, TINK USES HER **TINKER TALENT**...
...TO MAKE THE WATER COMING IN THROUGH THE ROOF...
...DRAIN AWAY WITHOUT FLOODING ALL THE ROOMS IN THE HOUSE!
FLITTERIFIC! EVERYTHING IS WORKING LIKE A CHARM, BUT...
...A NOISE DRAWS TINK'S ATTENTION...
...IT'S THE BUTTERFLY THAT DR. GRIFFITHS CAUGHT...
...BUT BUTTERFLIES NEED TO LIVE **FREE**!

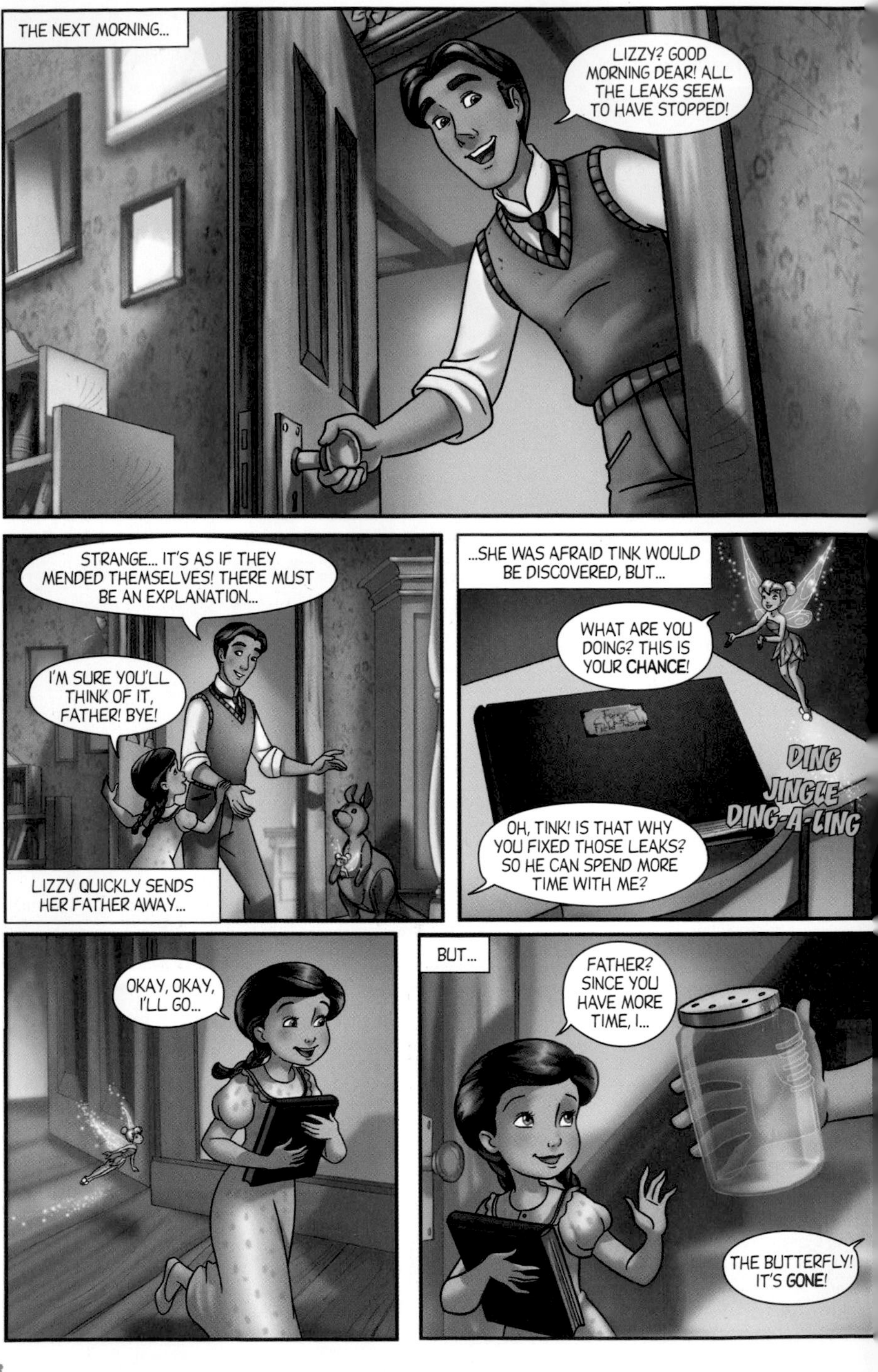
THE NEXT MORNING...
LIZZY? GOOD MORNING DEAR! ALL THE LEAKS SEEM TO HAVE STOPPED!
STRANGE... IT'S AS IF THEY MENDED THEMSELVES! THERE MUST BE AN EXPLANATION...
I'M SURE YOU'LL THINK OF IT, FATHER! BYE!
LIZZY QUICKLY SENDS HER FATHER AWAY...
...SHE WAS AFRAID TINK WOULD BE DISCOVERED, BUT...
WHAT ARE YOU DOING? THIS IS YOUR CHANCE!
DING
JINGLE
DING-A-LING
OH, TINK! IS THAT WHY YOU FIXED THOSE LEAKS? SO HE CAN SPEND MORE TIME WITH ME?
OKAY, OKAY, I'LL GO...
BUT...
FATHER? SINCE YOU HAVE MORE TIME, I...
THE BUTTERFLY! IT'S GONE!

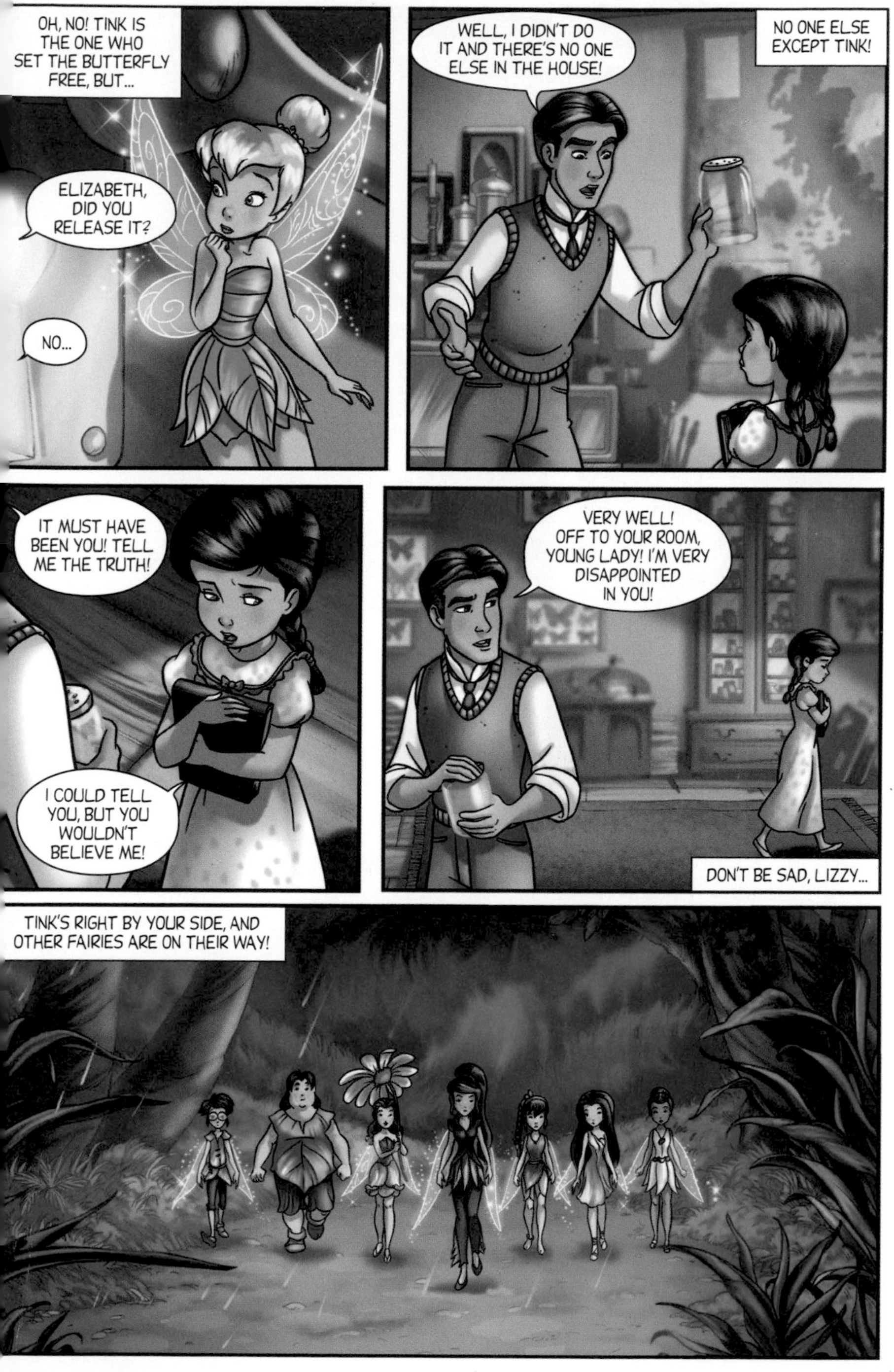
OH, NO! TINK IS THE ONE WHO SET THE BUTTERFLY FREE, BUT...
ELIZABETH, DID YOU RELEASE IT?
NO...
WELL, I DIDN'T DO IT AND THERE'S NO ONE ELSE IN THE HOUSE!
NO ONE ELSE EXCEPT TINK!
IT MUST HAVE BEEN YOU! TELL ME THE TRUTH!
I COULD TELL YOU, BUT YOU WOULDN'T BELIEVE ME!
VERY WELL! OFF TO YOUR ROOM, YOUNG LADY! I'M VERY DISAPPOINTED IN YOU!
DON'T BE SAD, LIZZY...
TINK'S RIGHT BY YOUR SIDE, AND OTHER FAIRIES ARE ON THEIR WAY!

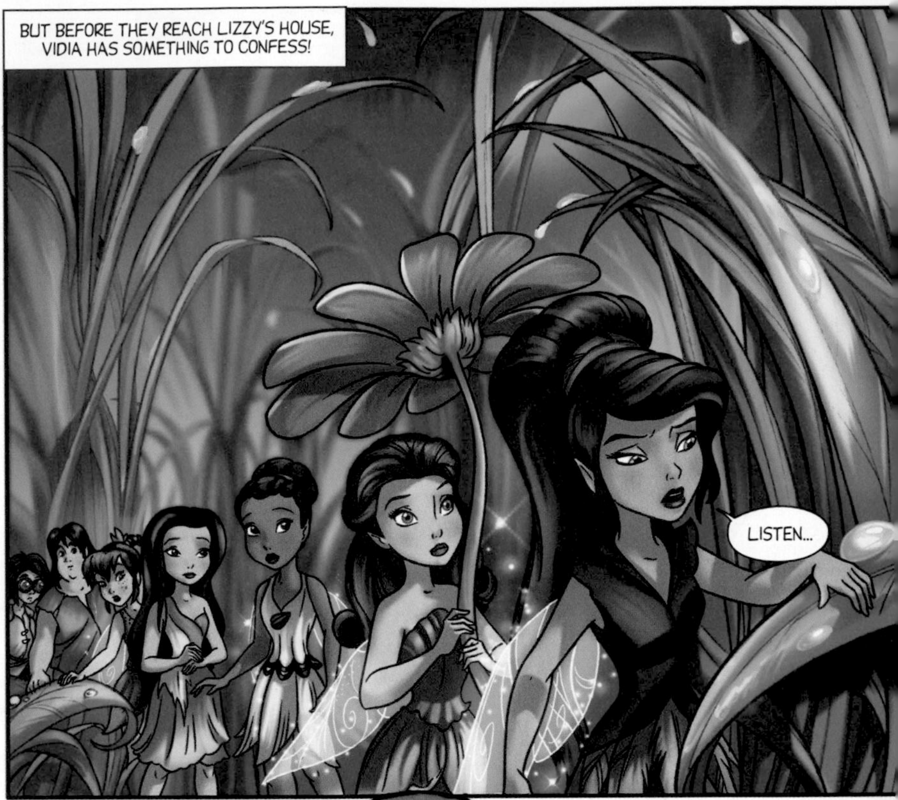
BUT BEFORE THEY REACH LIZZY'S HOUSE, VIDIA HAS SOMETHING TO CONFESS!
LISTEN...

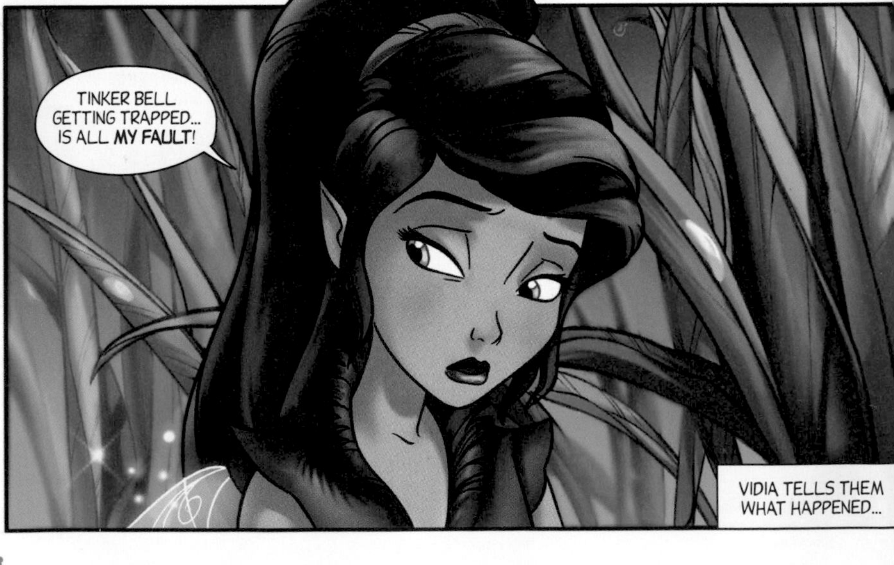
TINKER BELL GETTING TRAPPED... IS ALL **MY FAULT**!
VIDIA TELLS THEM WHAT HAPPENED...

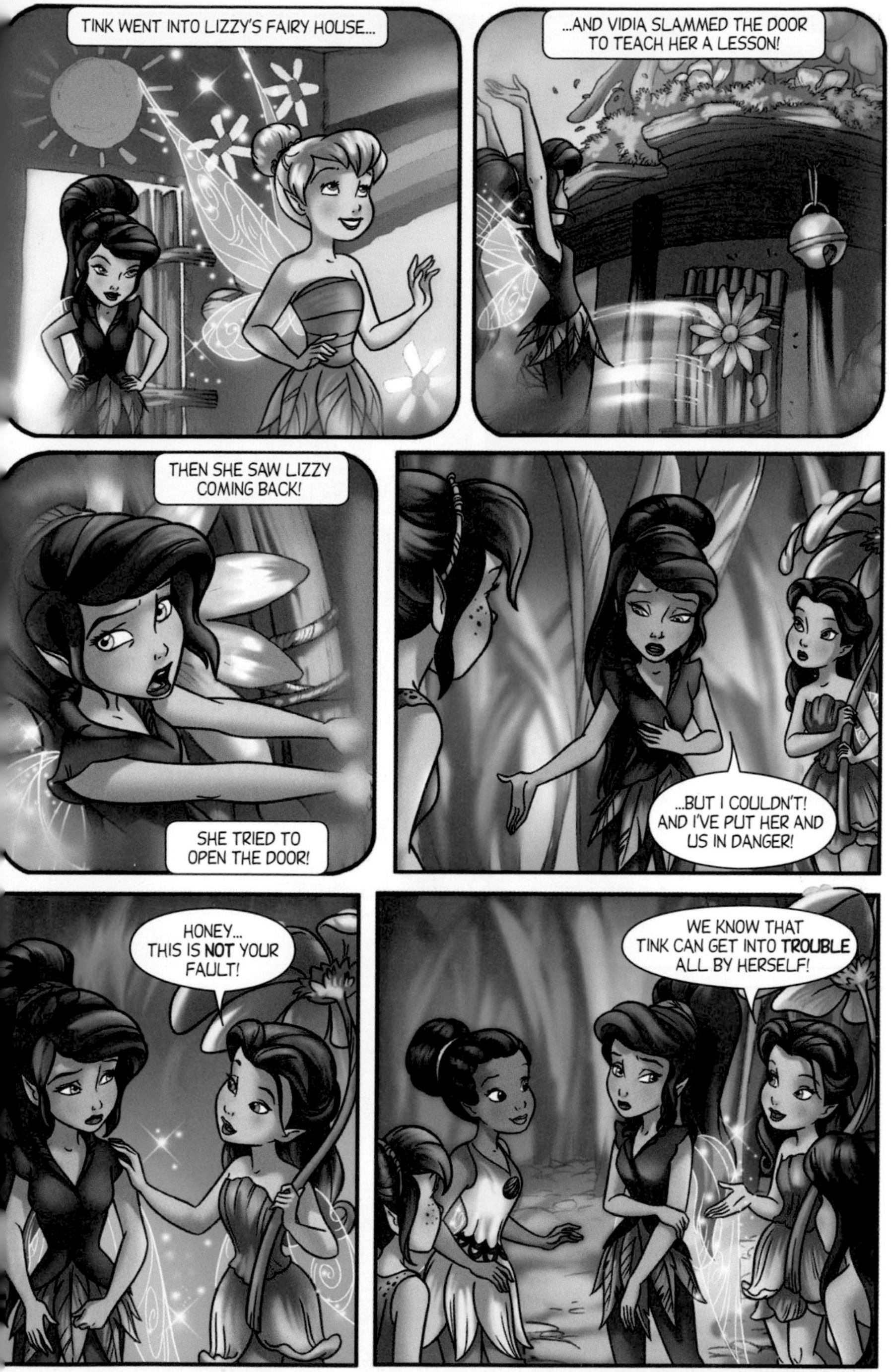
TINK WENT INTO LIZZY'S FAIRY HOUSE...
...AND VIDIA SLAMMED THE DOOR TO TEACH HER A LESSON!
THEN SHE SAW LIZZY COMING BACK!
SHE TRIED TO OPEN THE DOOR!
...BUT I COULDN'T! AND I'VE PUT HER AND US IN DANGER!
HONEY... THIS IS **NOT** YOUR FAULT!
WE KNOW THAT TINK CAN GET INTO **TROUBLE** ALL BY HERSELF!

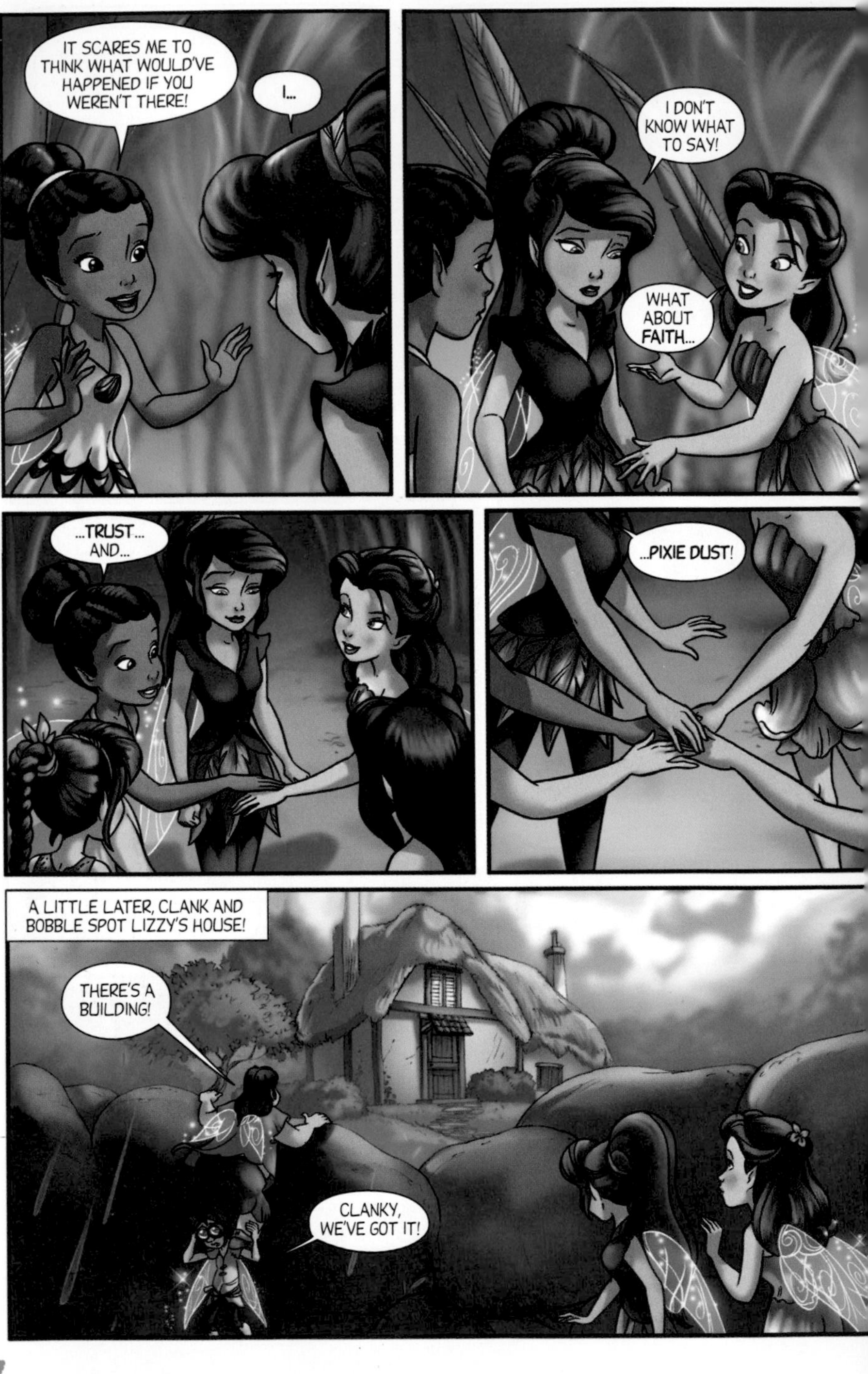
IT SCARES ME TO THINK WHAT WOULD'VE HAPPENED IF YOU WEREN'T THERE!
I...
I DON'T KNOW WHAT TO SAY!
WHAT ABOUT FAITH...
...TRUST... AND...
...PIXIE DUST!
A LITTLE LATER, CLANK AND BOBBLE SPOT LIZZY'S HOUSE!
THERE'S A BUILDING!
CLANKY, WE'VE GOT IT!

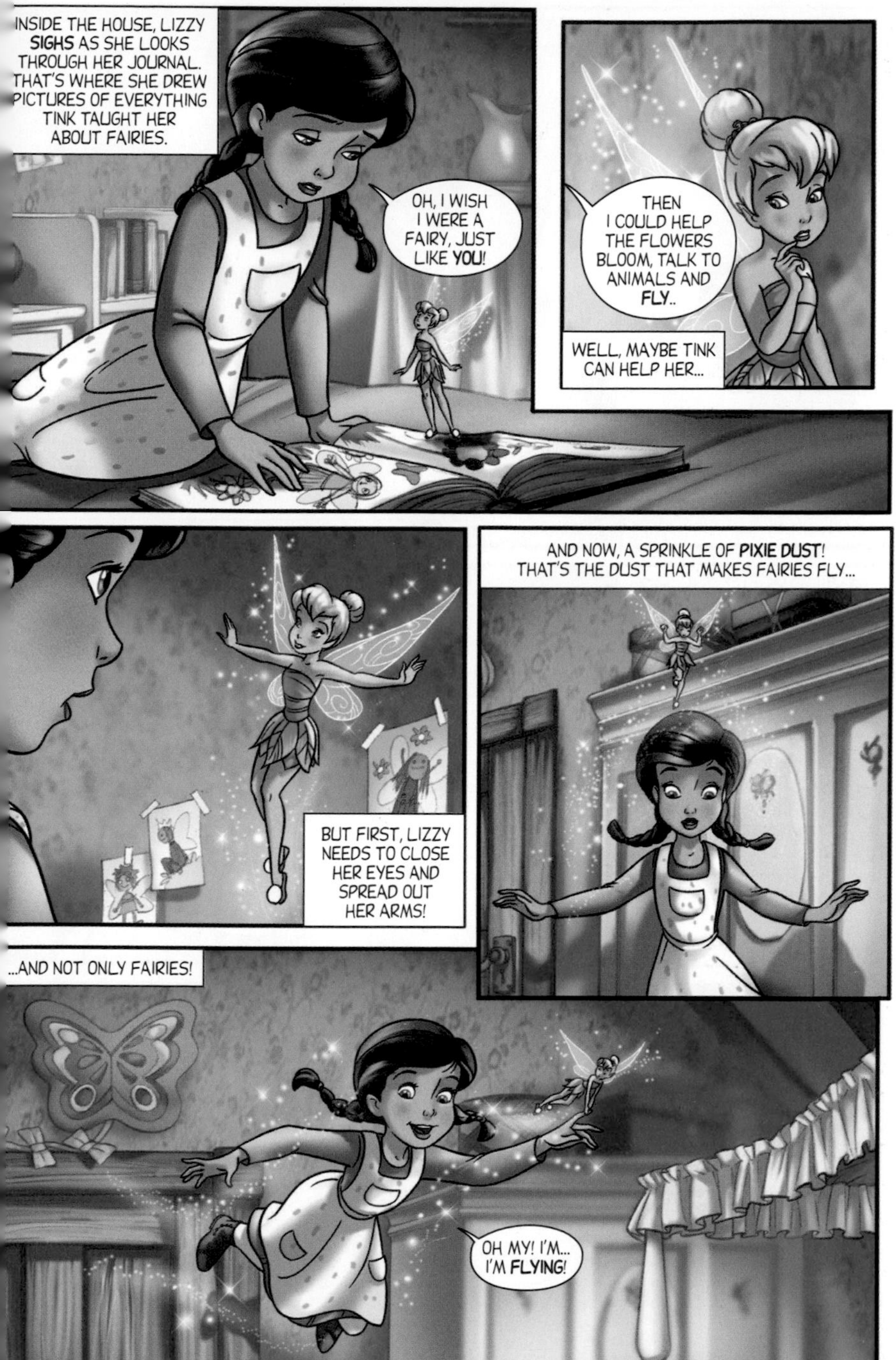
INSIDE THE HOUSE, LIZZY SIGHS AS SHE LOOKS THROUGH HER JOURNAL. THAT'S WHERE SHE DREW PICTURES OF EVERYTHING TINK TAUGHT HER ABOUT FAIRIES.
OH, I WISH I WERE A FAIRY, JUST LIKE YOU!
THEN I COULD HELP THE FLOWERS BLOOM, TALK TO ANIMALS AND FLY..
WELL, MAYBE TINK CAN HELP HER...
BUT FIRST, LIZZY NEEDS TO CLOSE HER EYES AND SPREAD OUT HER ARMS!
AND NOW, A SPRINKLE OF PIXIE DUST! THAT'S THE DUST THAT MAKES FAIRIES FLY...
...AND NOT ONLY FAIRIES!
OH MY! I'M... I'M FLYING!

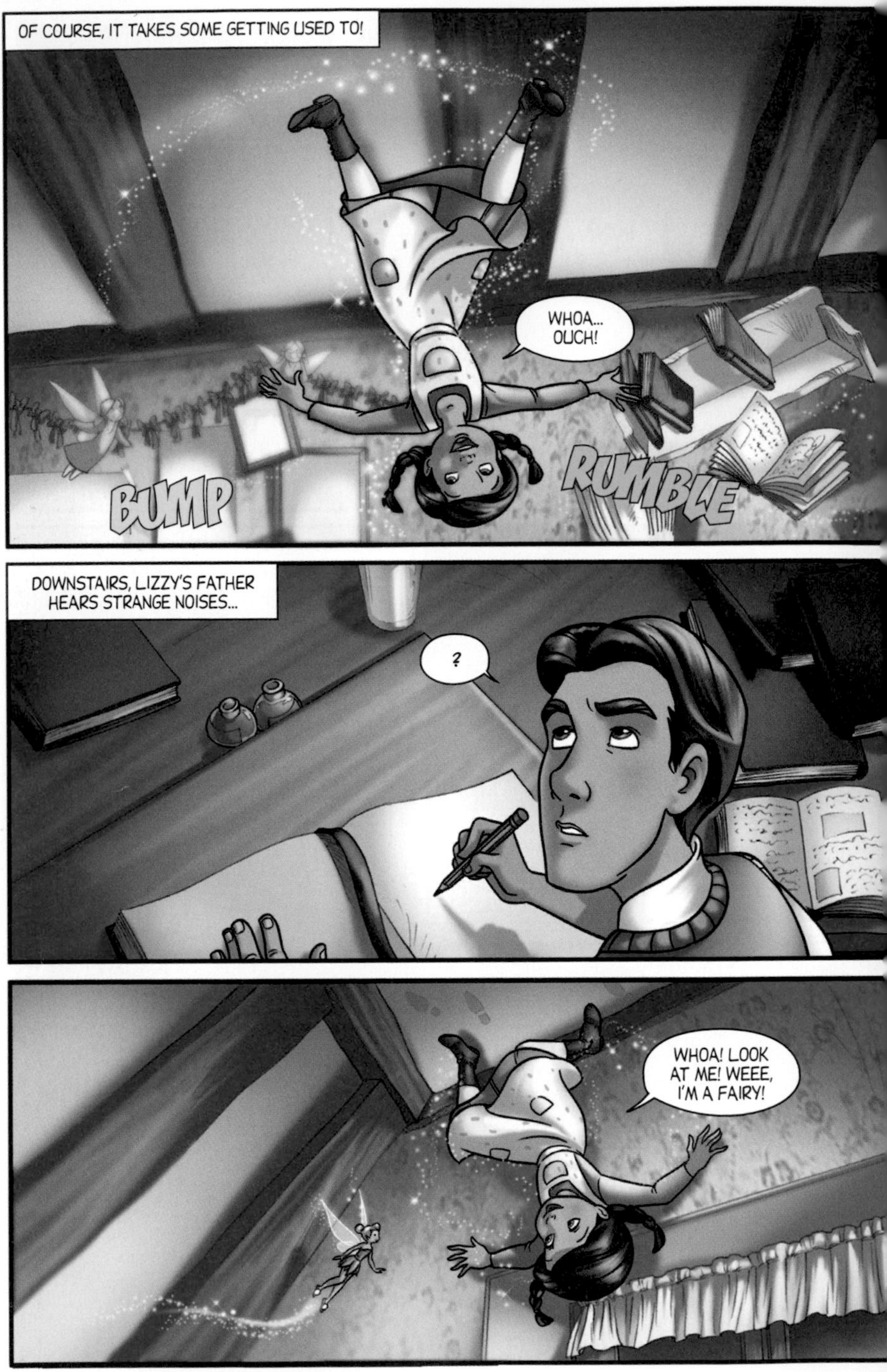
OF COURSE, IT TAKES SOME GETTING USED TO!
WHOA... OUCH!
BUMP
RUMBLE
DOWNSTAIRS, LIZZY'S FATHER HEARS STRANGE NOISES...
?
WHOA! LOOK AT ME! WEEE, I'M A FAIRY!

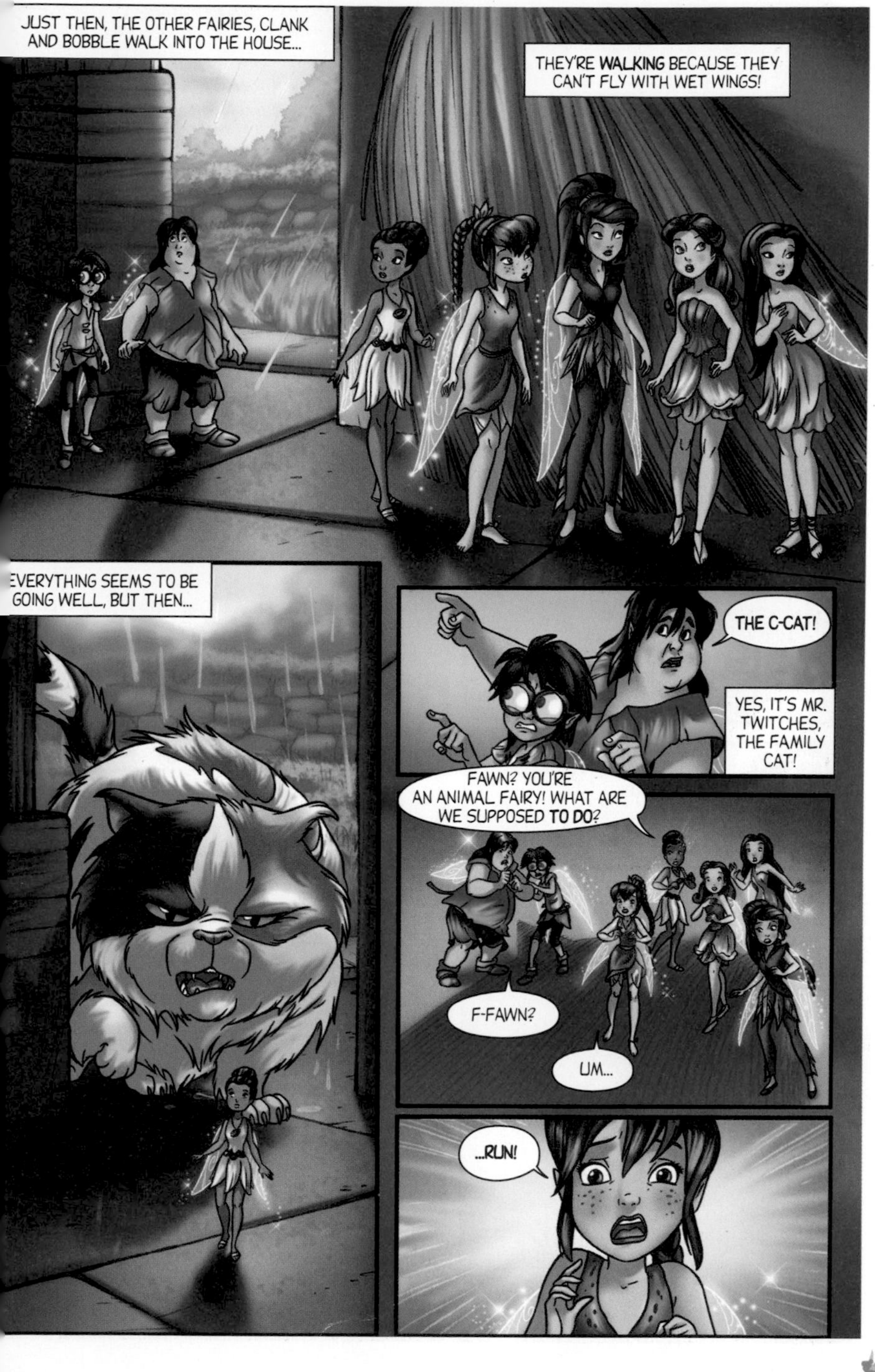
JUST THEN, THE OTHER FAIRIES, CLANK AND BOBBLE WALK INTO THE HOUSE...
THEY'RE **WALKING** BECAUSE THEY CAN'T FLY WITH WET WINGS!
EVERYTHING SEEMS TO BE GOING WELL, BUT THEN...
THE C-CAT!
YES, IT'S MR. TWITCHES, THE FAMILY CAT!
FAWN? YOU'RE AN ANIMAL FAIRY! WHAT ARE WE SUPPOSED **TO DO**?
F-FAWN?
UM...
...RUN!

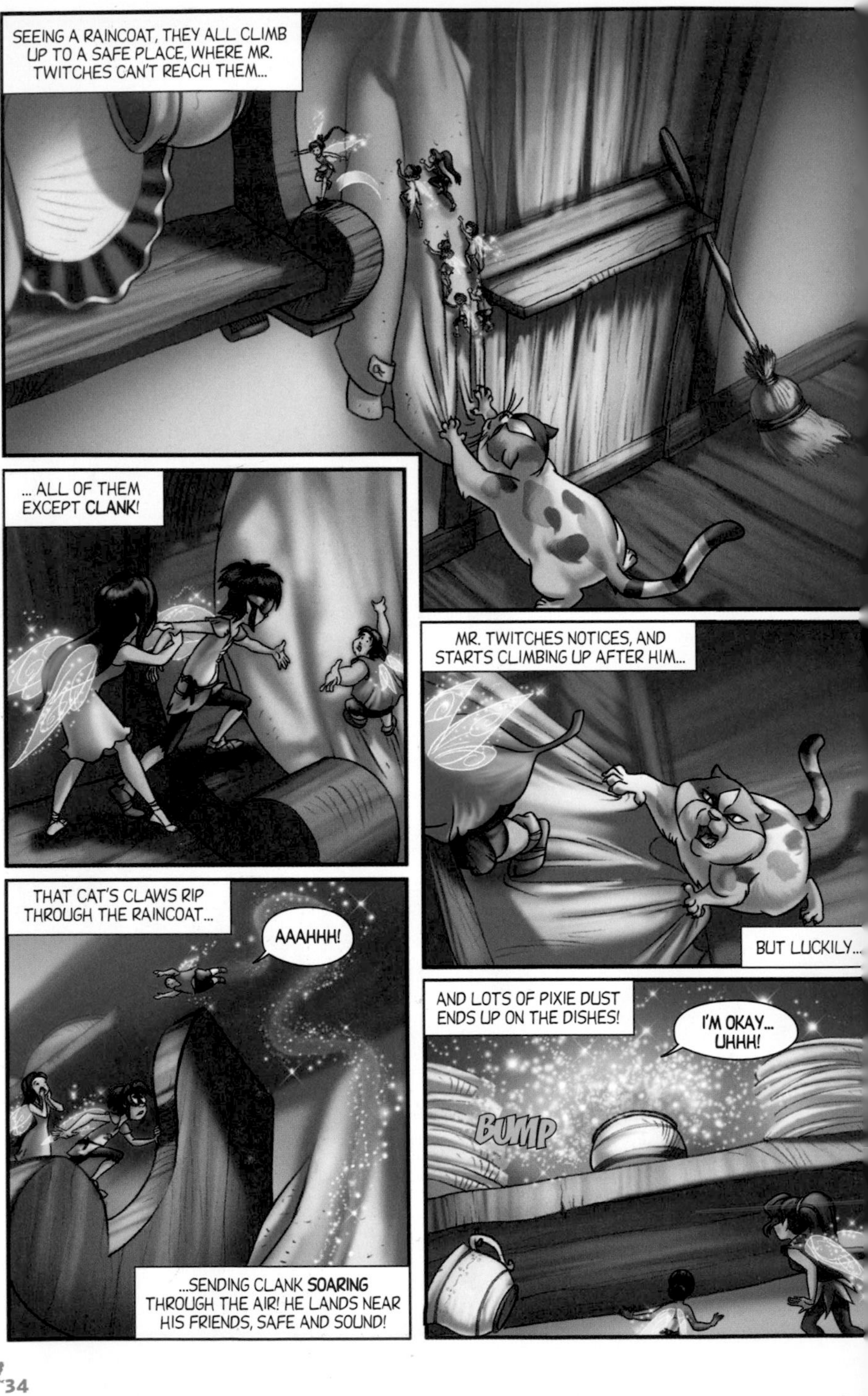
SEEING A RAINCOAT, THEY ALL CLIMB UP TO A SAFE PLACE, WHERE MR. TWITCHES CAN'T REACH THEM...
... ALL OF THEM EXCEPT **CLANK**!
MR. TWITCHES NOTICES, AND STARTS CLIMBING UP AFTER HIM...
BUT LUCKILY...
THAT CAT'S CLAWS RIP THROUGH THE RAINCOAT...
AAAHHH!
...SENDING CLANK **SOARING** THROUGH THE AIR! HE LANDS NEAR HIS FRIENDS, SAFE AND SOUND!
AND LOTS OF PIXIE DUST ENDS UP ON THE DISHES!
I'M OKAY... UHHH!
BUMP

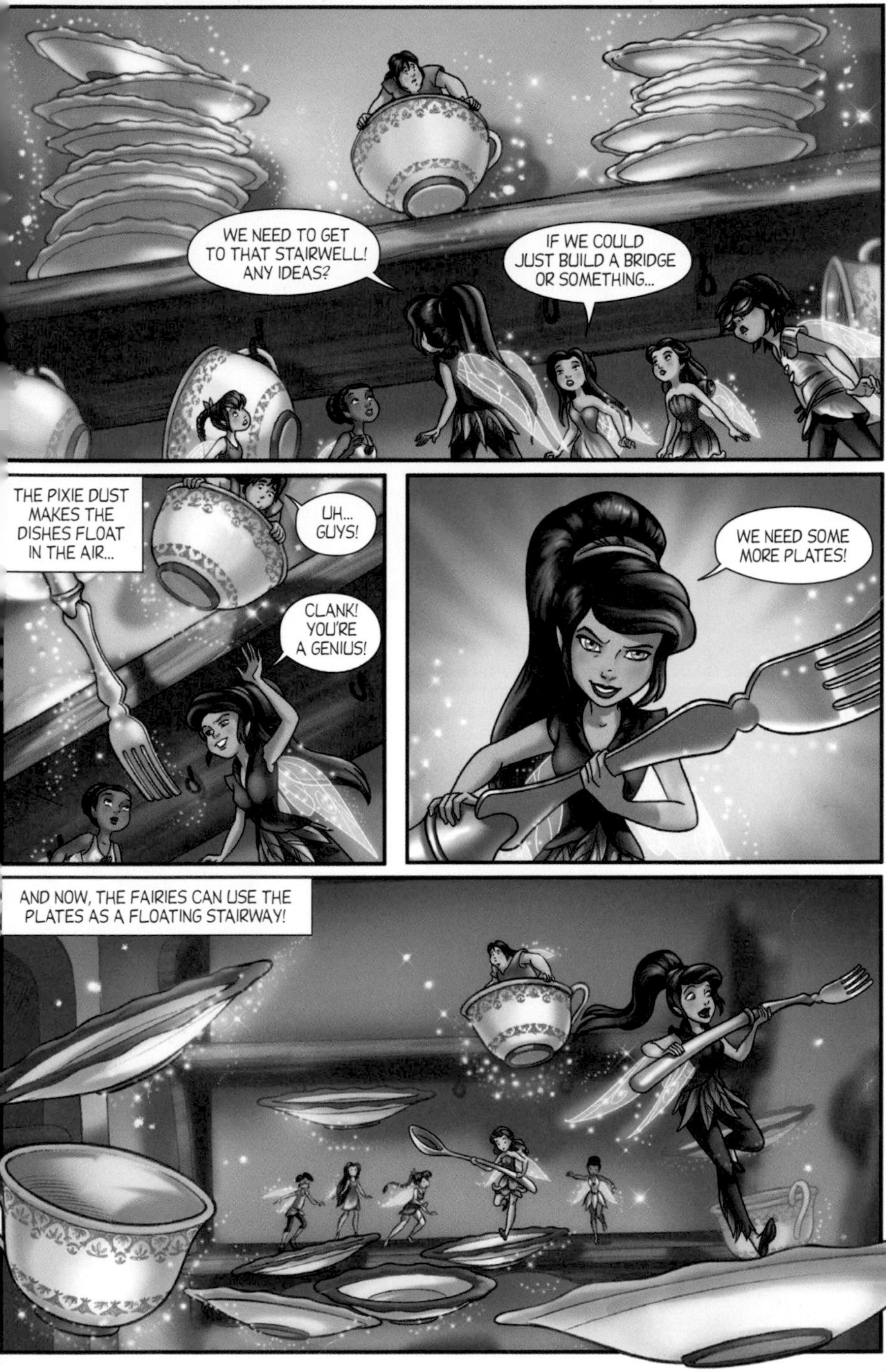
WE NEED TO GET TO THAT STAIRWELL! ANY IDEAS?
IF WE COULD JUST BUILD A BRIDGE OR SOMETHING...
THE PIXIE DUST MAKES THE DISHES FLOAT IN THE AIR...
UH... GUYS!
CLANK! YOU'RE A GENIUS!
WE NEED SOME MORE PLATES!
AND NOW, THE FAIRIES CAN USE THE PLATES AS A FLOATING STAIRWAY!

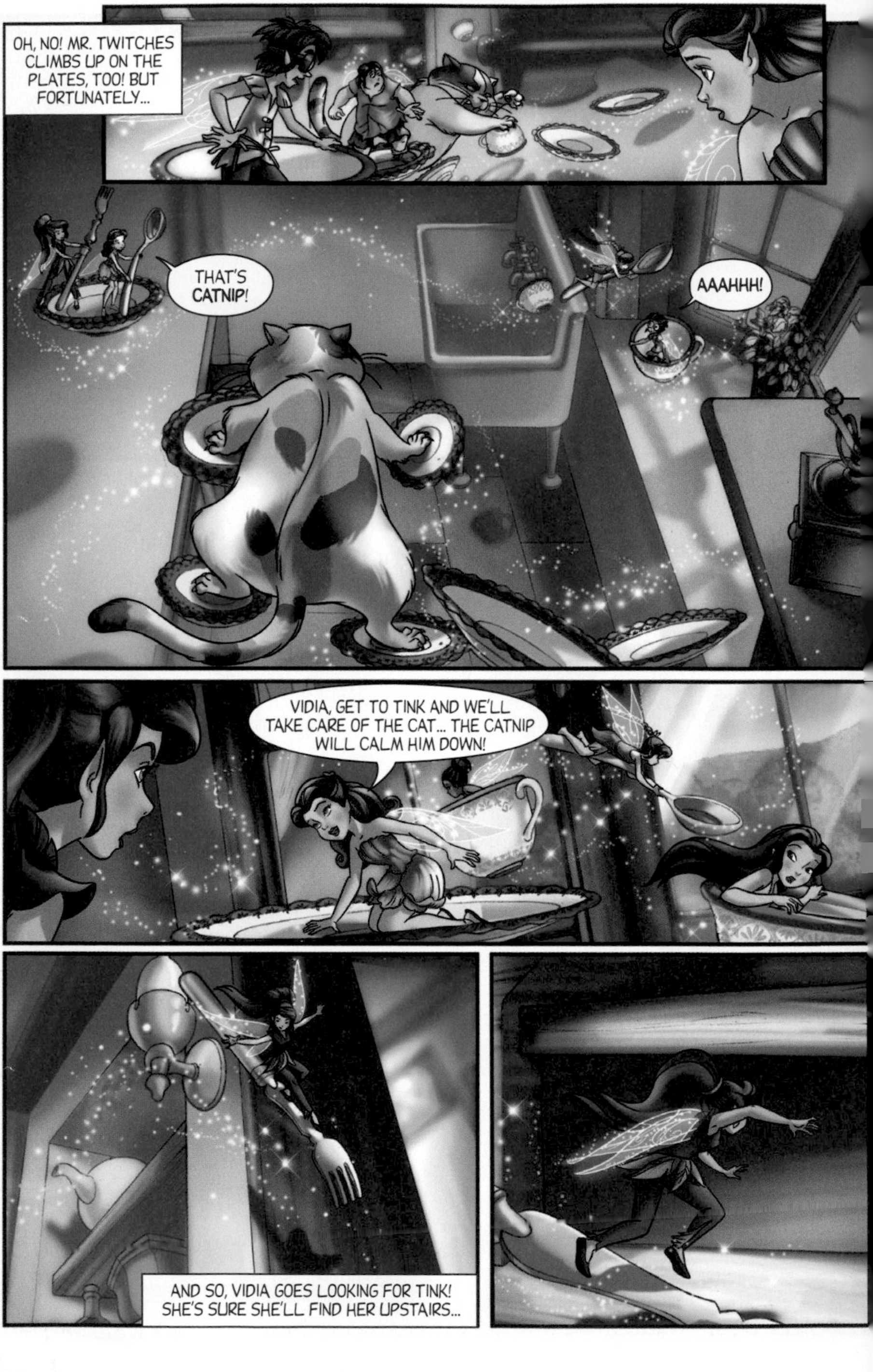
OH, NO! MR. TWITCHES CLIMBS UP ON THE PLATES, TOO! BUT FORTUNATELY...
THAT'S CATNIP!
AAAHHH!
VIDIA, GET TO TINK AND WE'LL TAKE CARE OF THE CAT... THE CATNIP WILL CALM HIM DOWN!
AND SO, VIDIA GOES LOOKING FOR TINK! SHE'S SURE SHE'LL FIND HER UPSTAIRS...

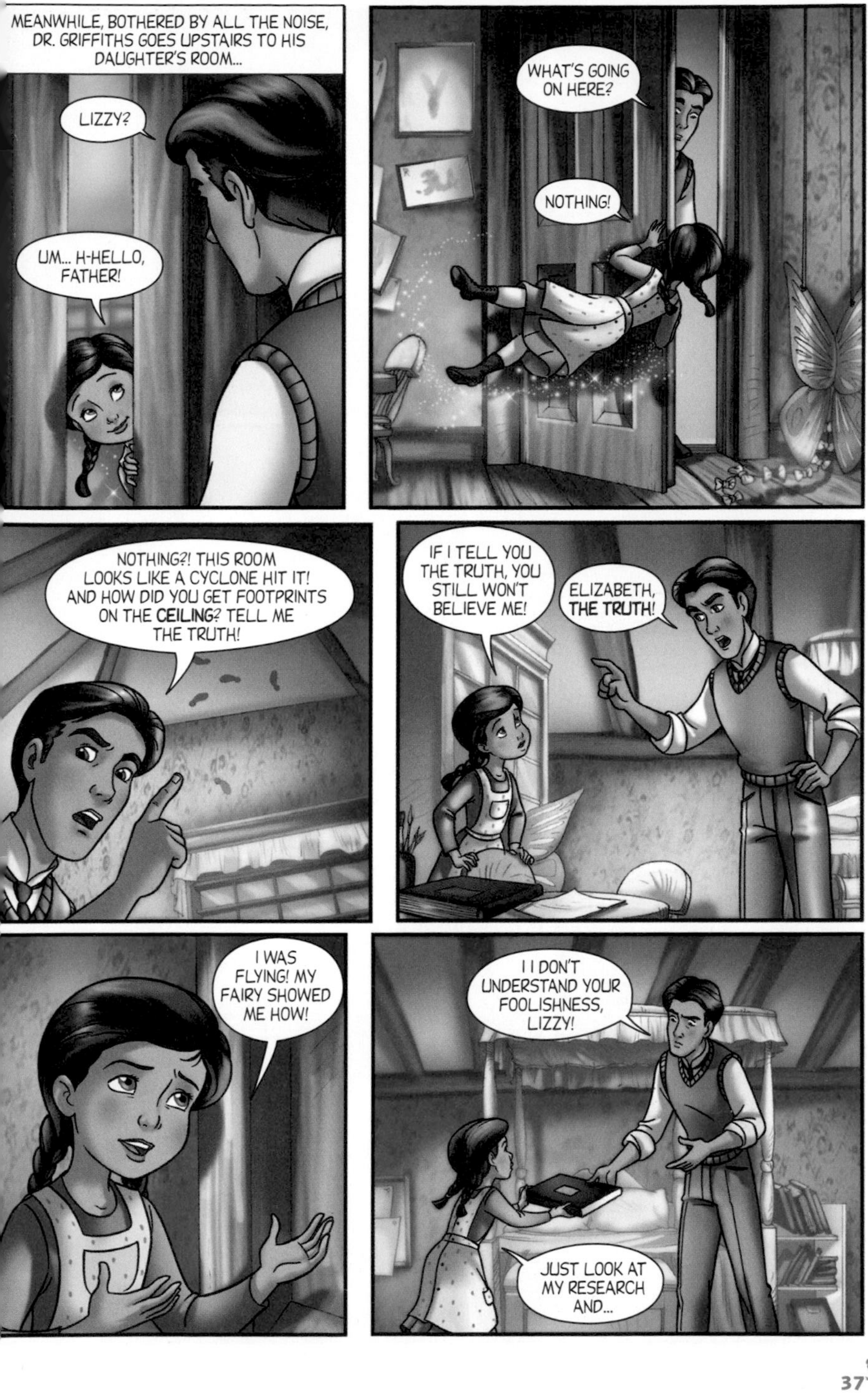
MEANWHILE, BOTHERED BY ALL THE NOISE, DR. GRIFFITHS GOES UPSTAIRS TO HIS DAUGHTER'S ROOM...
LIZZY?
UM... H-HELLO, FATHER!
WHAT'S GOING ON HERE?
NOTHING!
NOTHING?! THIS ROOM LOOKS LIKE A CYCLONE HIT IT! AND HOW DID YOU GET FOOTPRINTS ON THE CEILING? TELL ME THE TRUTH!
IF I TELL YOU THE TRUTH, YOU STILL WON'T BELIEVE ME!
ELIZABETH, THE TRUTH!
I WAS FLYING! MY FAIRY SHOWED ME HOW!
I I DON'T UNDERSTAND YOUR FOOLISHNESS, LIZZY!
JUST LOOK AT MY RESEARCH AND...

I KNOW THIS IS DIFFICULT FOR YOU TO UNDERSTAND, BUT THIS IS ALL **MAKE-BELIEVE!**

NO, THEY'RE REAL!

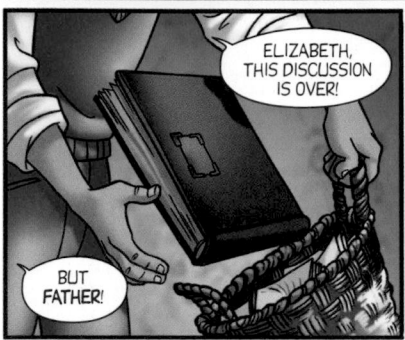

ELIZABETH, THIS DISCUSSION IS OVER!

BUT FATHER!

TINK IS HIDING IN THE FAIRY HOUSE... AND SHE'S VERY, VERY ANGRY!

SO ANGRY THAT SHE COMES OUT IN THE OPEN!

!

SEE? FAIRIES ARE REAL!

DING JINGLE DING-A-LING

A LITTLE LATER...

ISN'T SHE MAGICAL?

IT'S... IT'S EXTRAORDINARY! THIS IS GOING TO BE THE DISCOVERY OF THE CENTURY!

HER WINGS NOW DRY, VIDIA FINALLY MAKES IT TO LIZZY'S ROOM... JUST IN TIME TO SEE THAT...

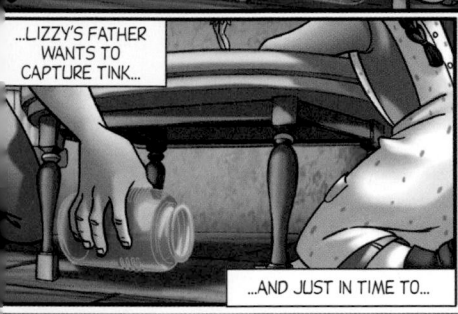

...LIZZY'S FATHER WANTS TO CAPTURE TINK...

...AND JUST IN TIME TO...

...FLY TO HER FRIEND'S RESCUE...

TINK! GET OUT OF THE WAY!

BUT NOW, IT'S VIDIA WHO'S BEEN CAPTURED!

FLUMP

OH, NO! THE FACT THAT FAIRIES EXIST NEEDS TO BE KEPT SECRET, BUT...

I MUST GET THIS TO THE MUSEUM RIGHT AWAY!

FATHER, NO! PLEASE, FATHER! PLEASE!

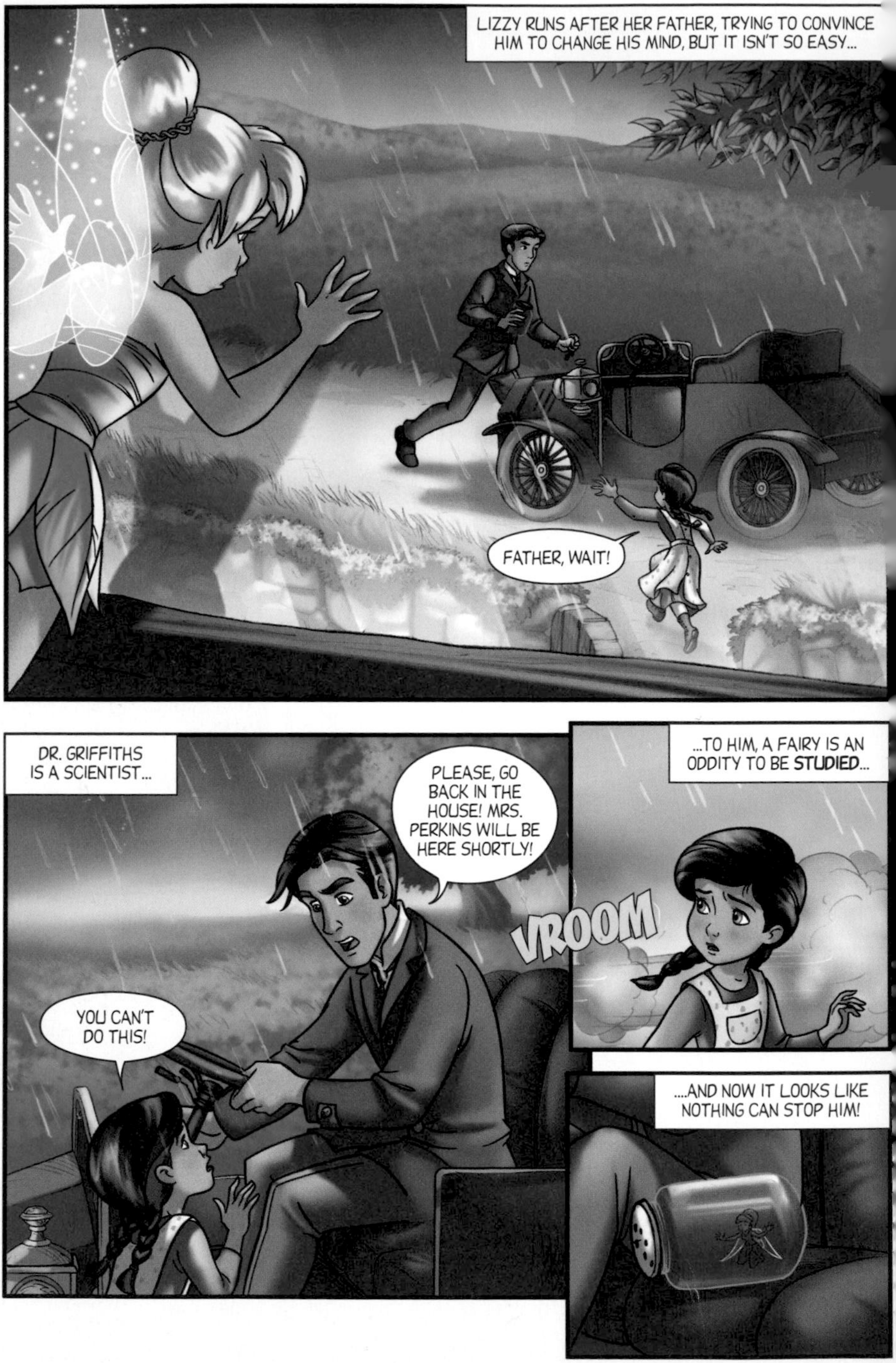
LIZZY RUNS AFTER HER FATHER, TRYING TO CONVINCE HIM TO CHANGE HIS MIND, BUT IT ISN'T SO EASY...
FATHER, WAIT!
DR. GRIFFITHS IS A SCIENTIST...
PLEASE, GO BACK IN THE HOUSE! MRS. PERKINS WILL BE HERE SHORTLY!
YOU CAN'T DO THIS!
...TO HIM, A FAIRY IS AN ODDITY TO BE **STUDIED**...
VROOM
...AND NOW IT LOOKS LIKE NOTHING CAN STOP HIM!

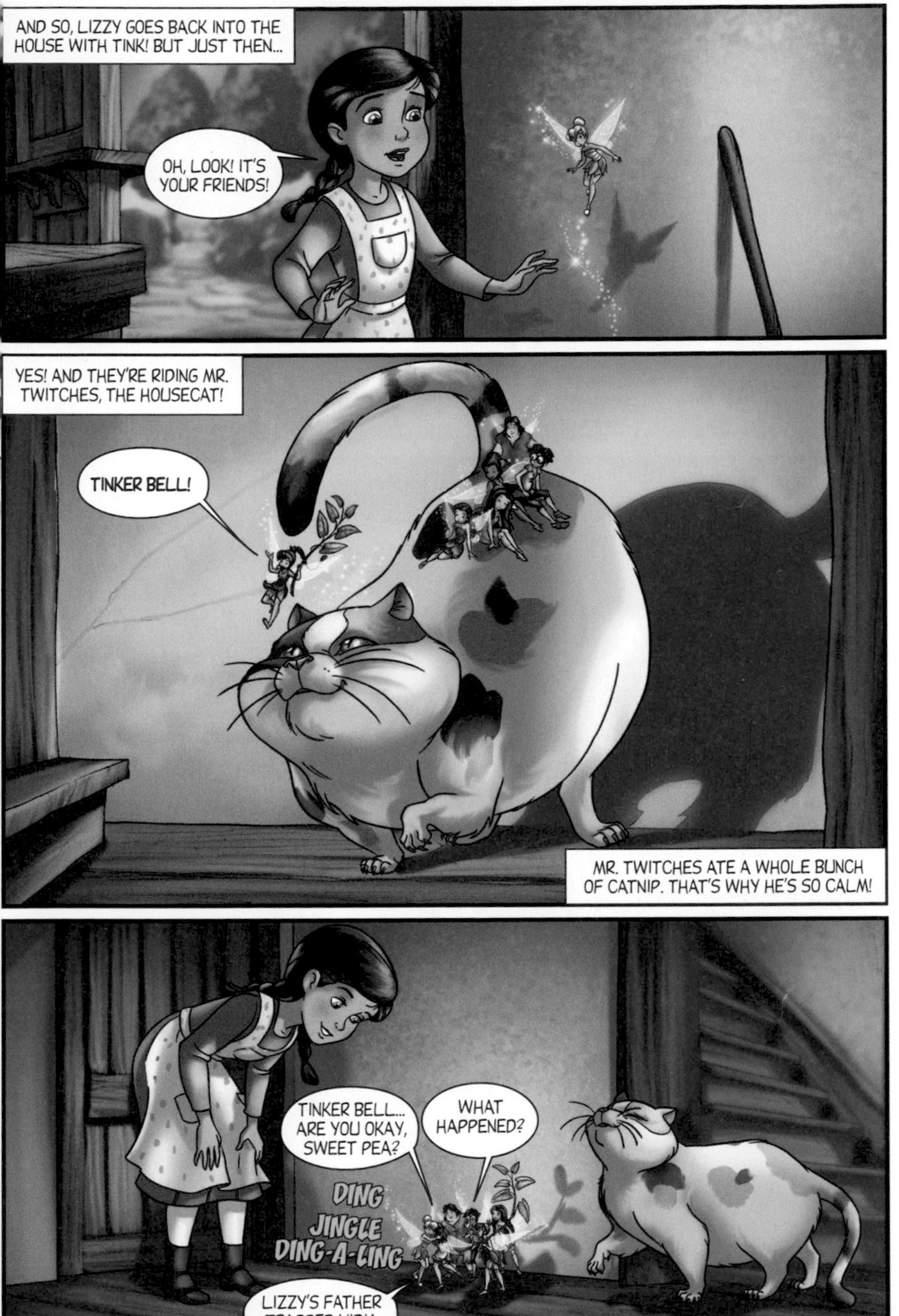
AND SO, LIZZY GOES BACK INTO THE HOUSE WITH TINK! BUT JUST THEN...
OH, LOOK! IT'S YOUR FRIENDS!
YES! AND THEY'RE RIDING MR. TWITCHES, THE HOUSECAT!
TINKER BELL!
MR. TWITCHES ATE A WHOLE BUNCH OF CATNIP. THAT'S WHY HE'S SO CALM!
TINKER BELL... ARE YOU OKAY, SWEET PEA?
WHAT HAPPENED?
DING
JINGLE
DING-A-LING
LIZZY'S FATHER TRAPPED VIDIA IN A JAR!

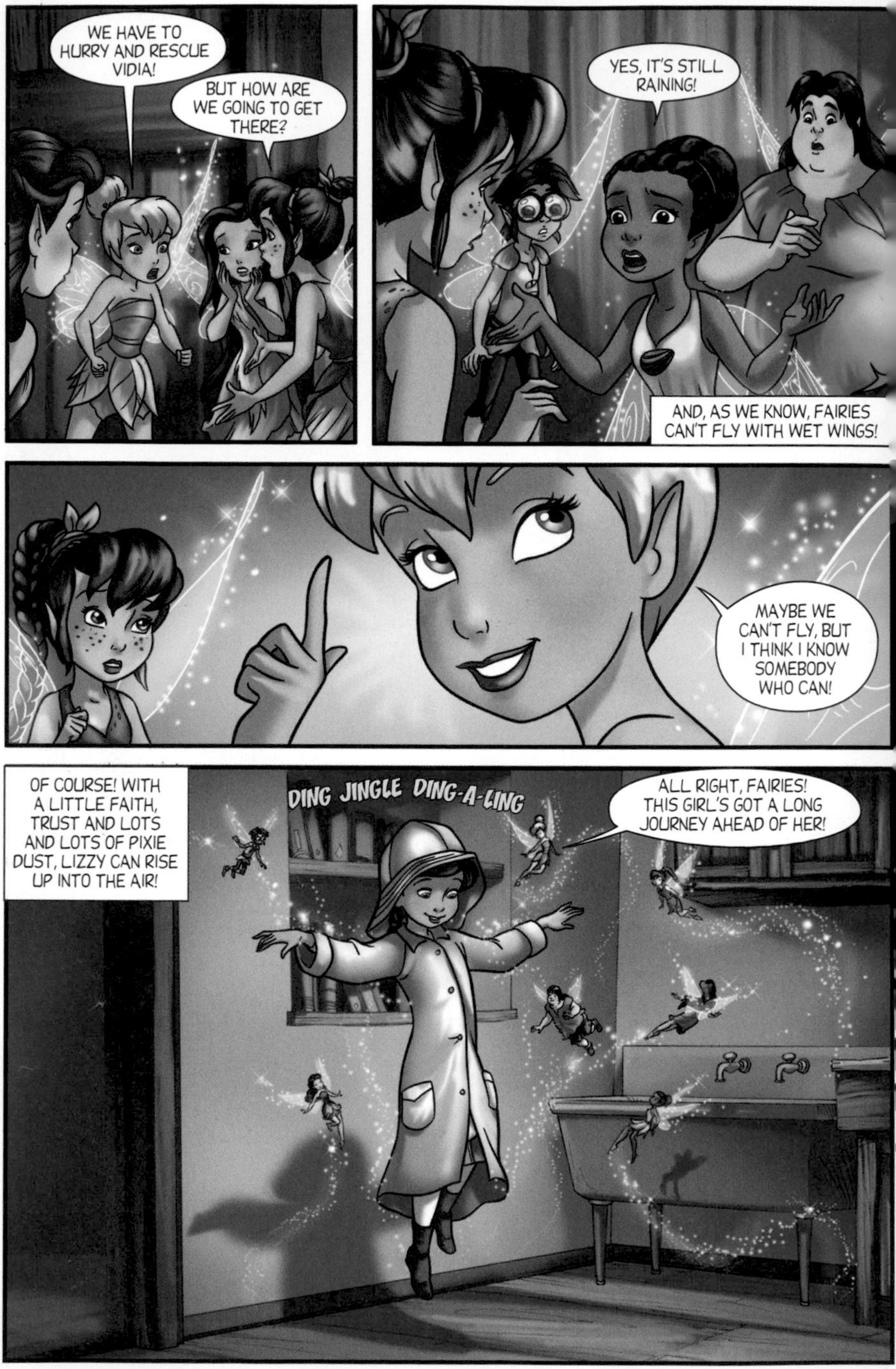

WE HAVE TO HURRY AND RESCUE VIDIA!
BUT HOW ARE WE GOING TO GET THERE?
YES, IT'S STILL RAINING!
AND, AS WE KNOW, FAIRIES CAN'T FLY WITH WET WINGS!
MAYBE WE CAN'T FLY, BUT I THINK I KNOW SOMEBODY WHO CAN!
OF COURSE! WITH A LITTLE FAITH, TRUST AND LOTS AND LOTS OF PIXIE DUST, LIZZY CAN RISE UP INTO THE AIR!
DING JINGLE DING-A-LING
ALL RIGHT, FAIRIES! THIS GIRL'S GOT A LONG JOURNEY AHEAD OF HER!

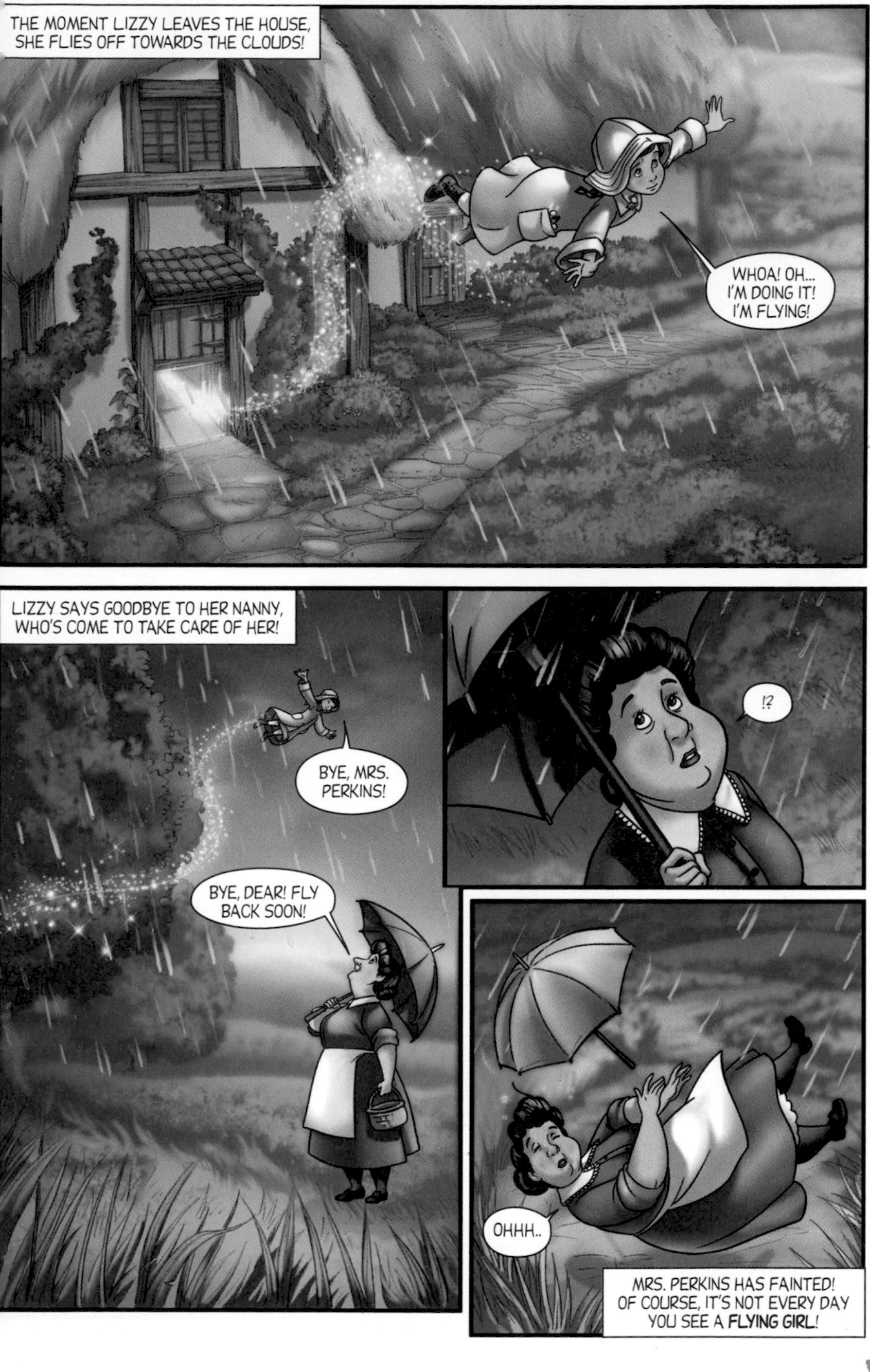
THE MOMENT LIZZY LEAVES THE HOUSE, SHE FLIES OFF TOWARDS THE CLOUDS!
WHOA! OH... I'M DOING IT! I'M FLYING!
LIZZY SAYS GOODBYE TO HER NANNY, WHO'S COME TO TAKE CARE OF HER!
BYE, MRS. PERKINS!
BYE, DEAR! FLY BACK SOON!
!?
OHHH..
MRS. PERKINS HAS FAINTED! OF COURSE, IT'S NOT EVERY DAY YOU SEE A **FLYING GIRL**!

MEANWHILE, VIDIA IS TRYING TO KNOCK OVER THE JAR SHE'S TRAPPED IN! MAYBE THAT WAY IT'LL OPEN UP...

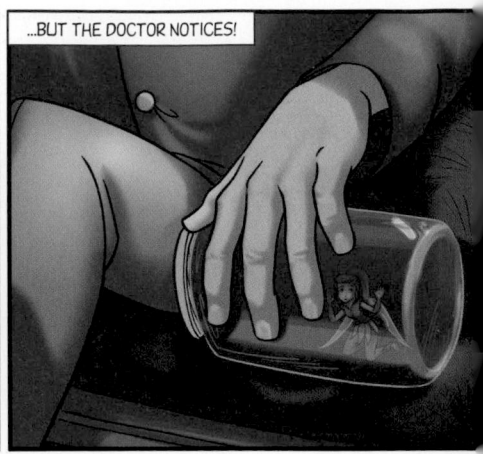

...BUT THE DOCTOR NOTICES!

SOON, HE'S DRIVING INTO THE CITY...

DR. GRIFFITHS HAS ALMOST REACHED THE MUSEUM... AND LIZZY SEES HIM!

TINK, I CAN'T KEEP UP! HE'S TOO FAST!

BUT FAIRIES ARE FAST, TOO! TINK DIVES DOWN WITHOUT A MOMENT'S HESITATION!

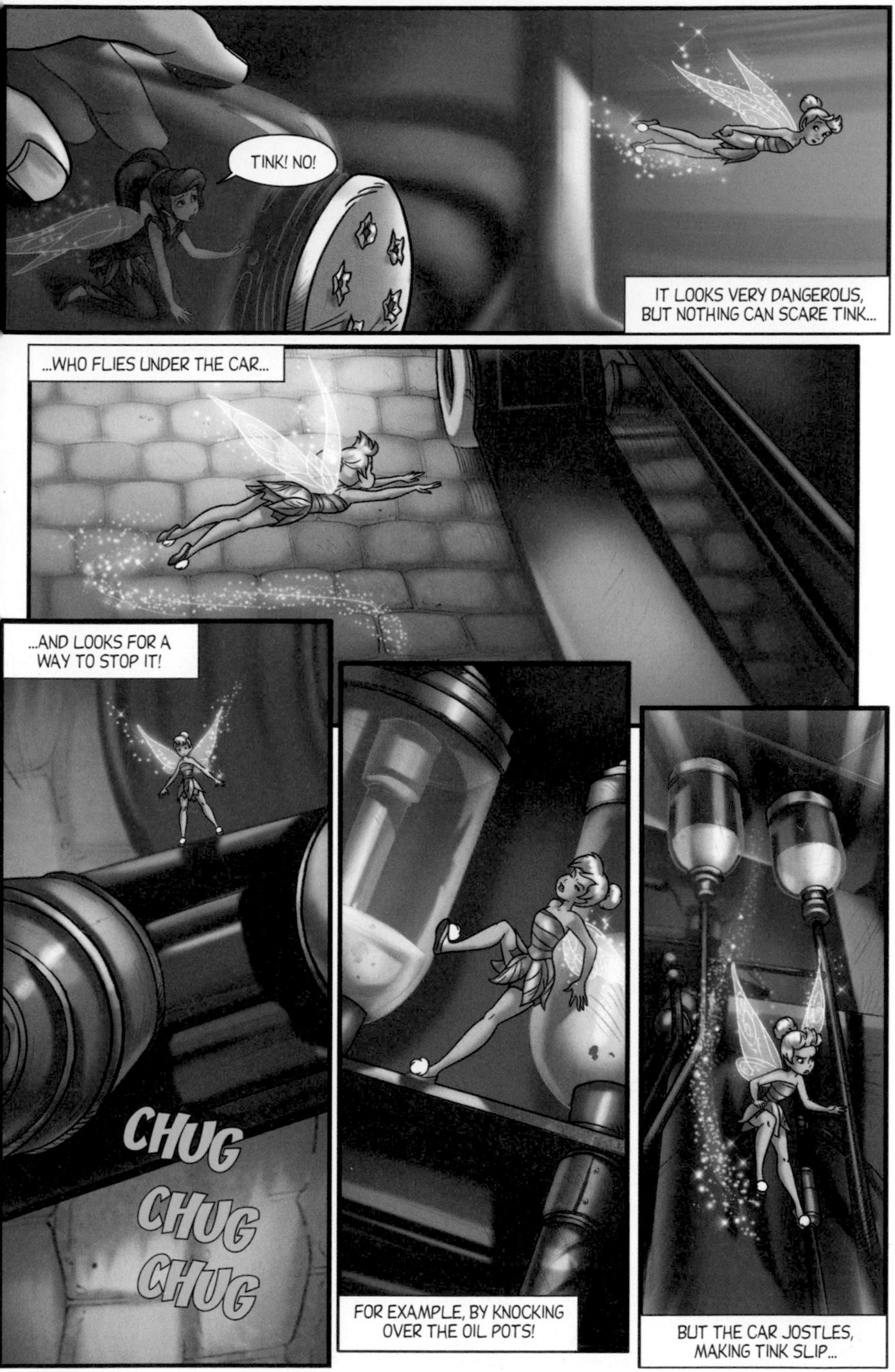
TINK! NO!
IT LOOKS VERY DANGEROUS, BUT NOTHING CAN SCARE TINK...
...WHO FLIES UNDER THE CAR...
...AND LOOKS FOR A WAY TO STOP IT!
CHUG
CHUG
CHUG
FOR EXAMPLE, BY KNOCKING OVER THE OIL POTS!
BUT THE CAR JOSTLES, MAKING TINK SLIP...

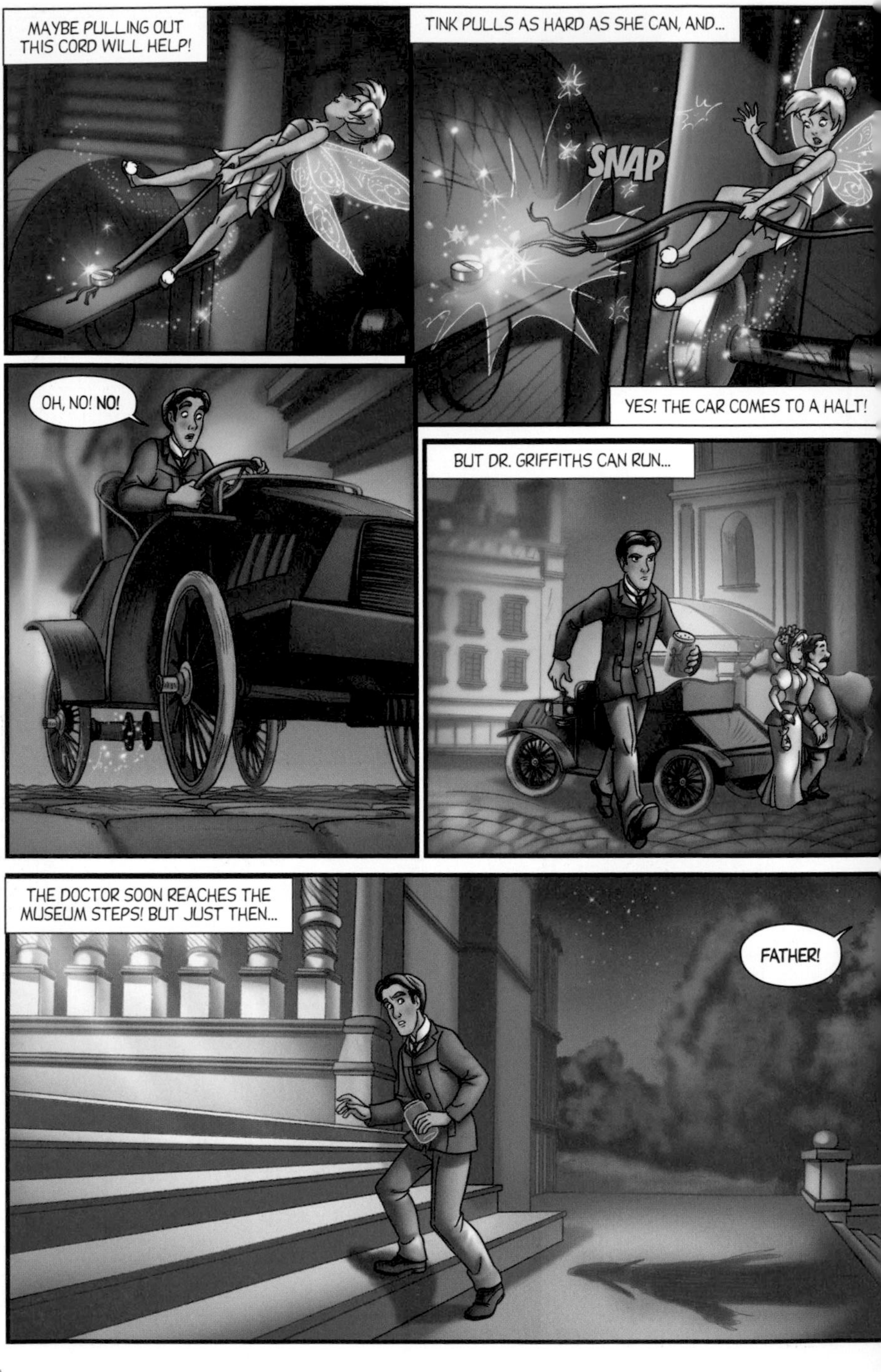
MAYBE PULLING OUT THIS CORD WILL HELP!
TINK PULLS AS HARD AS SHE CAN, AND...
SNAP
YES! THE CAR COMES TO A HALT!
OH, NO! **NO!**
BUT DR. GRIFFITHS CAN RUN...
THE DOCTOR SOON REACHES THE MUSEUM STEPS! BUT JUST THEN...
FATHER!

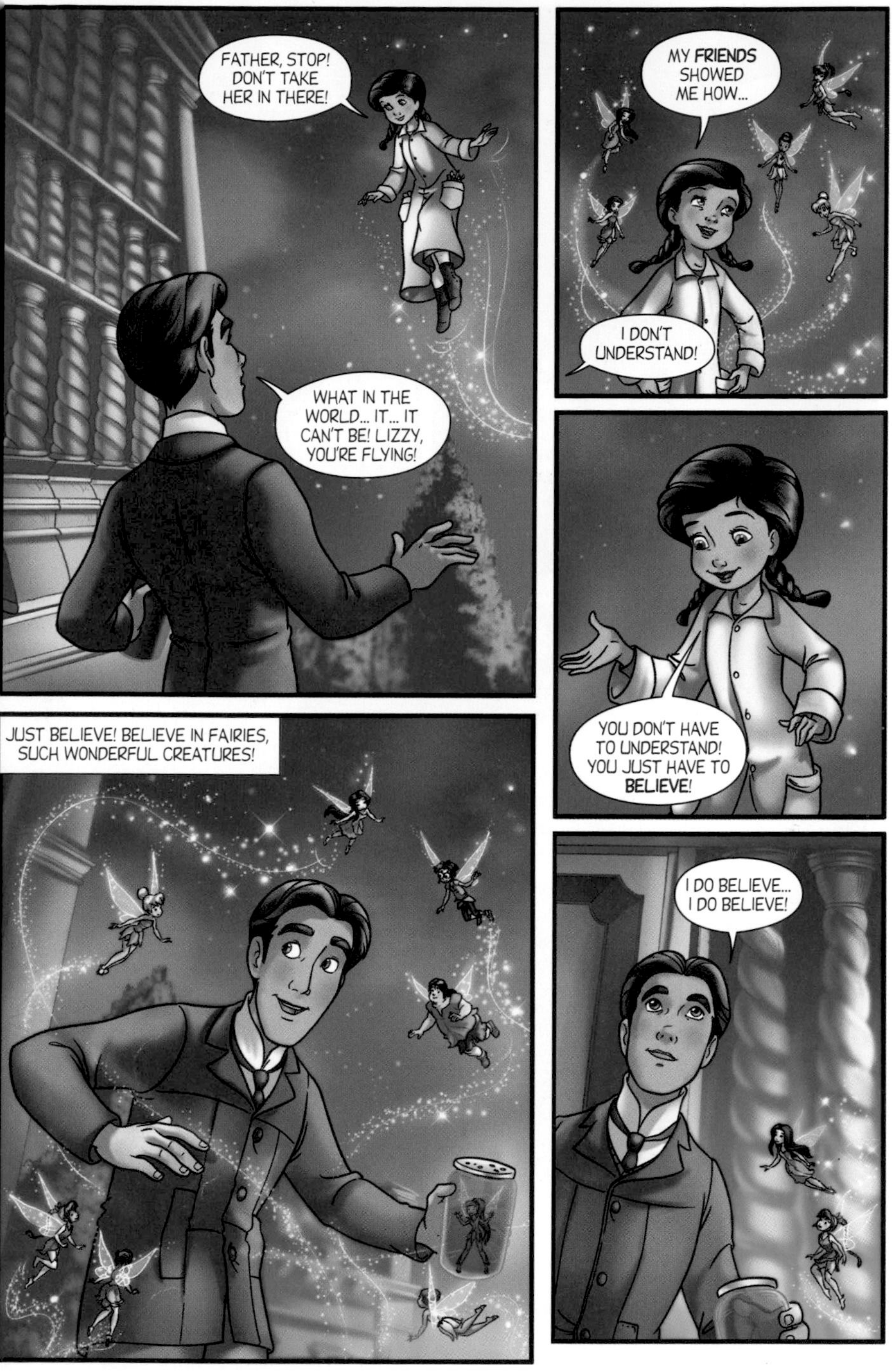
FATHER, STOP! DON'T TAKE HER IN THERE!
WHAT IN THE WORLD... IT... IT CAN'T BE! LIZZY, YOU'RE FLYING!
MY **FRIENDS** SHOWED ME HOW...
I DON'T UNDERSTAND!
YOU DON'T HAVE TO UNDERSTAND! YOU JUST HAVE TO **BELIEVE**!
JUST BELIEVE! BELIEVE IN FAIRIES, SUCH WONDERFUL CREATURES!
I DO BELIEVE... I DO BELIEVE!

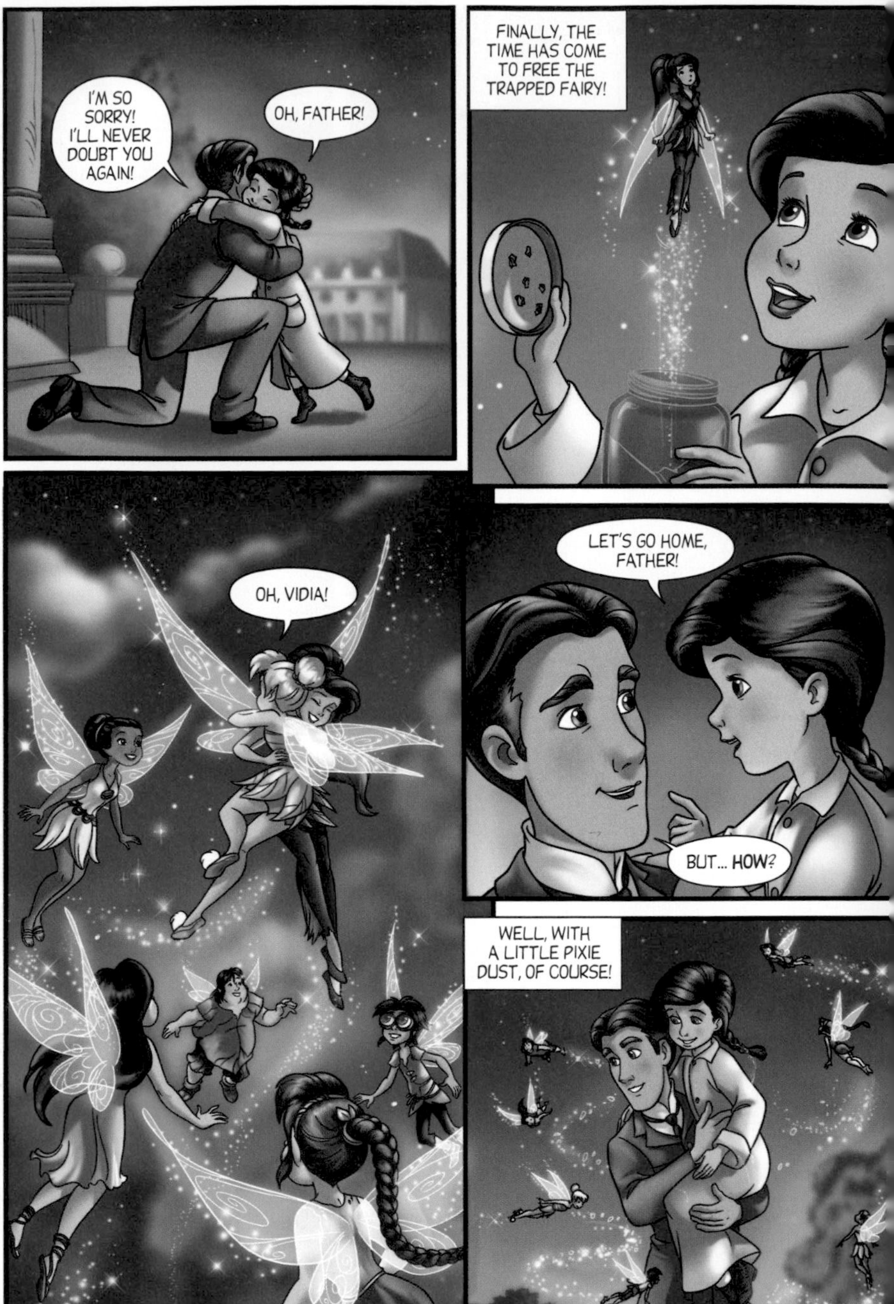
I'M SO SORRY! I'LL NEVER DOUBT YOU AGAIN!
OH, FATHER!
FINALLY, THE TIME HAS COME TO FREE THE TRAPPED FAIRY!
OH, VIDIA!
LET'S GO HOME, FATHER!
BUT... HOW?
WELL, WITH A LITTLE PIXIE DUST, OF COURSE!

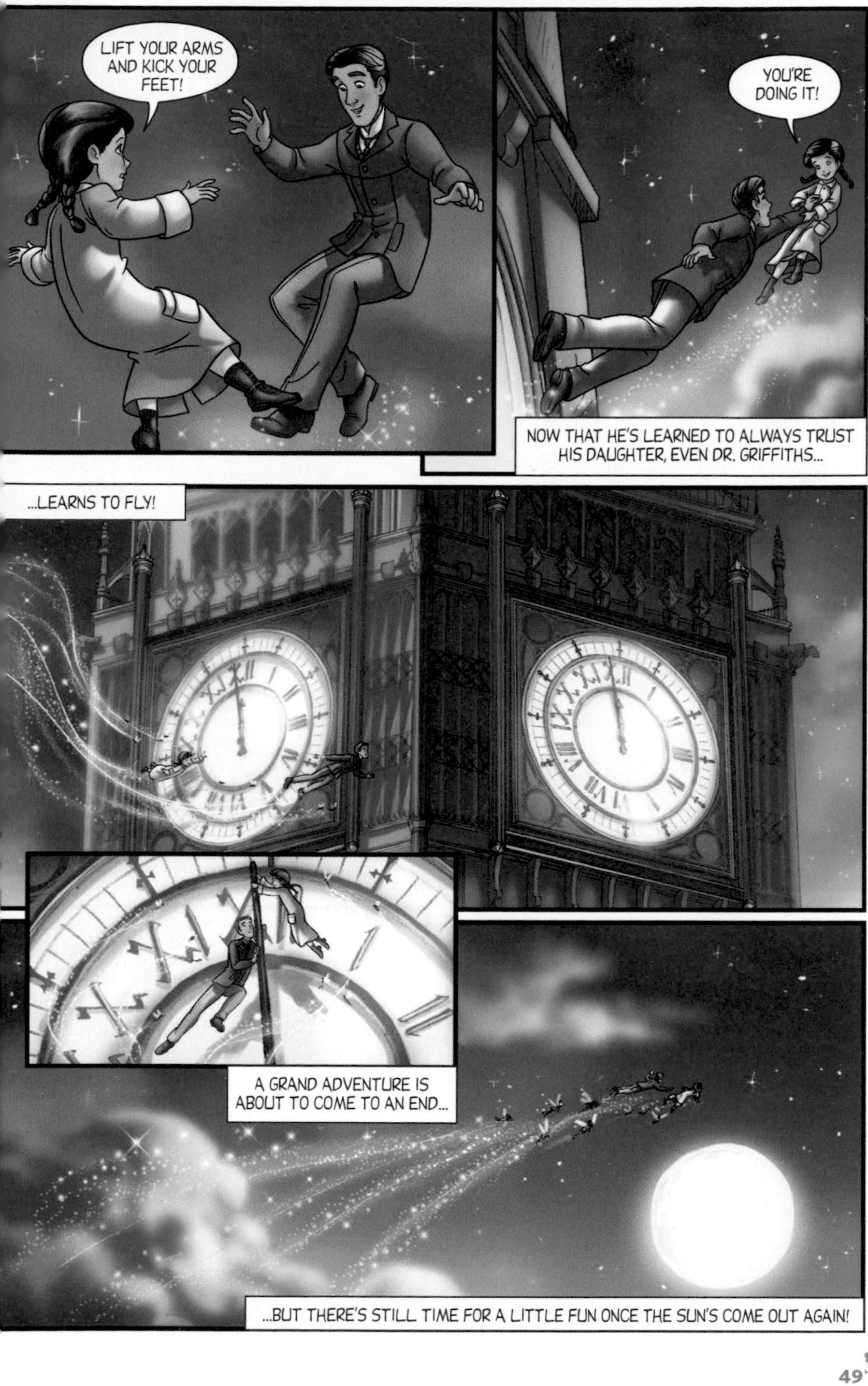
LIFT YOUR ARMS AND KICK YOUR FEET!
YOU'RE DOING IT!
NOW THAT HE'S LEARNED TO ALWAYS TRUST HIS DAUGHTER, EVEN DR. GRIFFITHS...
...LEARNS TO FLY!
A GRAND ADVENTURE IS ABOUT TO COME TO AN END...
...BUT THERE'S STILL TIME FOR A LITTLE FUN ONCE THE SUN'S COME OUT AGAIN!

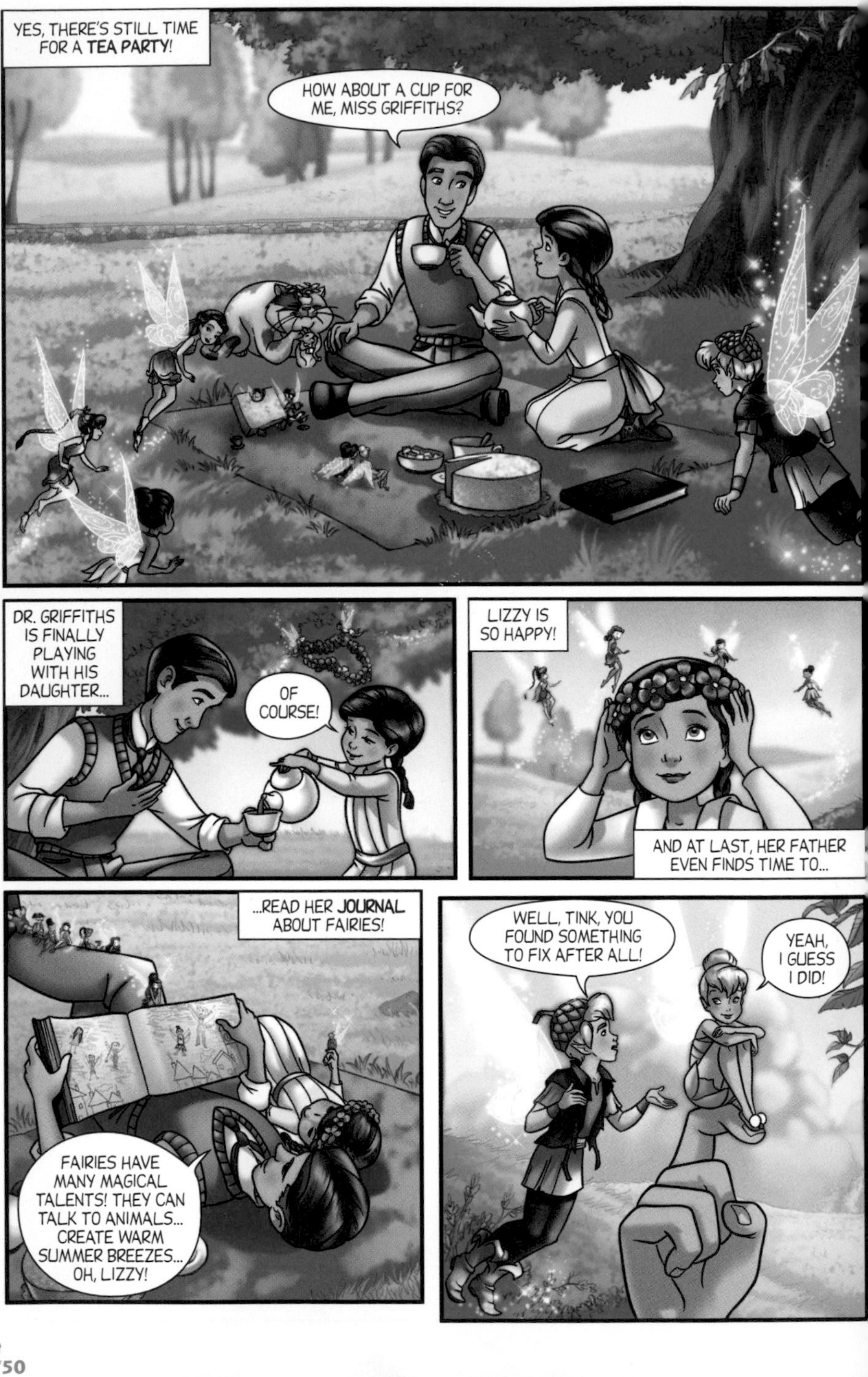
YES, THERE'S STILL TIME FOR A **TEA PARTY**!
HOW ABOUT A CUP FOR ME, MISS GRIFFITHS?
DR. GRIFFITHS IS FINALLY PLAYING WITH HIS DAUGHTER...
OF COURSE!
LIZZY IS SO HAPPY!
AND AT LAST, HER FATHER EVEN FINDS TIME TO...
...READ HER **JOURNAL** ABOUT FAIRIES!
FAIRIES HAVE MANY MAGICAL TALENTS! THEY CAN TALK TO ANIMALS... CREATE WARM SUMMER BREEZES... OH, LIZZY!
WELL, TINK, YOU FOUND SOMETHING TO FIX AFTER ALL!
YEAH, I GUESS I DID!

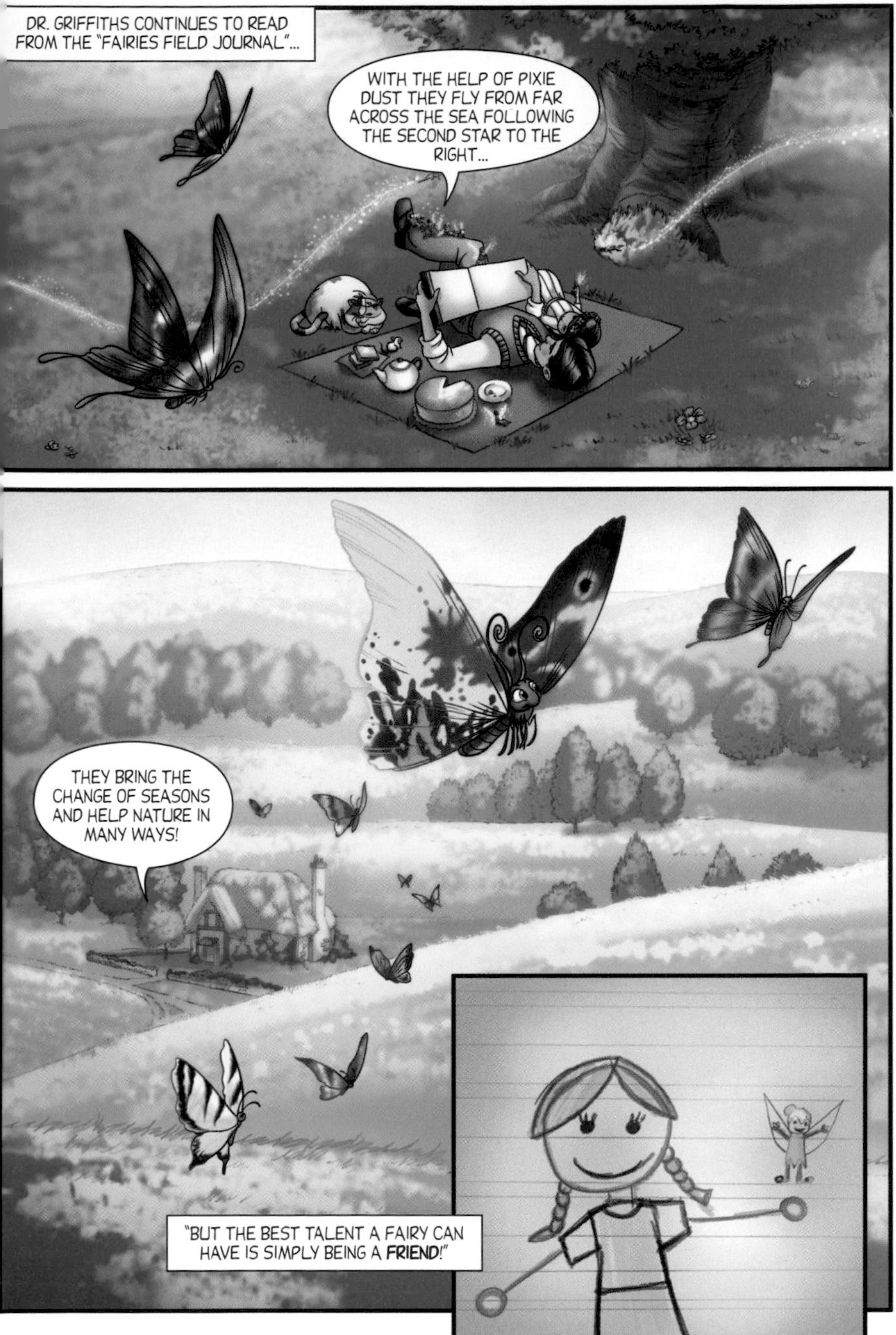
DR. GRIFFITHS CONTINUES TO READ FROM THE "FAIRIES FIELD JOURNAL"...
WITH THE HELP OF PIXIE DUST THEY FLY FROM FAR ACROSS THE SEA FOLLOWING THE SECOND STAR TO THE RIGHT...
THEY BRING THE CHANGE OF SEASONS AND HELP NATURE IN MANY WAYS!
"BUT THE BEST TALENT A FAIRY CAN HAVE IS SIMPLY BEING A **FRIEND**!"

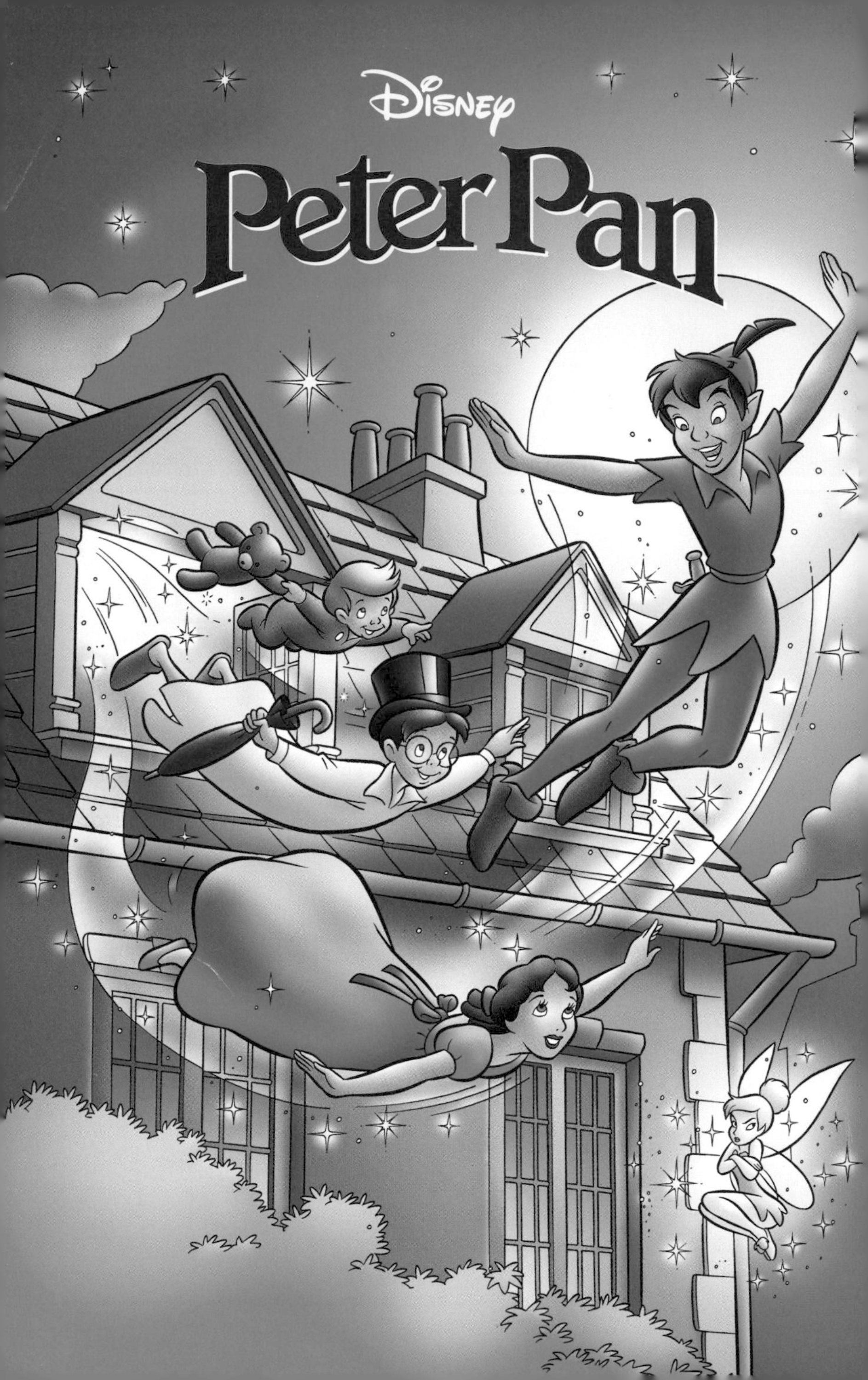
Disney
Peter Pan

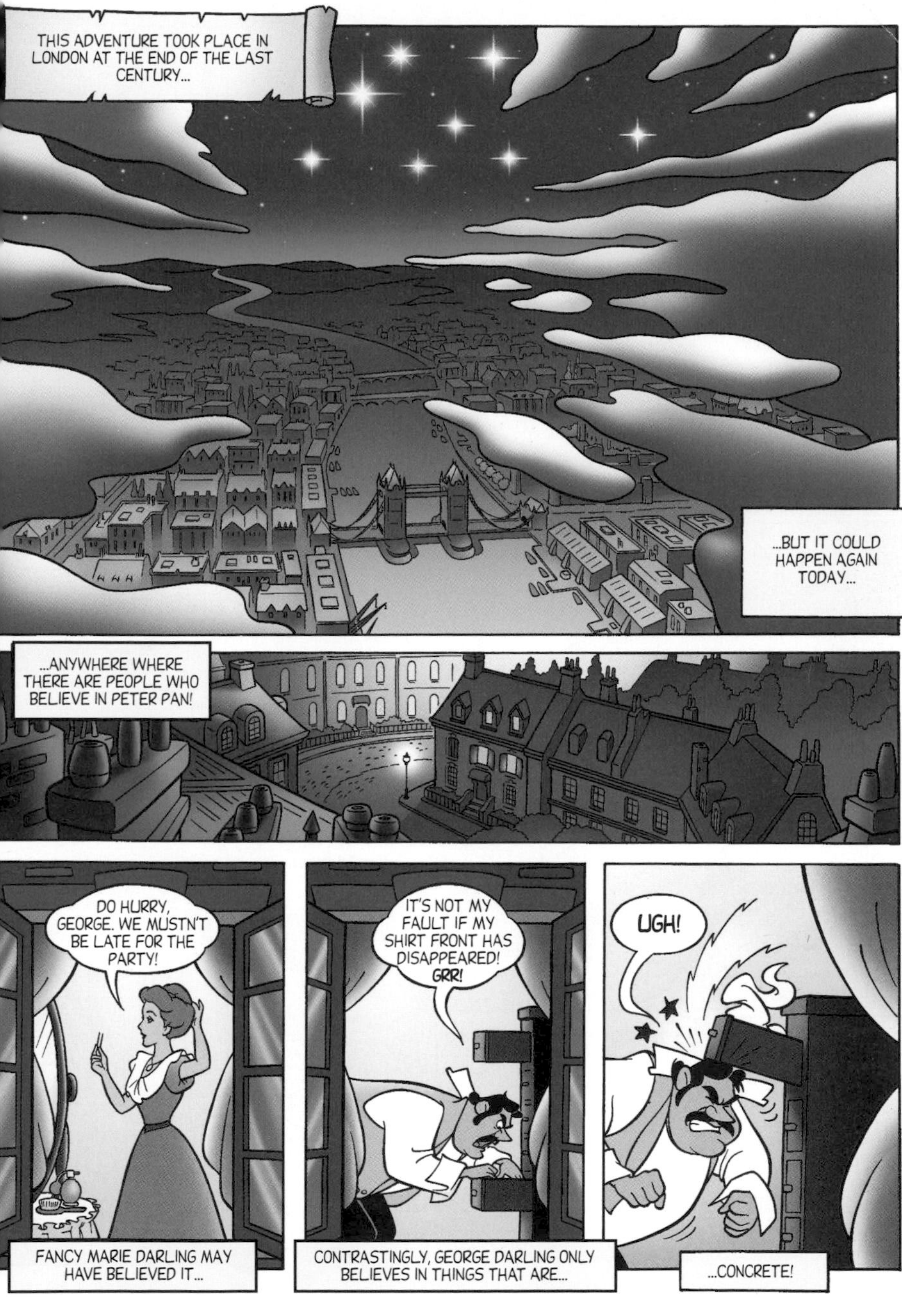
THIS ADVENTURE TOOK PLACE IN LONDON AT THE END OF THE LAST CENTURY...
...BUT IT COULD HAPPEN AGAIN TODAY...
...ANYWHERE WHERE THERE ARE PEOPLE WHO BELIEVE IN PETER PAN!
DO HURRY, GEORGE. WE MUSTN'T BE LATE FOR THE PARTY!
FANCY MARIE DARLING MAY HAVE BELIEVED IT...
IT'S NOT MY FAULT IF MY SHIRT FRONT HAS DISAPPEARED! GRR!
CONTRASTINGLY, GEORGE DARLING ONLY BELIEVES IN THINGS THAT ARE...
UGH!
...CONCRETE!

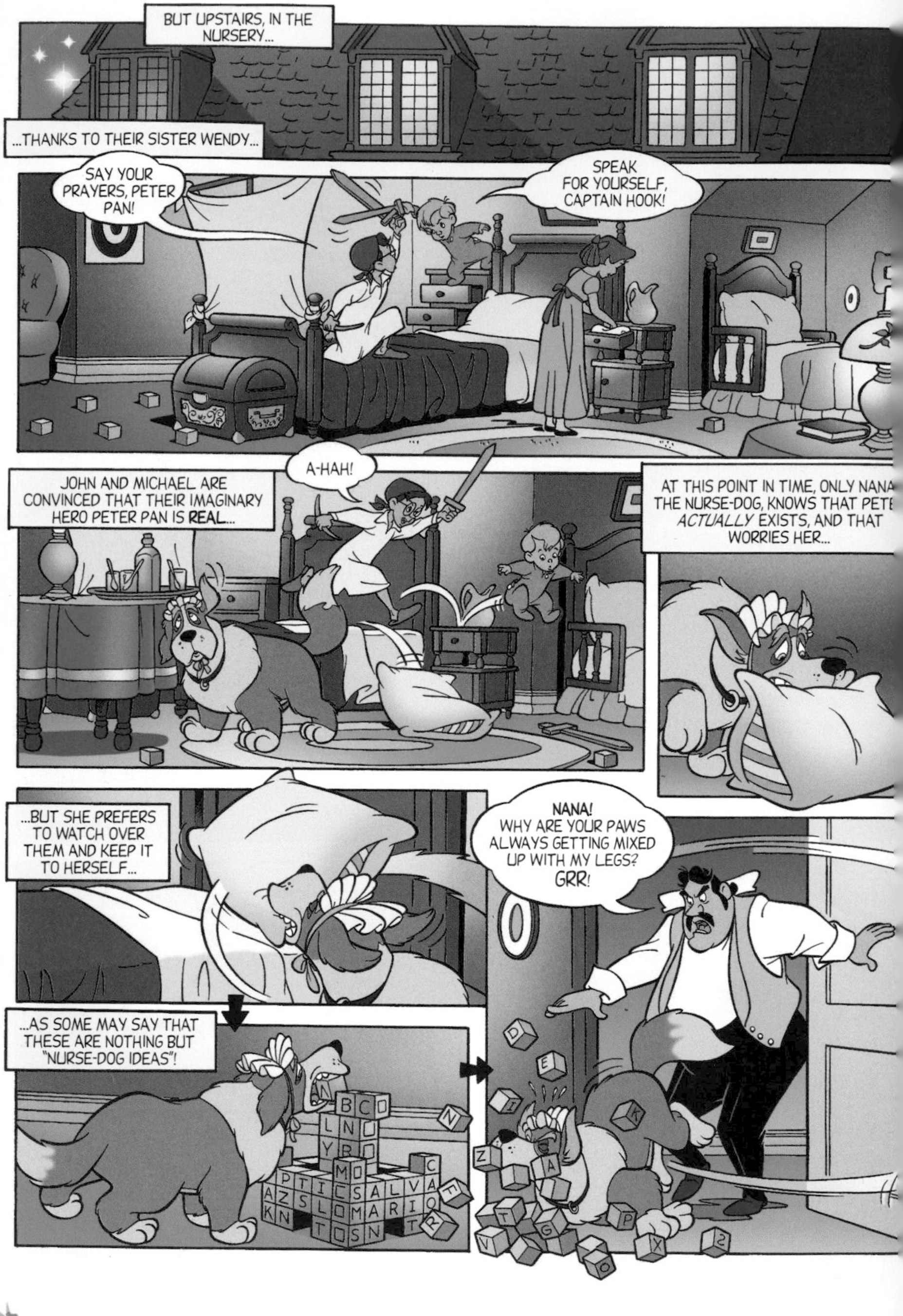

BUT UPSTAIRS, IN THE NURSERY...
...THANKS TO THEIR SISTER WENDY...
SAY YOUR PRAYERS, PETER PAN!
SPEAK FOR YOURSELF, CAPTAIN HOOK!
JOHN AND MICHAEL ARE CONVINCED THAT THEIR IMAGINARY HERO PETER PAN IS **REAL**...
A-HAH!
AT THIS POINT IN TIME, ONLY NANA THE NURSE-DOG, KNOWS THAT PETE *ACTUALLY* EXISTS, AND THAT WORRIES HER...
...BUT SHE PREFERS TO WATCH OVER THEM AND KEEP IT TO HERSELF...
NANA! WHY ARE YOUR PAWS ALWAYS GETTING MIXED UP WITH MY LEGS? GRR!
...AS SOME MAY SAY THAT THESE ARE NOTHING BUT "NURSE-DOG IDEAS"!

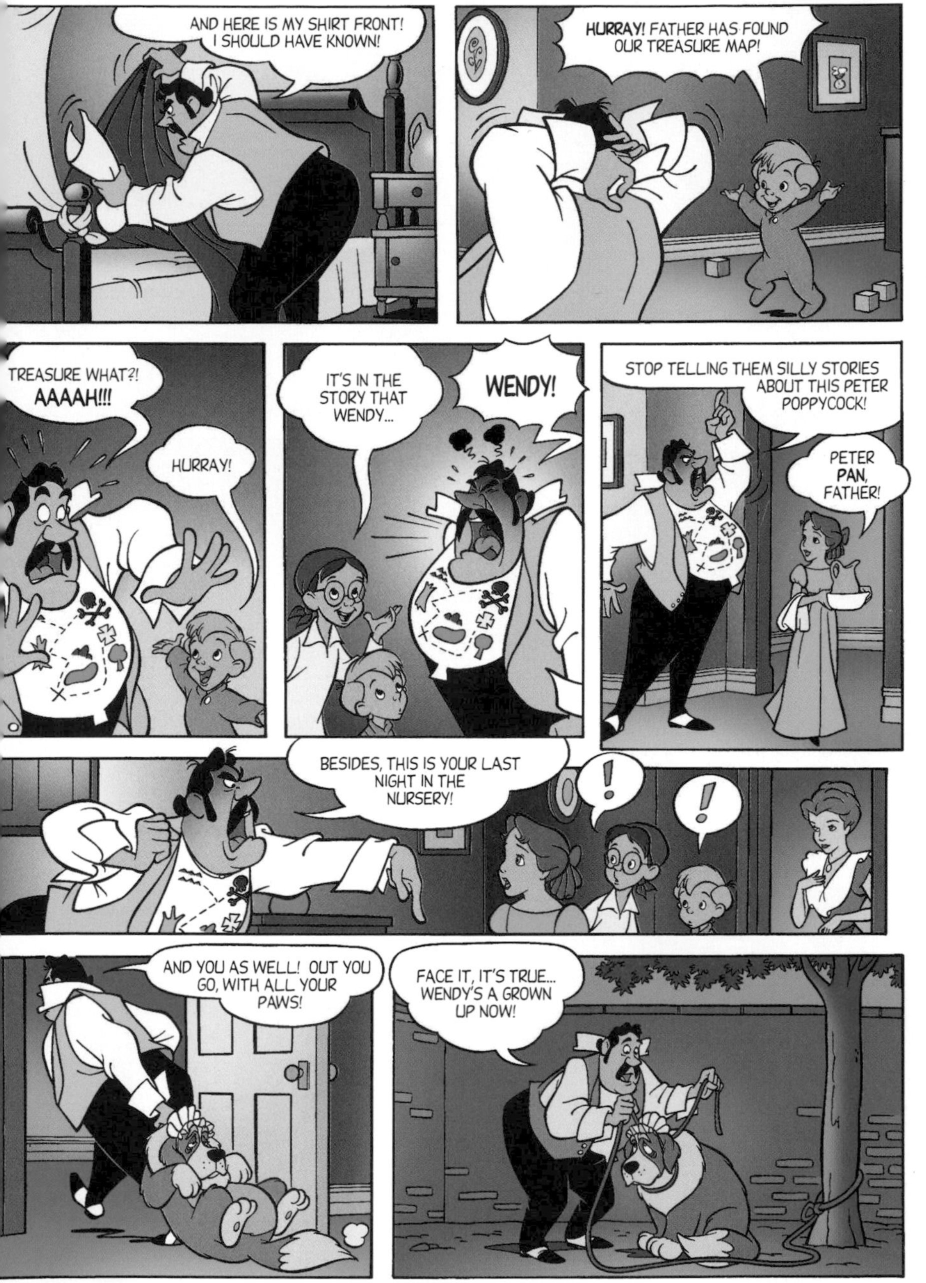
AND HERE IS MY SHIRT FRONT! I SHOULD HAVE KNOWN!
HURRAY! FATHER HAS FOUND OUR TREASURE MAP!
TREASURE WHAT?! AAAAH!!!
HURRAY!
IT'S IN THE STORY THAT WENDY...
WENDY!
STOP TELLING THEM SILLY STORIES ABOUT THIS PETER POPPYCOCK!
PETER PAN, FATHER!
BESIDES, THIS IS YOUR LAST NIGHT IN THE NURSERY!
!
!
AND YOU AS WELL! OUT YOU GO, WITH ALL YOUR PAWS!
FACE IT, IT'S TRUE... WENDY'S A GROWN UP NOW!

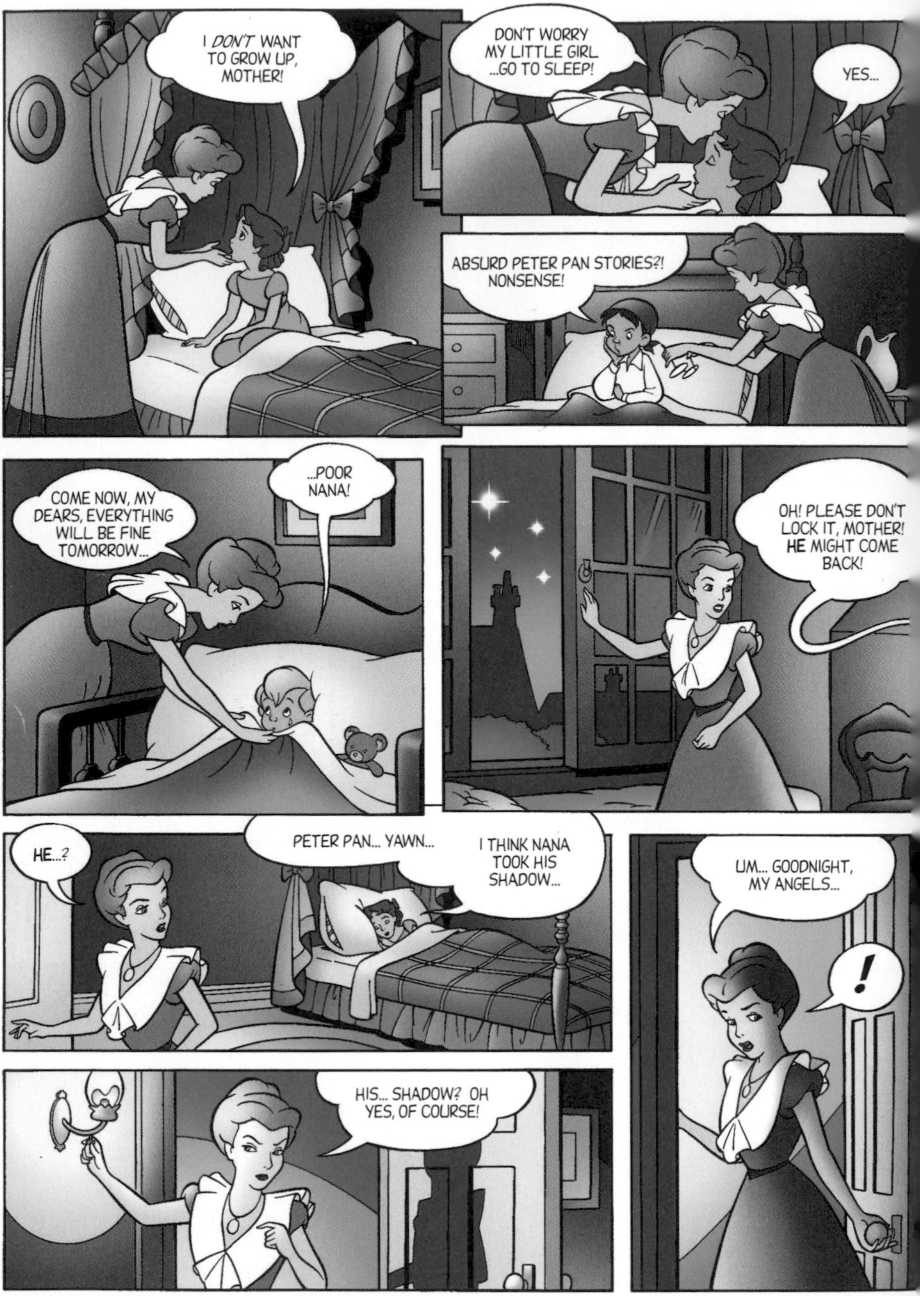
I *DON'T* WANT TO GROW UP, MOTHER!
DON'T WORRY MY LITTLE GIRL ...GO TO SLEEP!
YES...
ABSURD PETER PAN STORIES?! NONSENSE!
COME NOW, MY DEARS, EVERYTHING WILL BE FINE TOMORROW...
...POOR NANA!
OH! PLEASE DON'T LOCK IT, MOTHER! **HE** MIGHT COME BACK!
HE...?
PETER PAN... YAWN...
I THINK NANA TOOK HIS SHADOW...
UM... GOODNIGHT, MY ANGELS...
!
HIS... SHADOW? OH YES, OF COURSE!

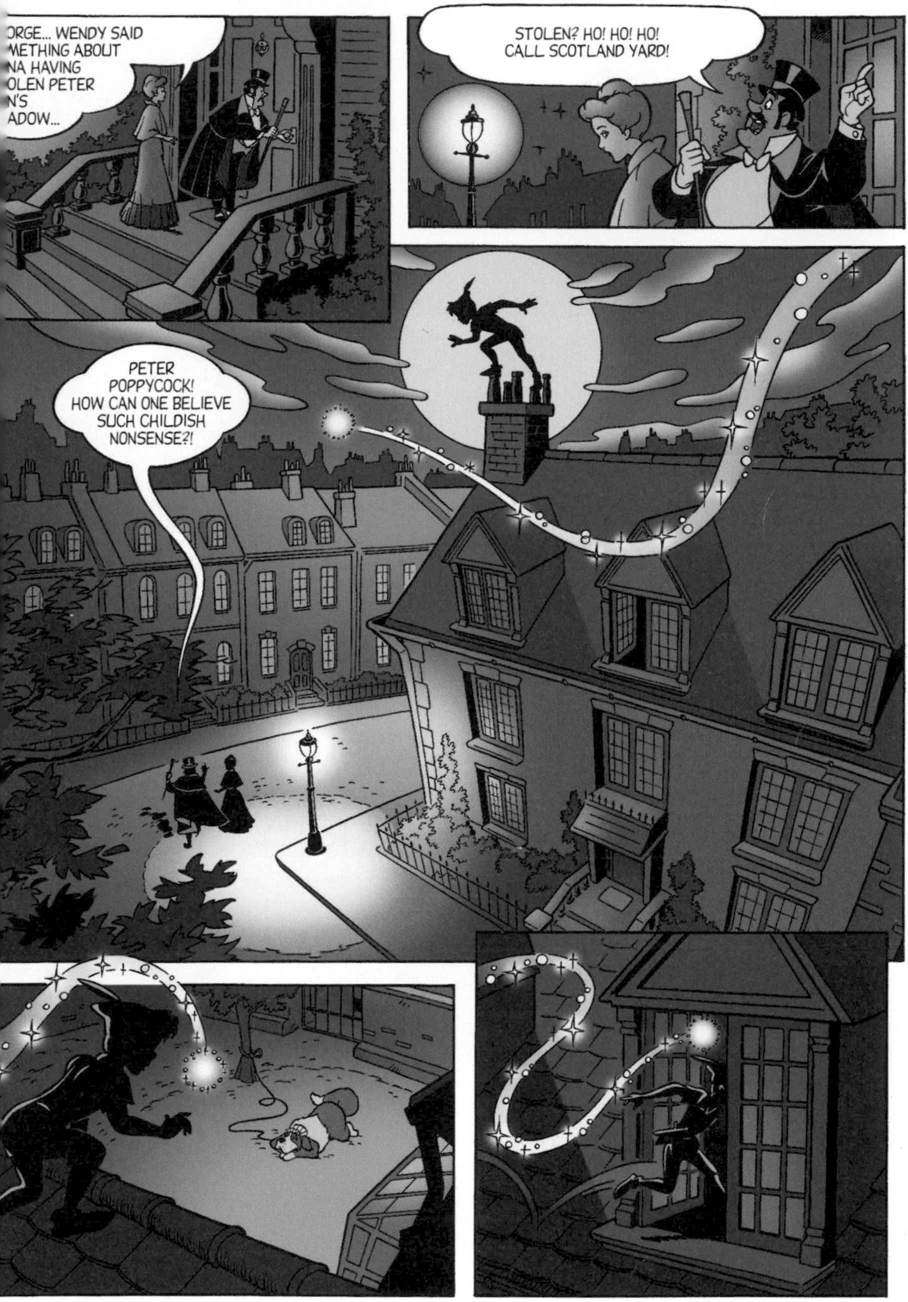
ORGE... WENDY SAID
METHING ABOUT
NA HAVING
OLEN PETER
N'S
ADOW...
STOLEN? HO! HO! HO!
CALL SCOTLAND YARD!
PETER
POPPYCOCK!
HOW CAN ONE BELIEVE
SUCH CHILDISH
NONSENSE?!

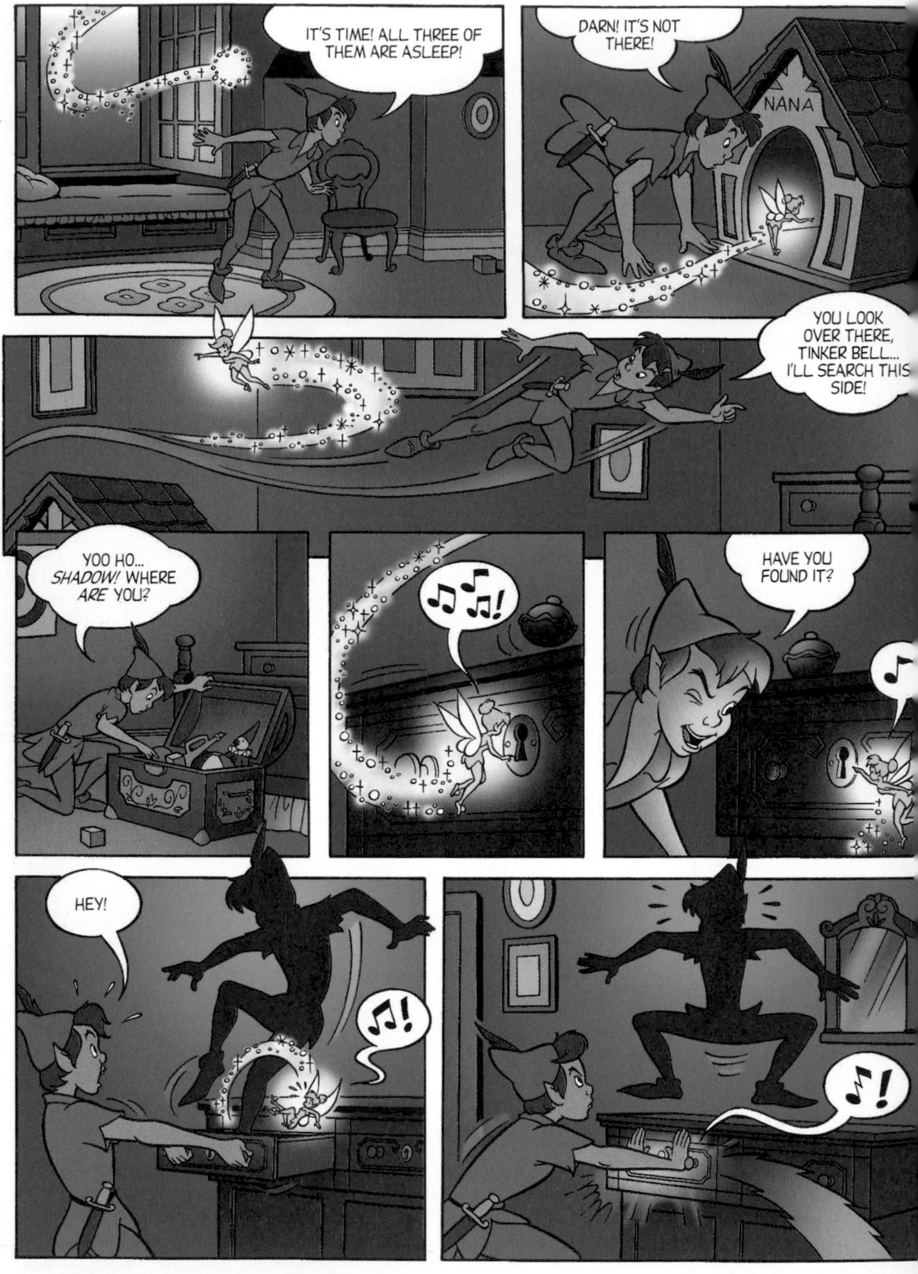
IT'S TIME! ALL THREE OF THEM ARE ASLEEP!
DARN! IT'S NOT THERE!
NANA
YOU LOOK OVER THERE, TINKER BELL... I'LL SEARCH THIS SIDE!
YOO HO... SHADOW! WHERE ARE YOU?
♫ ♫!
HAVE YOU FOUND IT?
♪
HEY!
♫!
♫!

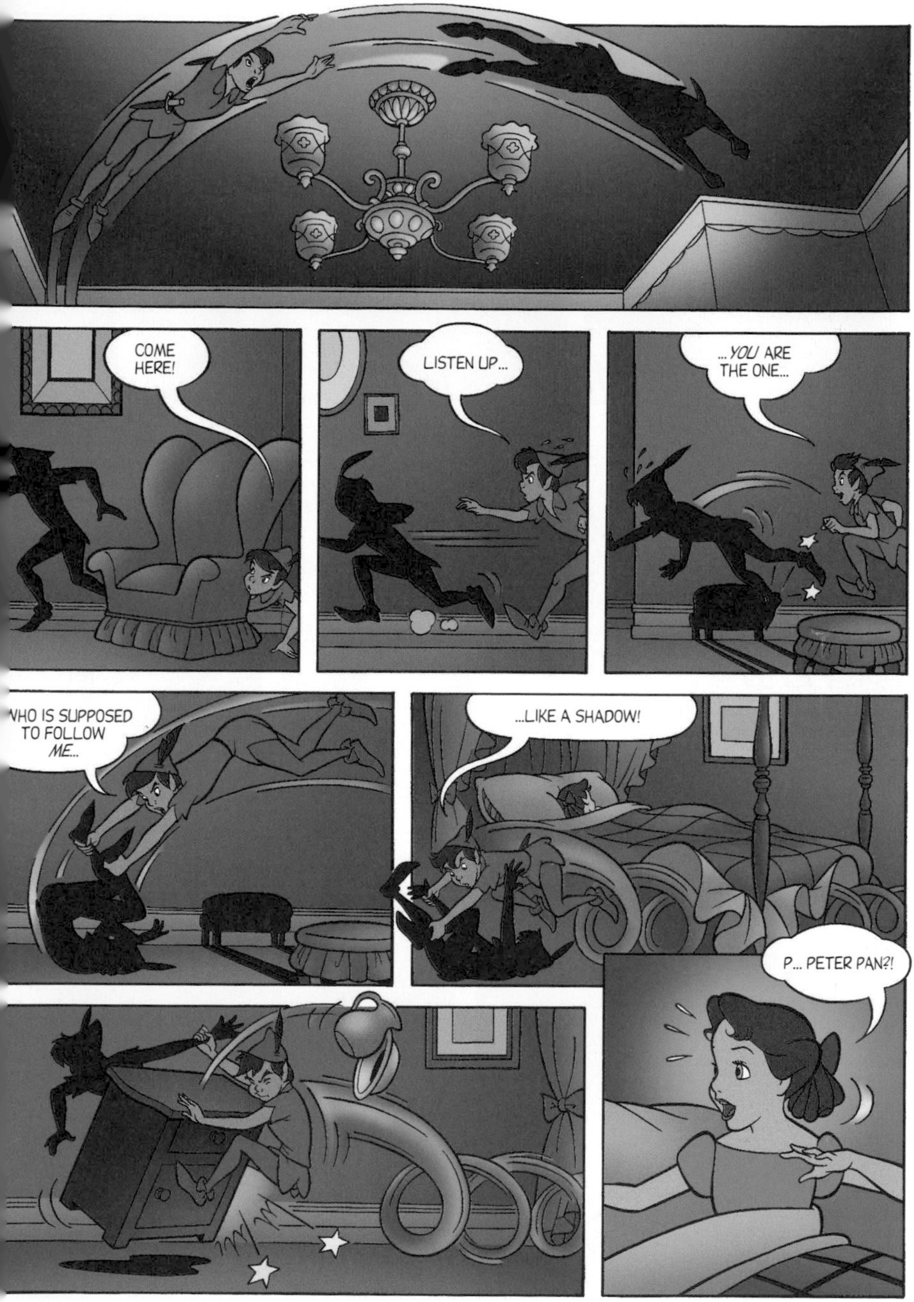
COME HERE!
LISTEN UP...
...*YOU* ARE THE ONE...
WHO IS SUPPOSED TO FOLLOW *ME*...
...LIKE A SHADOW!
P... PETER PAN?!

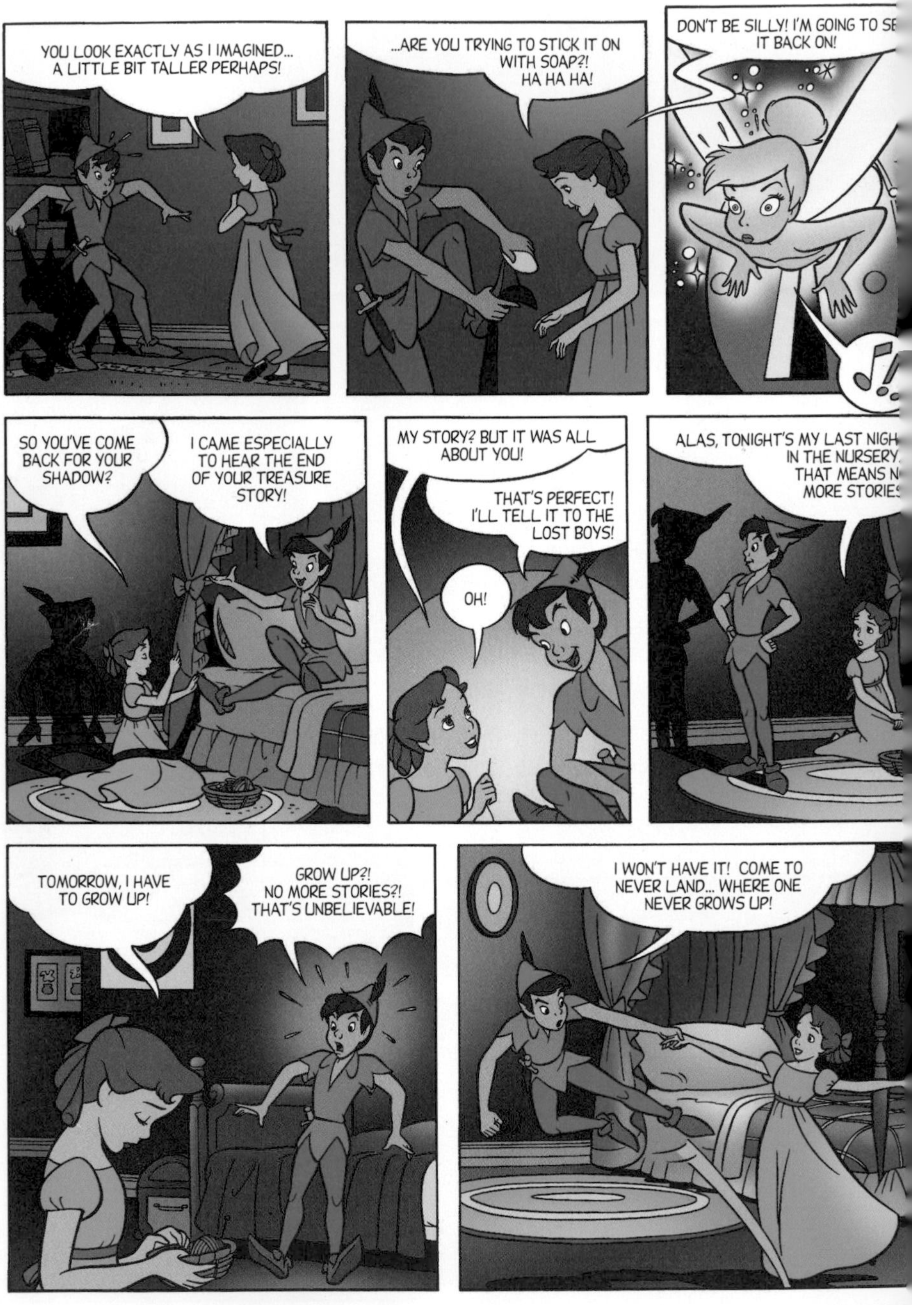
YOU LOOK EXACTLY AS I IMAGINED... A LITTLE BIT TALLER PERHAPS!
...ARE YOU TRYING TO STICK IT ON WITH SOAP?! HA HA HA!
DON'T BE SILLY! I'M GOING TO SE IT BACK ON!
SO YOU'VE COME BACK FOR YOUR SHADOW?
I CAME ESPECIALLY TO HEAR THE END OF YOUR TREASURE STORY!
MY STORY? BUT IT WAS ALL ABOUT YOU!
THAT'S PERFECT! I'LL TELL IT TO THE LOST BOYS!
OH!
ALAS, TONIGHT'S MY LAST NIGH IN THE NURSERY THAT MEANS N MORE STORIE
TOMORROW, I HAVE TO GROW UP!
GROW UP?! NO MORE STORIES?! THAT'S UNBELIEVABLE!
I WON'T HAVE IT! COME TO NEVER LAND... WHERE ONE NEVER GROWS UP!

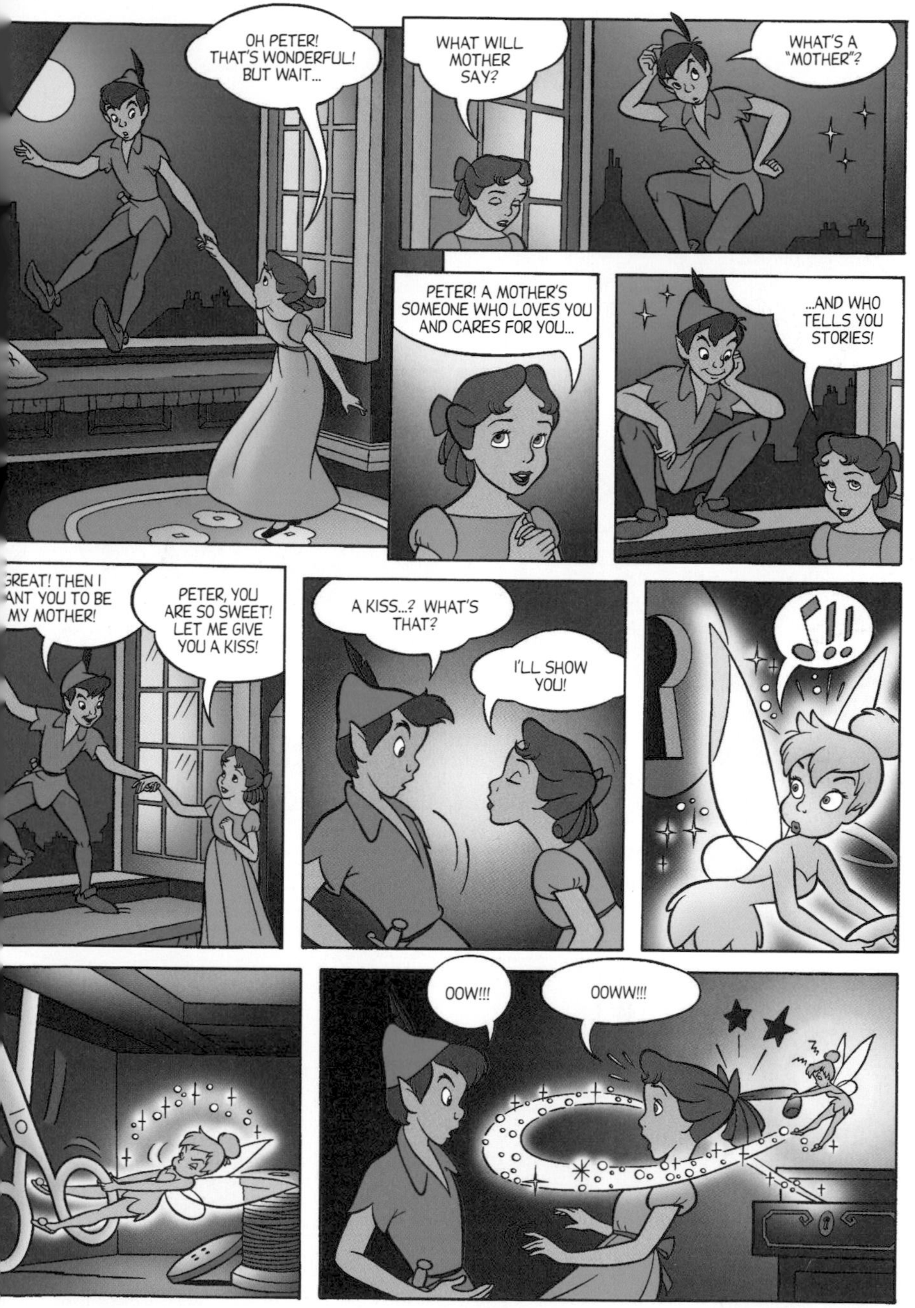
OH PETER! THAT'S WONDERFUL! BUT WAIT...
WHAT WILL MOTHER SAY?
WHAT'S A "MOTHER"?
PETER! A MOTHER'S SOMEONE WHO LOVES YOU AND CARES FOR YOU...
...AND WHO TELLS YOU STORIES!
GREAT! THEN I
ANT YOU TO BE MY MOTHER!
PETER, YOU ARE SO SWEET! LET ME GIVE YOU A KISS!
A KISS...? WHAT'S THAT?
I'LL SHOW YOU!
!!
OOW!!!
OOWW!!!

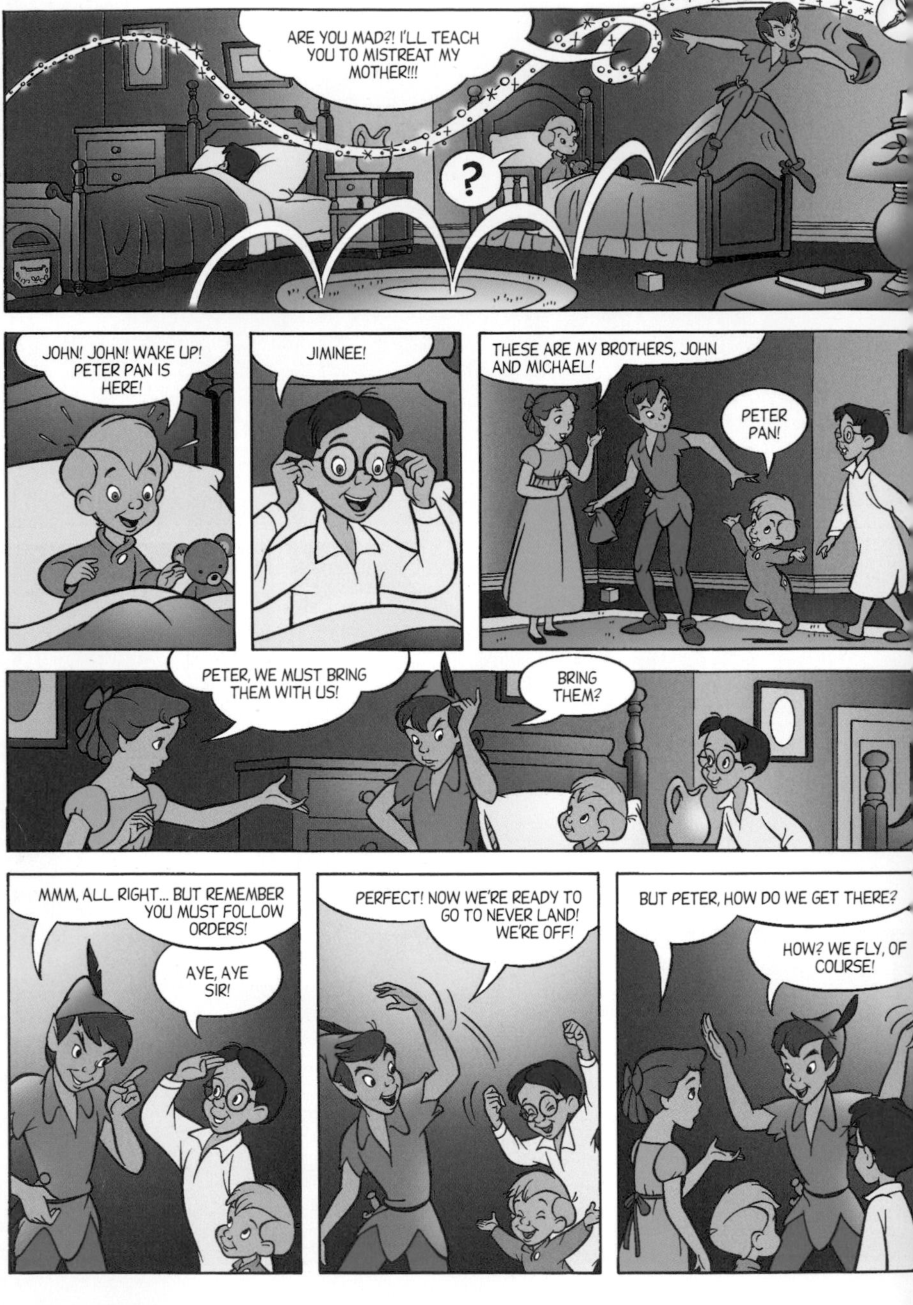

ARE YOU MAD?! I'LL TEACH YOU TO MISTREAT MY MOTHER!!!
?
JOHN! JOHN! WAKE UP! PETER PAN IS HERE!
JIMINEE!
THESE ARE MY BROTHERS, JOHN AND MICHAEL!
PETER PAN!
PETER, WE MUST BRING THEM WITH US!
BRING THEM?
MMM, ALL RIGHT... BUT REMEMBER YOU MUST FOLLOW ORDERS!
AYE, AYE SIR!
PERFECT! NOW WE'RE READY TO GO TO NEVER LAND! WE'RE OFF!
BUT PETER, HOW DO WE GET THERE?
HOW? WE FLY, OF COURSE!

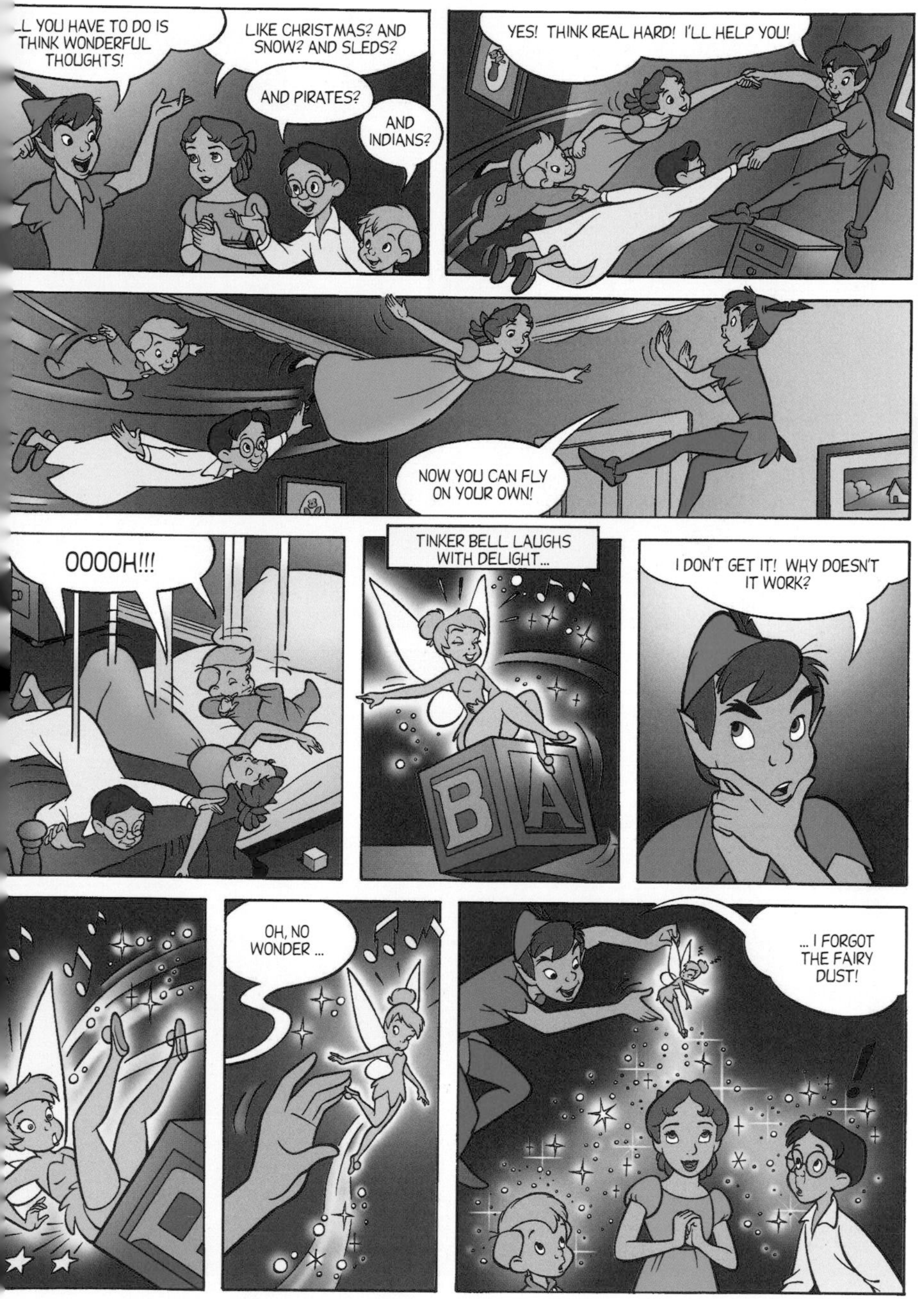

...LL YOU HAVE TO DO IS THINK WONDERFUL THOUGHTS!
LIKE CHRISTMAS? AND SNOW? AND SLEDS?
AND PIRATES?
AND INDIANS?
YES! THINK REAL HARD! I'LL HELP YOU!
NOW YOU CAN FLY ON YOUR OWN!
OOOOH!!!
TINKER BELL LAUGHS WITH DELIGHT...
I DON'T GET IT! WHY DOESN'T IT WORK?
OH, NO WONDER ...
... I FORGOT THE FAIRY DUST!

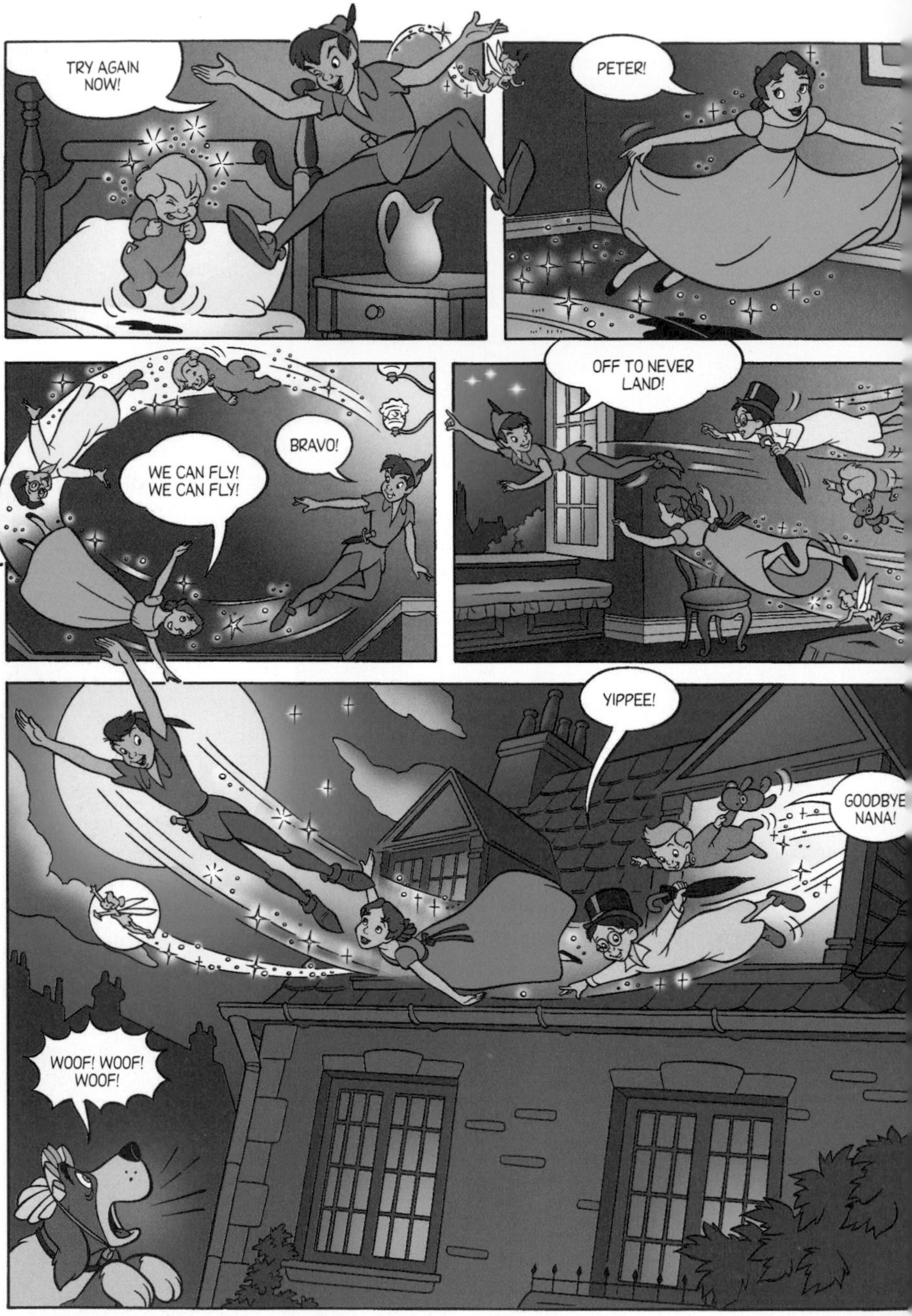
TRY AGAIN NOW!
PETER!
WE CAN FLY! WE CAN FLY!
BRAVO!
OFF TO NEVER LAND!
YIPPEE!
GOODBYE NANA!
WOOF! WOOF! WOOF!

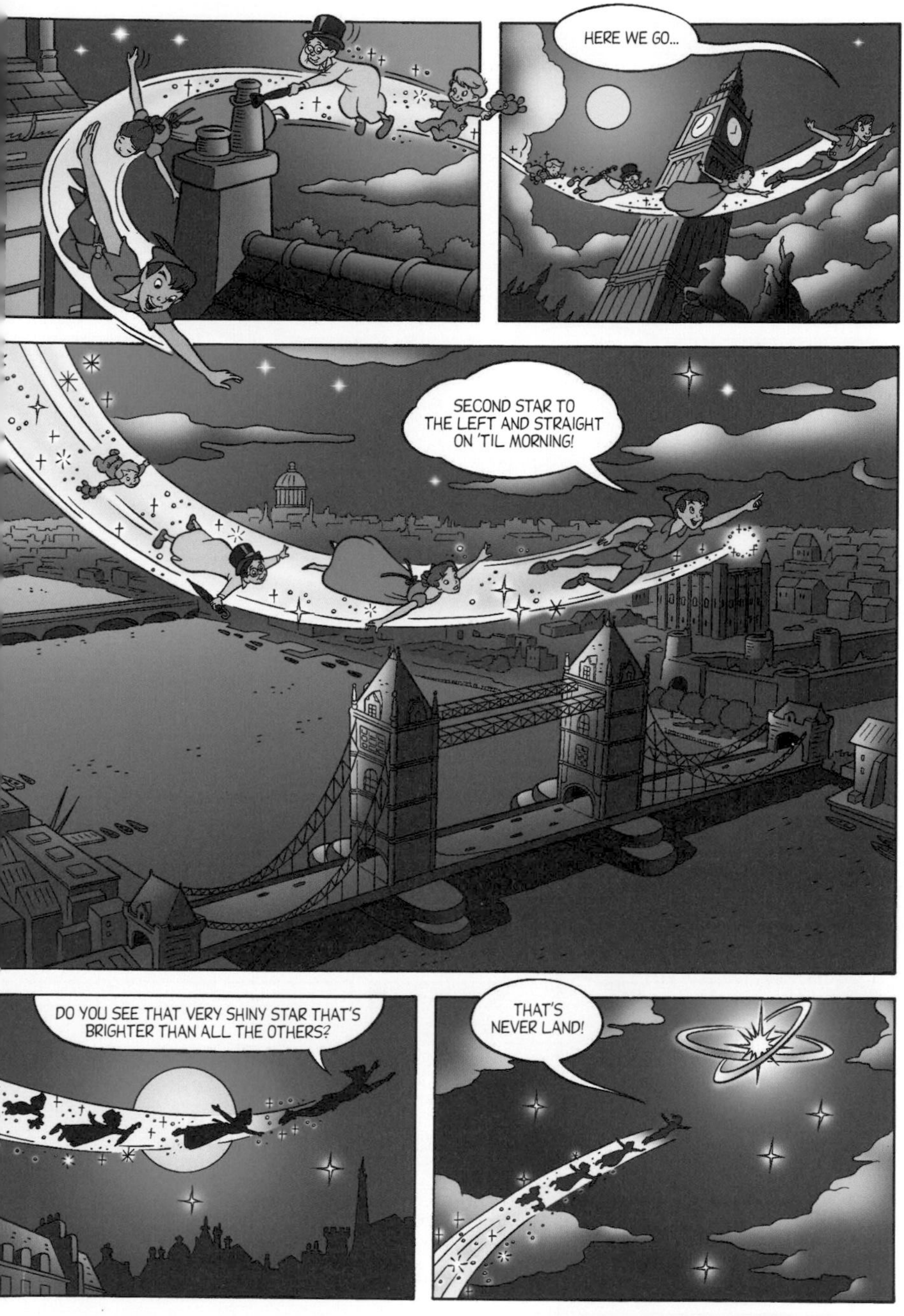
HERE WE GO...
SECOND STAR TO THE LEFT AND STRAIGHT ON 'TIL MORNING!
DO YOU SEE THAT VERY SHINY STAR THAT'S BRIGHTER THAN ALL THE OTHERS?
THAT'S NEVER LAND!

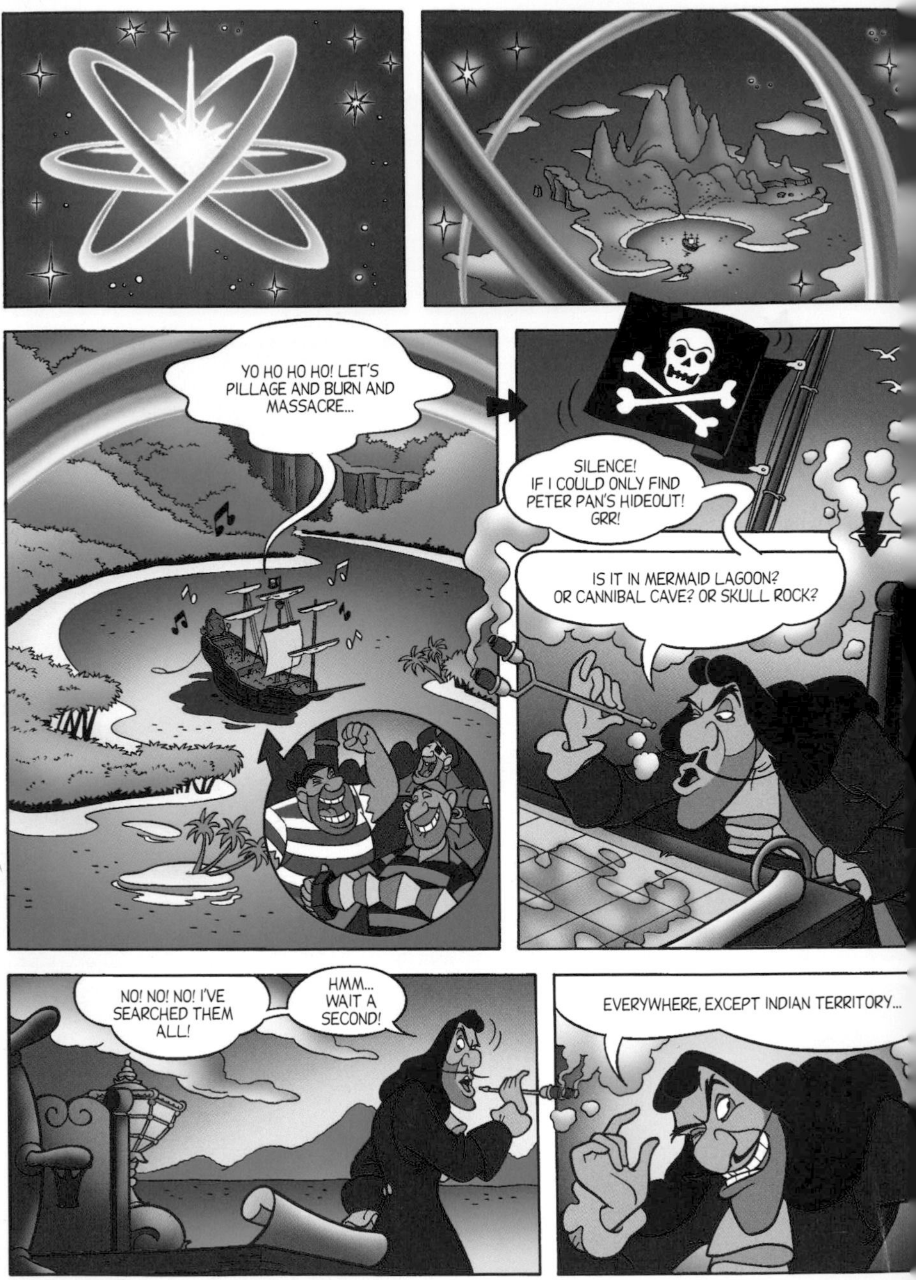
YO HO HO HO! LET'S PILLAGE AND BURN AND MASSACRE...
SILENCE! IF I COULD ONLY FIND PETER PAN'S HIDEOUT! GRR!
IS IT IN MERMAID LAGOON? OR CANNIBAL CAVE? OR SKULL ROCK?
NO! NO! NO! I'VE SEARCHED THEM ALL!
HMM... WAIT A SECOND!
EVERYWHERE, EXCEPT INDIAN TERRITORY...

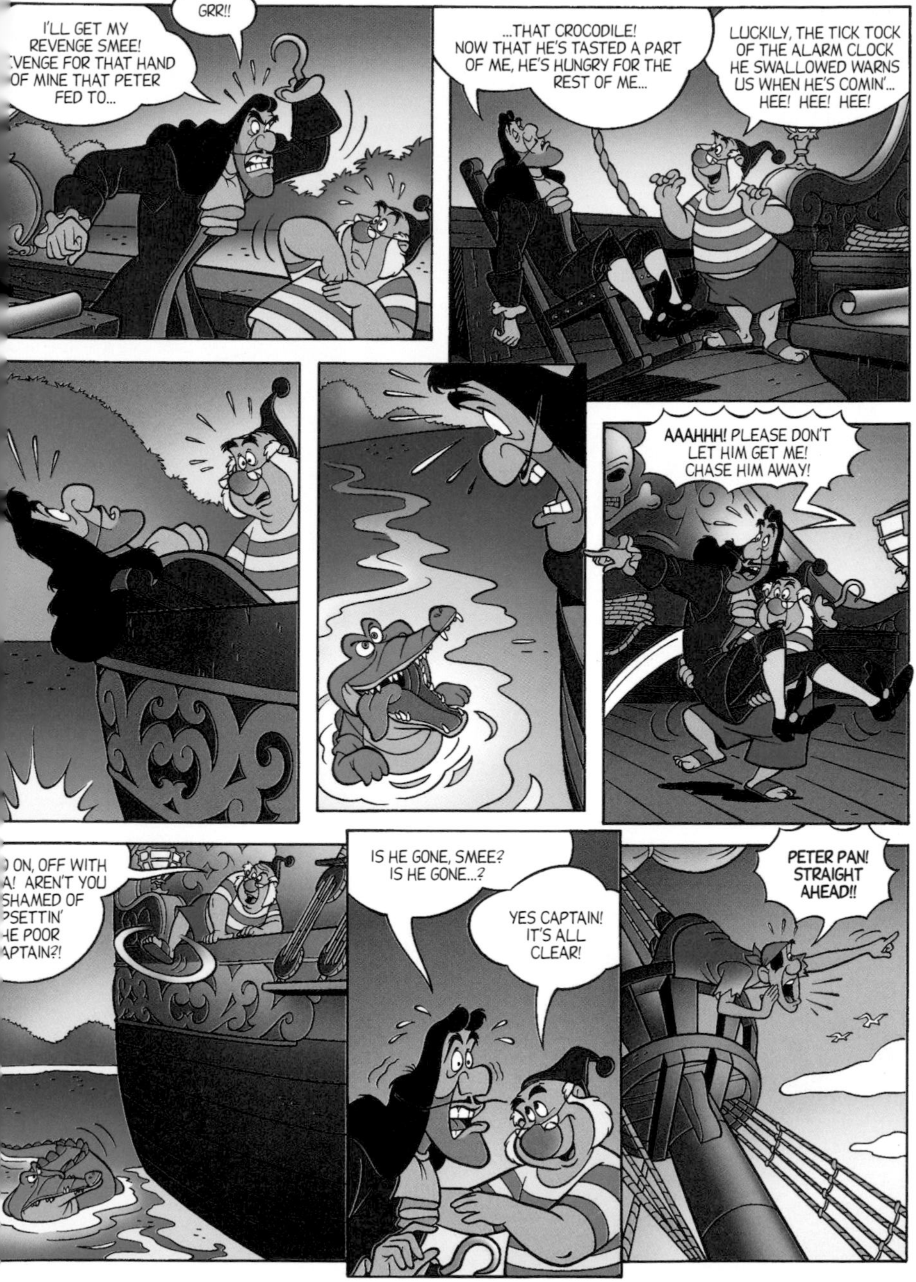
I'LL GET MY REVENGE SMEE! EVENGE FOR THAT HAND OF MINE THAT PETER FED TO...
GRR!!
...THAT CROCODILE! NOW THAT HE'S TASTED A PART OF ME, HE'S HUNGRY FOR THE REST OF ME...
LUCKILY, THE TICK TOCK OF THE ALARM CLOCK HE SWALLOWED WARNS US WHEN HE'S COMIN'... HEE! HEE! HEE!
AAAHHH! PLEASE DON'T LET HIM GET ME! CHASE HIM AWAY!
ON, OFF WITH A! AREN'T YOU SHAMED OF PSETTIN' HE POOR APTAIN?!
IS HE GONE, SMEE? IS HE GONE...?
YES CAPTAIN! IT'S ALL CLEAR!
PETER PAN! STRAIGHT AHEAD!!

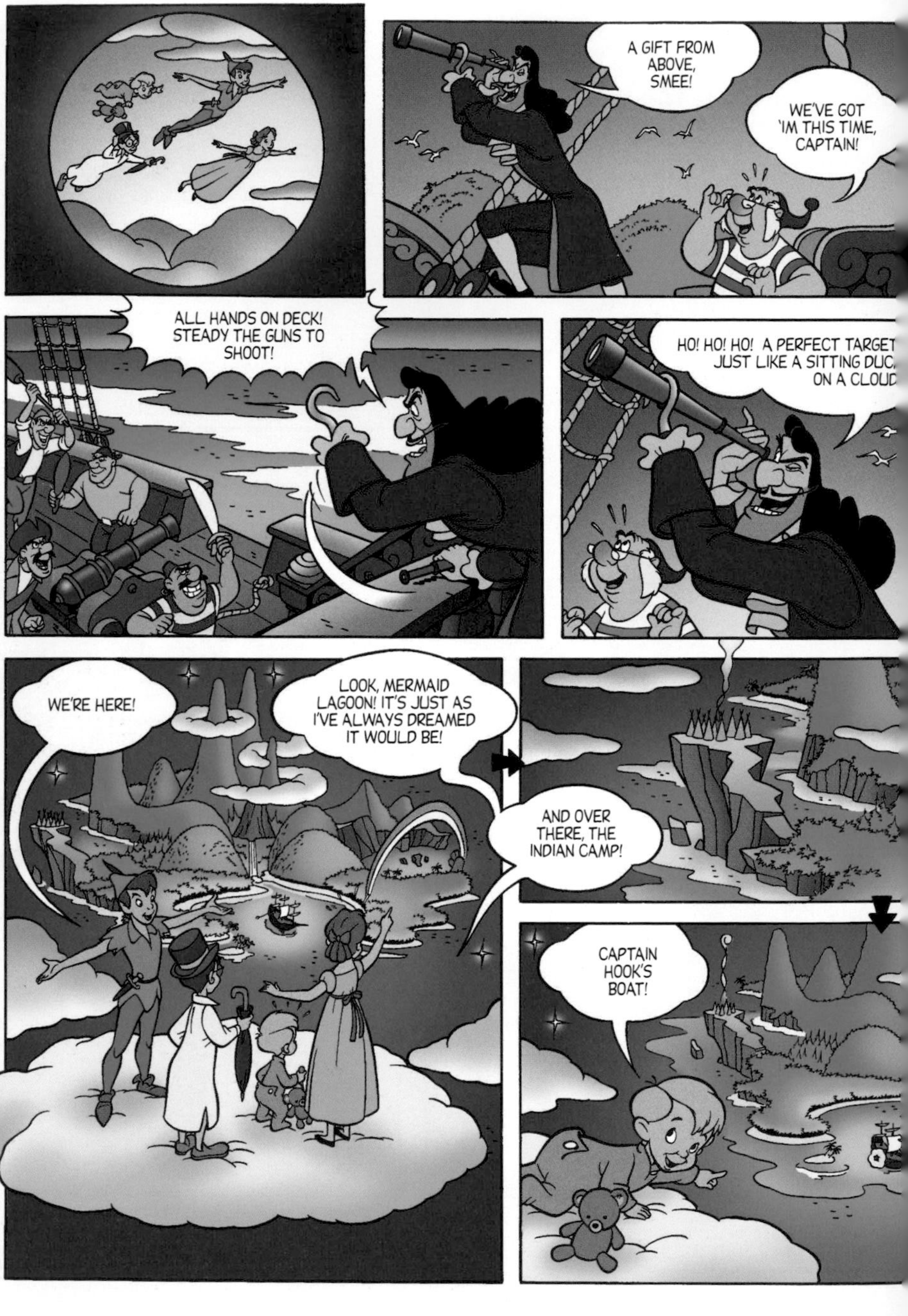

A GIFT FROM ABOVE, SMEE!
WE'VE GOT 'IM THIS TIME, CAPTAIN!
ALL HANDS ON DECK! STEADY THE GUNS TO SHOOT!
HO! HO! HO! A PERFECT TARGET JUST LIKE A SITTING DUC ON A CLOUD
WE'RE HERE!
LOOK, MERMAID LAGOON! IT'S JUST AS I'VE ALWAYS DREAMED IT WOULD BE!
AND OVER THERE, THE INDIAN CAMP!
CAPTAIN HOOK'S BOAT!

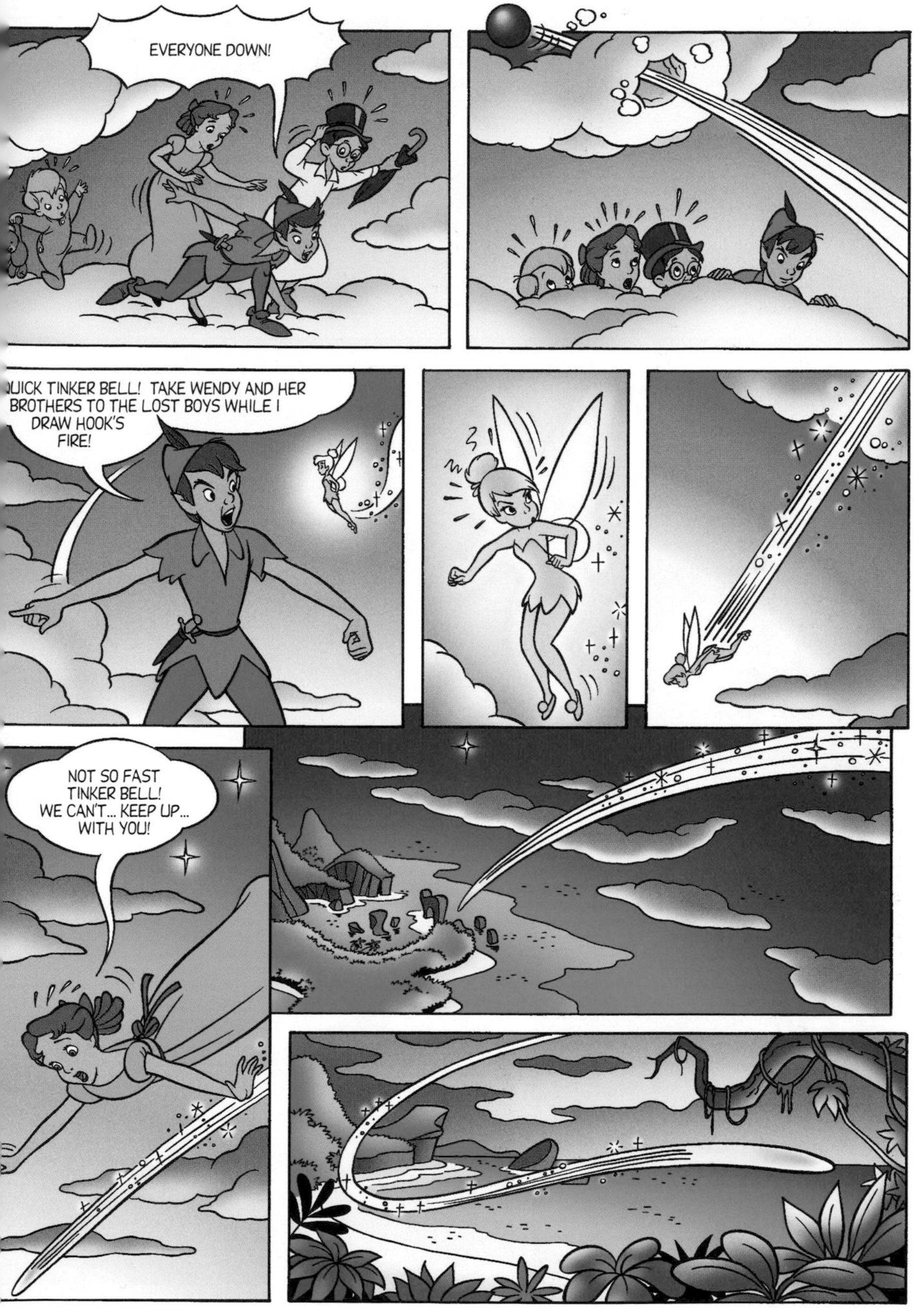
EVERYONE DOWN!
QUICK TINKER BELL! TAKE WENDY AND HER BROTHERS TO THE LOST BOYS WHILE I DRAW HOOK'S FIRE!
NOT SO FAST TINKER BELL! WE CAN'T... KEEP UP... WITH YOU!

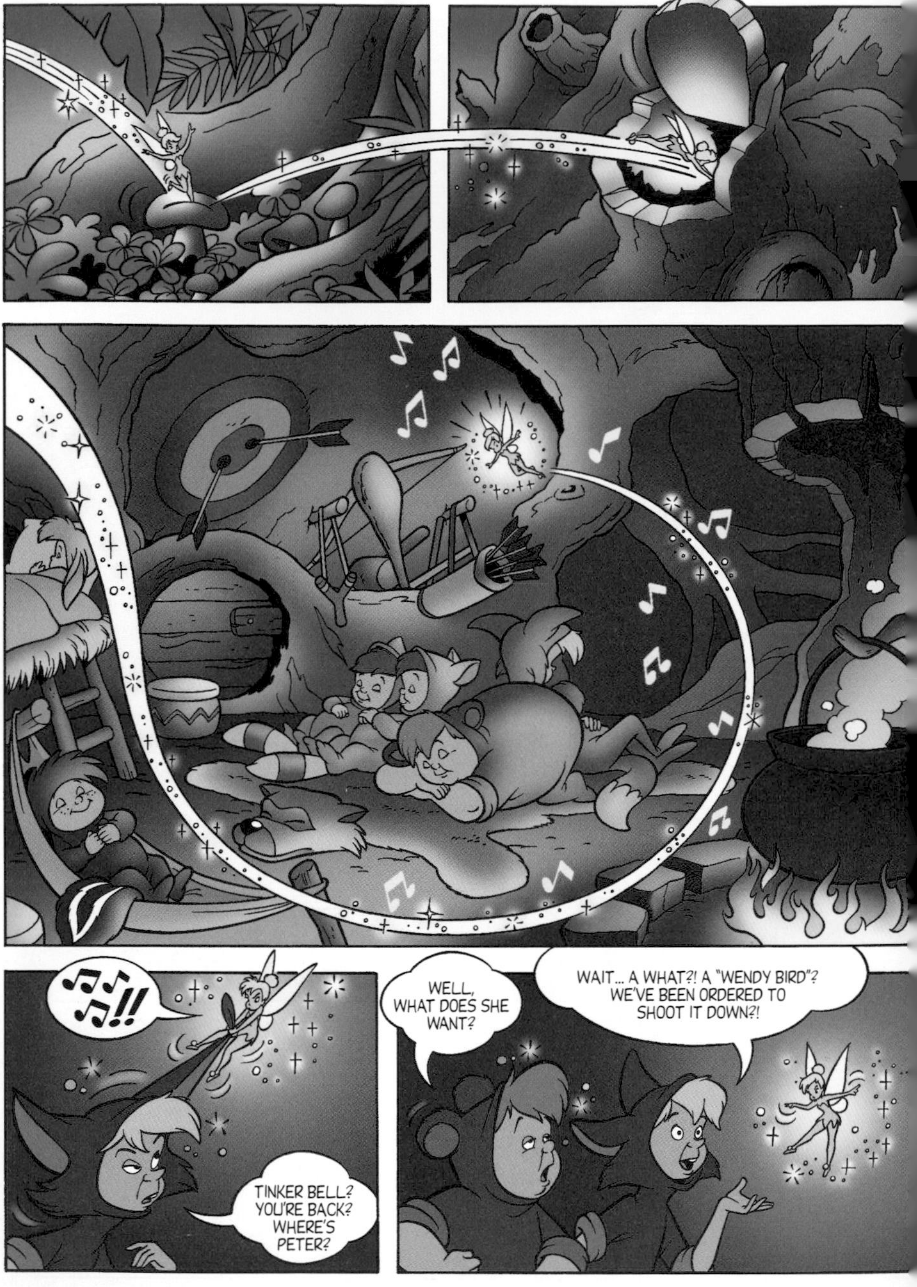
♫♪♫!!
TINKER BELL? YOU'RE BACK? WHERE'S PETER?
WELL, WHAT DOES SHE WANT?
WAIT... A WHAT?! A "WENDY BIRD"? WE'VE BEEN ORDERED TO SHOOT IT DOWN?!

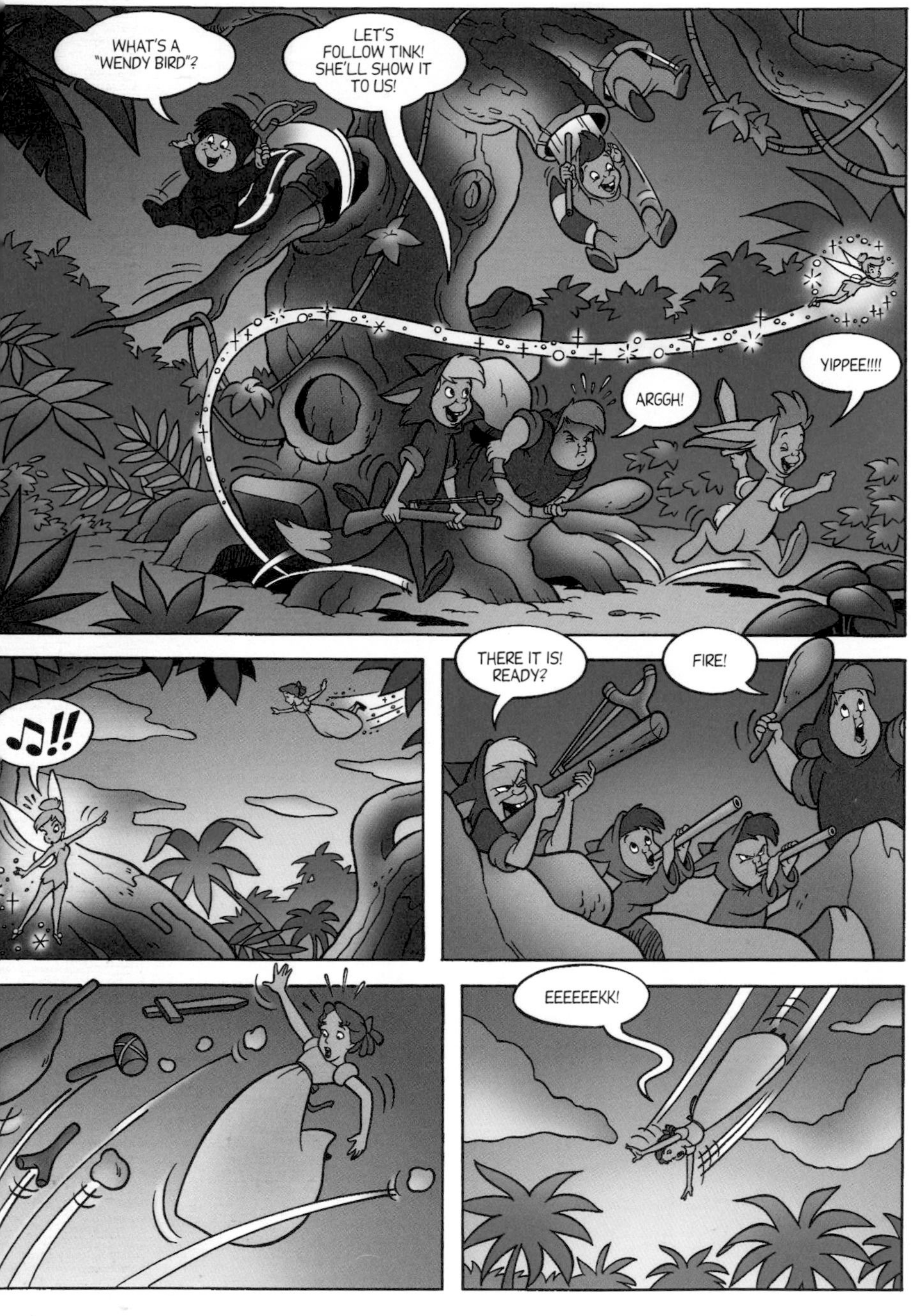
WHAT'S A "WENDY BIRD"?
LET'S FOLLOW TINK! SHE'LL SHOW IT TO US!
ARGGH!
YIPPEE!!!!
♫!!
THERE IT IS! READY?
FIRE!
EEEEEEKK!

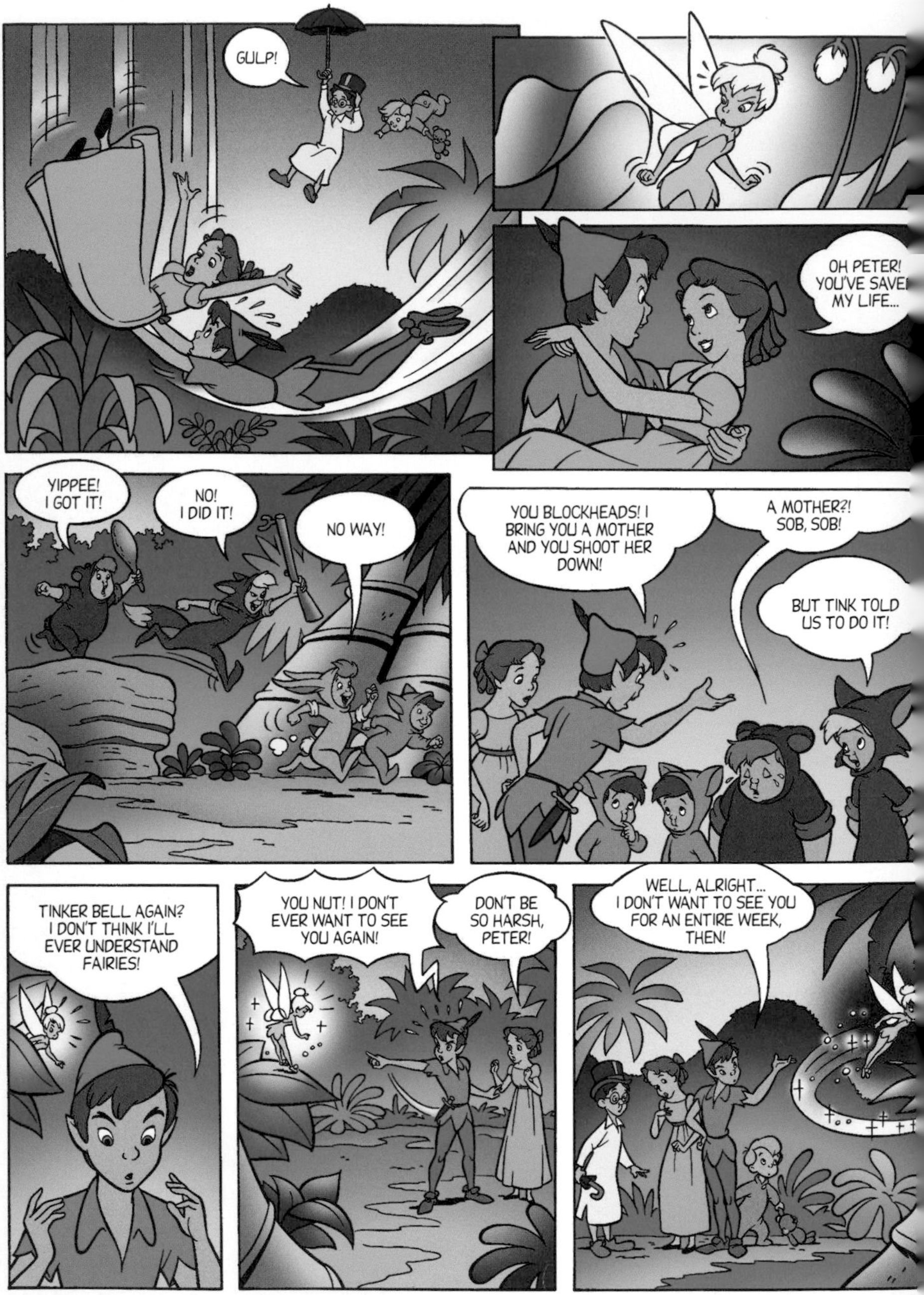
GULP!
OH PETER! YOU'VE SAVE MY LIFE...
YIPPEE! I GOT IT!
NO! I DID IT!
NO WAY!
YOU BLOCKHEADS! I BRING YOU A MOTHER AND YOU SHOOT HER DOWN!
A MOTHER?! SOB, SOB!
BUT TINK TOLD US TO DO IT!
TINKER BELL AGAIN? I DON'T THINK I'LL EVER UNDERSTAND FAIRIES!
YOU NUT! I DON'T EVER WANT TO SEE YOU AGAIN!
DON'T BE SO HARSH, PETER!
WELL, ALRIGHT... I DON'T WANT TO SEE YOU FOR AN ENTIRE WEEK, THEN!

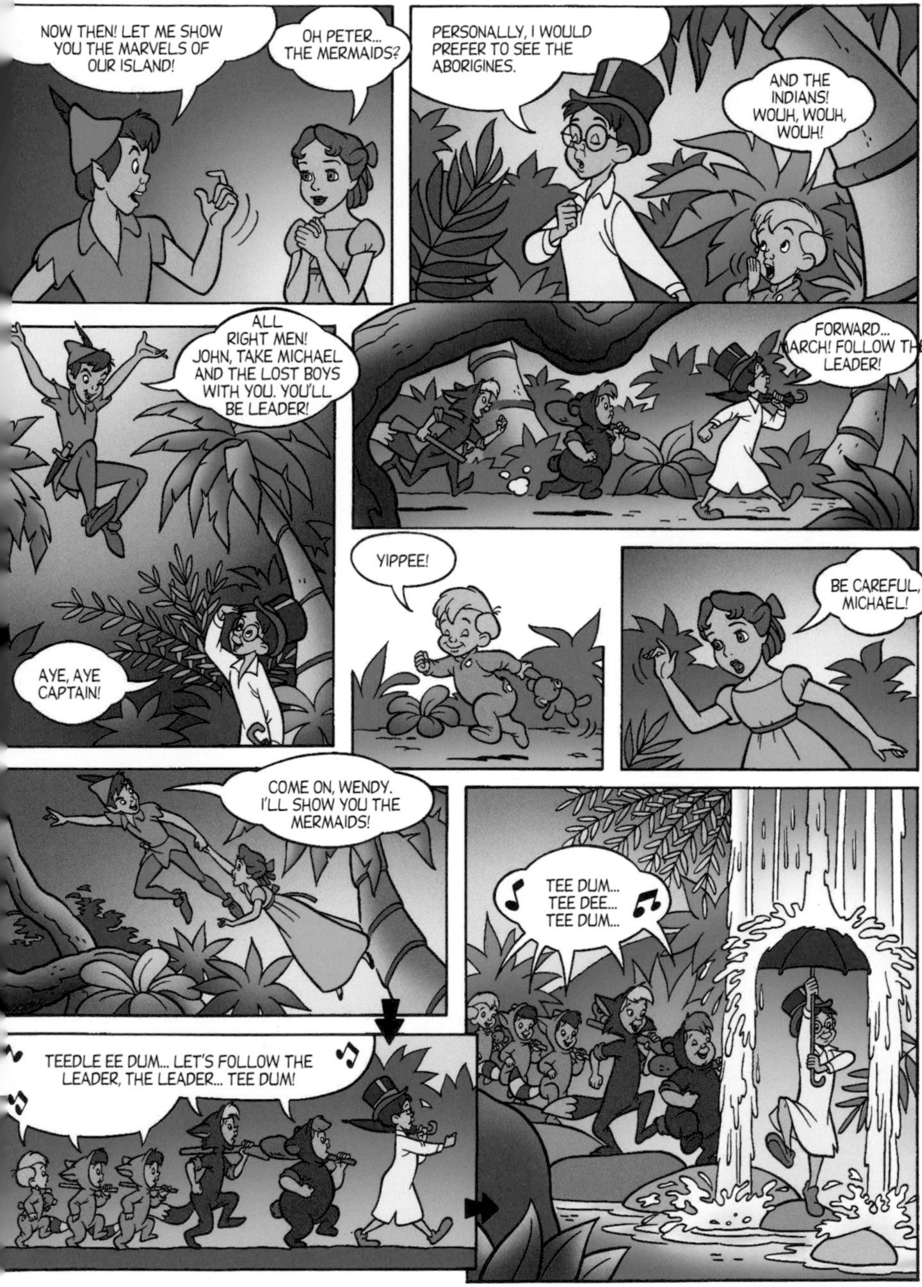
NOW THEN! LET ME SHOW YOU THE MARVELS OF OUR ISLAND!
OH PETER... THE MERMAIDS?
PERSONALLY, I WOULD PREFER TO SEE THE ABORIGINES.
AND THE INDIANS! WOUH, WOUH, WOUH!
ALL RIGHT MEN! JOHN, TAKE MICHAEL AND THE LOST BOYS WITH YOU. YOU'LL BE LEADER!
AYE, AYE CAPTAIN!
FORWARD... MARCH! FOLLOW THE LEADER!
YIPPEE!
BE CAREFUL, MICHAEL!
COME ON, WENDY. I'LL SHOW YOU THE MERMAIDS!
TEEDLE EE DUM... LET'S FOLLOW THE LEADER, THE LEADER... TEE DUM!
TEE DUM... TEE DEE... TEE DUM...

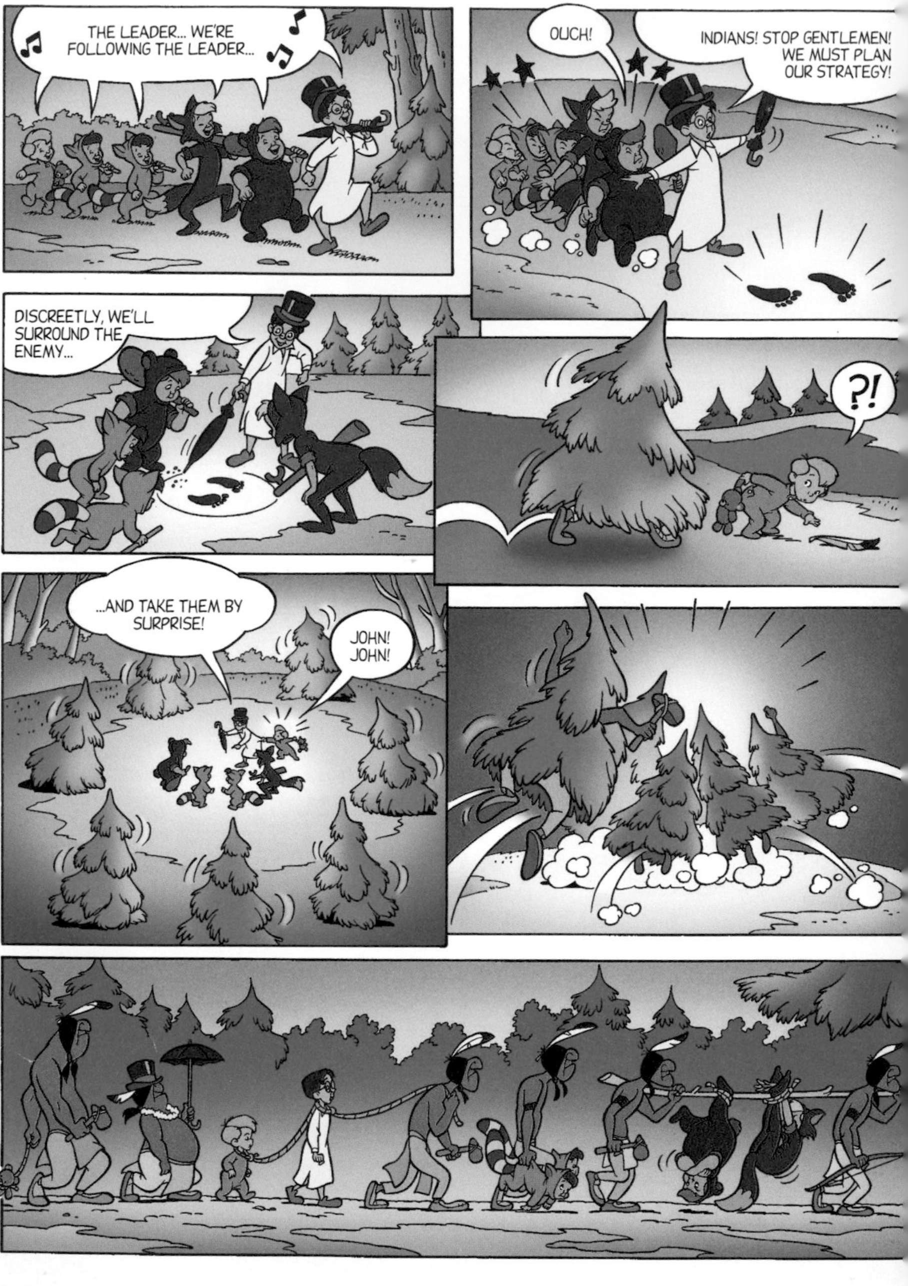

THE LEADER... WE'RE FOLLOWING THE LEADER...
OUCH!
INDIANS! STOP GENTLEMEN! WE MUST PLAN OUR STRATEGY!
DISCREETLY, WE'LL SURROUND THE ENEMY...
?!
...AND TAKE THEM BY SURPRISE!
JOHN! JOHN!

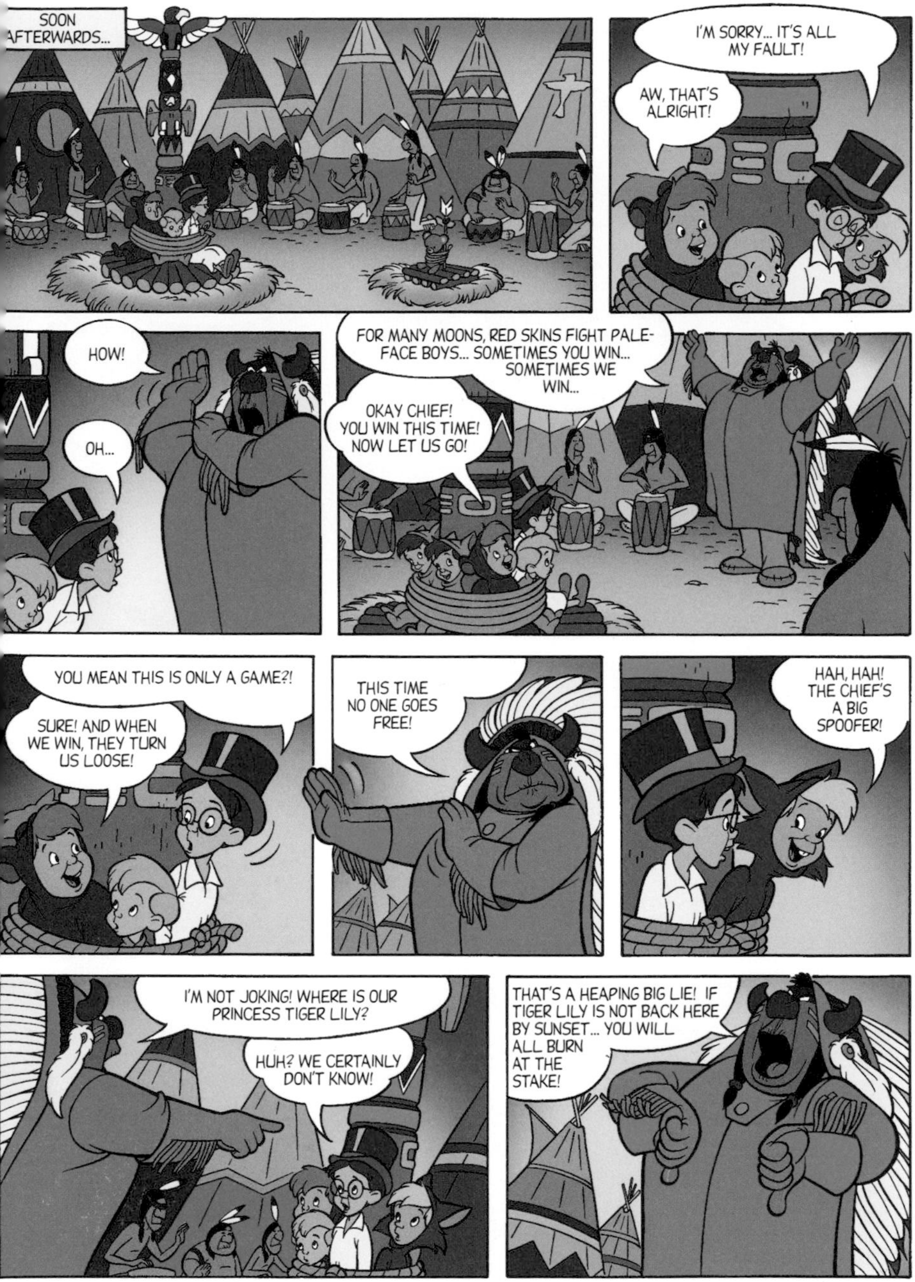
SOON AFTERWARDS...
I'M SORRY... IT'S ALL MY FAULT!
AW, THAT'S ALRIGHT!
HOW!
OH...
FOR MANY MOONS, RED SKINS FIGHT PALE-FACE BOYS... SOMETIMES YOU WIN... SOMETIMES WE WIN...
OKAY CHIEF! YOU WIN THIS TIME! NOW LET US GO!
YOU MEAN THIS IS ONLY A GAME?!
SURE! AND WHEN WE WIN, THEY TURN US LOOSE!
THIS TIME NO ONE GOES FREE!
HAH, HAH! THE CHIEF'S A BIG SPOOFER!
I'M NOT JOKING! WHERE IS OUR PRINCESS TIGER LILY?
HUH? WE CERTAINLY DON'T KNOW!
THAT'S A HEAPING BIG LIE! IF TIGER LILY IS NOT BACK HERE BY SUNSET... YOU WILL ALL BURN AT THE STAKE!

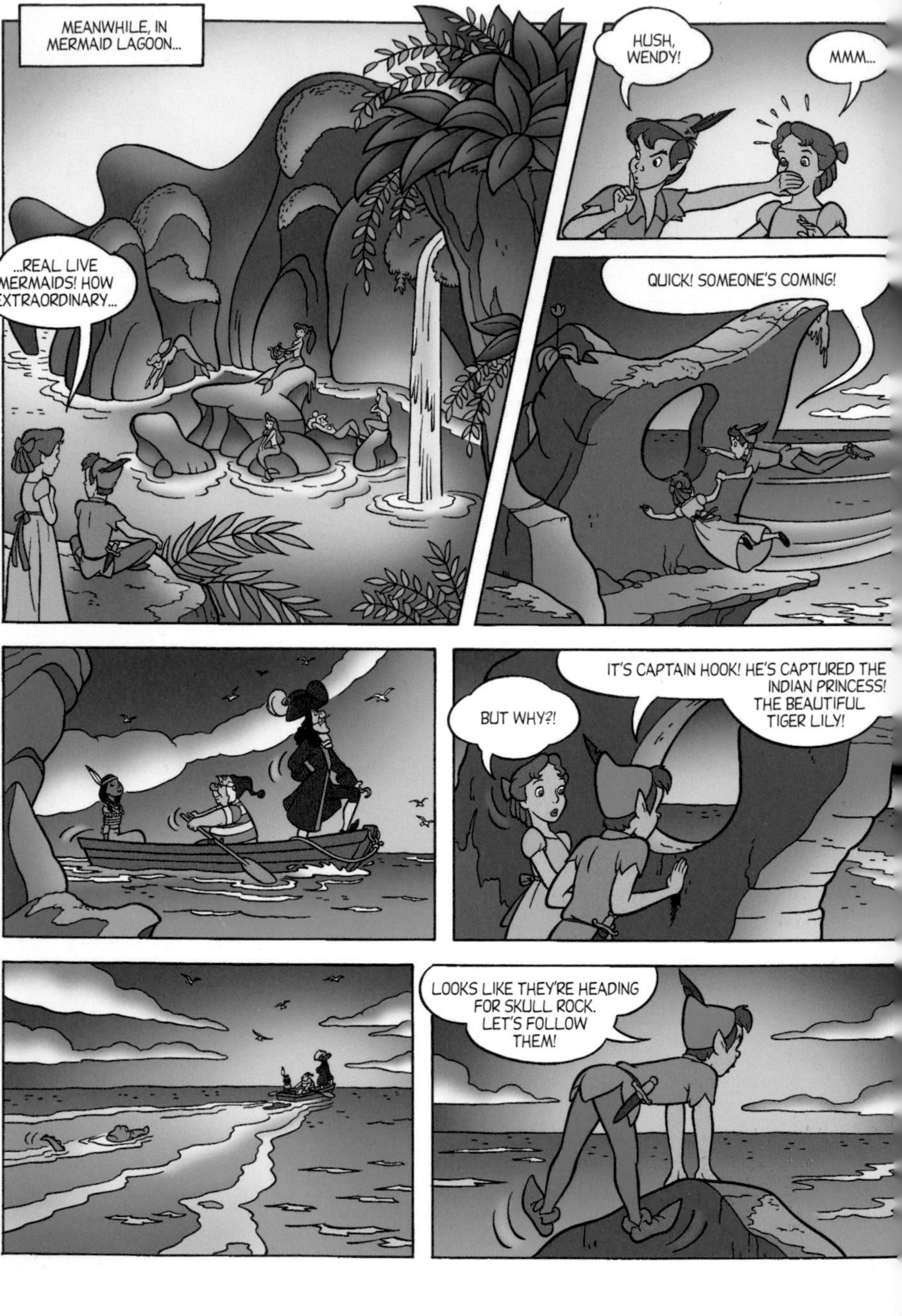
MEANWHILE, IN MERMAID LAGOON...
...REAL LIVE MERMAIDS! HOW EXTRAORDINARY...
HUSH, WENDY!
MMM...
QUICK! SOMEONE'S COMING!
BUT WHY?!
IT'S CAPTAIN HOOK! HE'S CAPTURED THE INDIAN PRINCESS! THE BEAUTIFUL TIGER LILY!
LOOKS LIKE THEY'RE HEADING FOR SKULL ROCK. LET'S FOLLOW THEM!

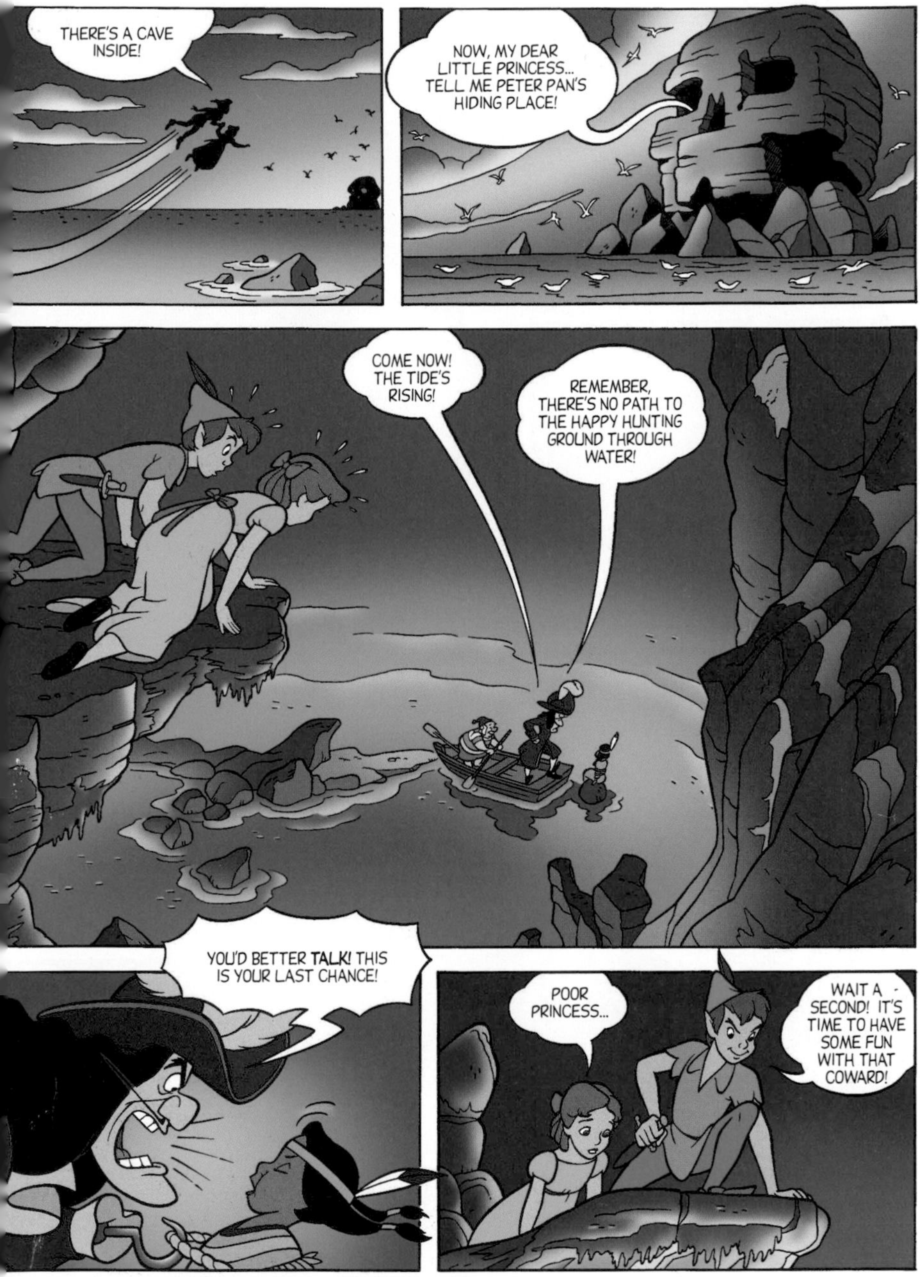
THERE'S A CAVE INSIDE!
NOW, MY DEAR LITTLE PRINCESS... TELL ME PETER PAN'S HIDING PLACE!
COME NOW! THE TIDE'S RISING!
REMEMBER, THERE'S NO PATH TO THE HAPPY HUNTING GROUND THROUGH WATER!
YOU'D BETTER **TALK!** THIS IS YOUR LAST CHANCE!
POOR PRINCESS...
WAIT A SECOND! IT'S TIME TO HAVE SOME FUN WITH THAT COWARD!

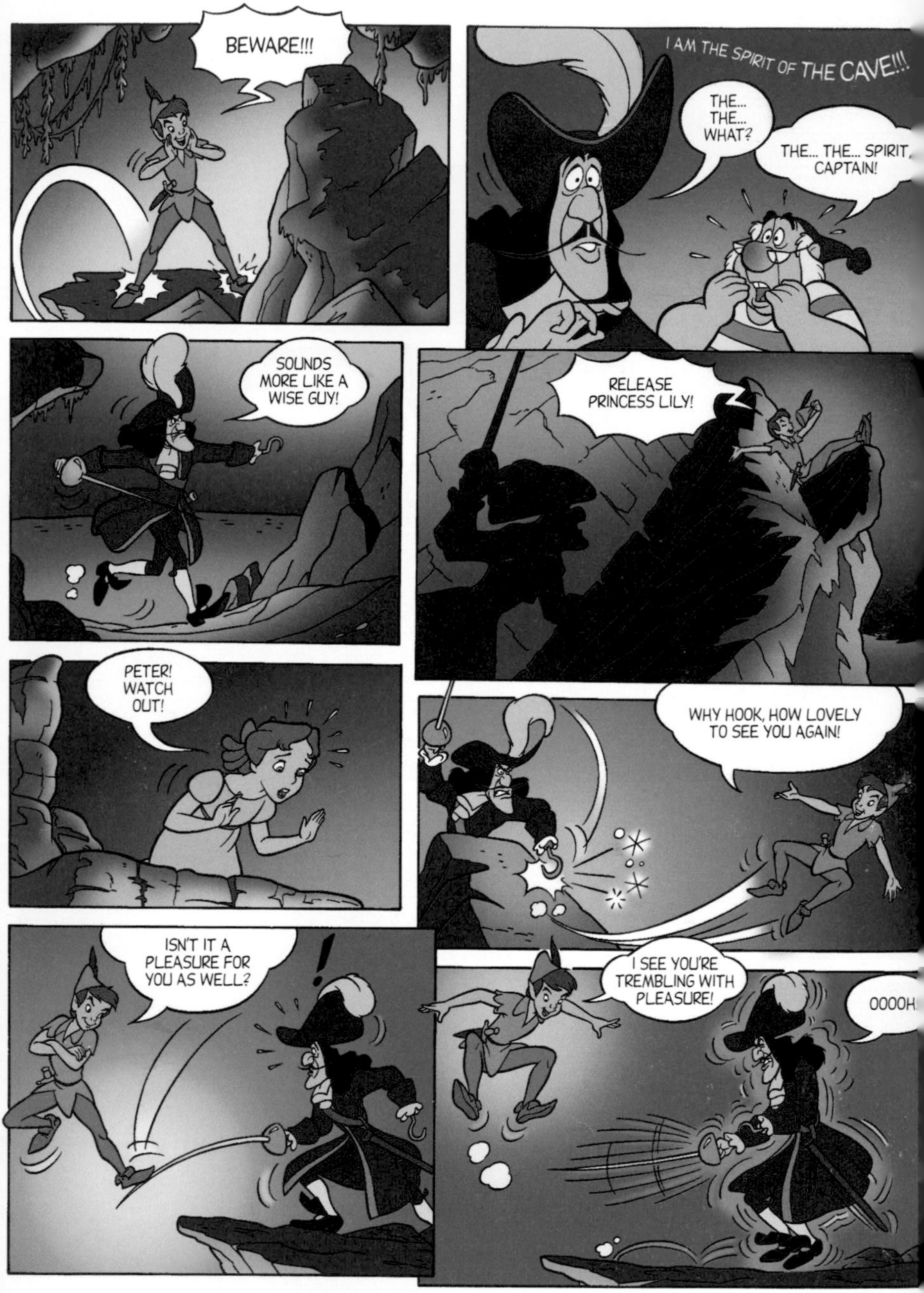
BEWARE!!!
I AM THE SPIRIT OF THE CAVE!!!
THE... THE... WHAT?
THE... THE... SPIRIT, CAPTAIN!
SOUNDS MORE LIKE A WISE GUY!
RELEASE PRINCESS LILY!
PETER! WATCH OUT!
WHY HOOK, HOW LOVELY TO SEE YOU AGAIN!
ISN'T IT A PLEASURE FOR YOU AS WELL?
I SEE YOU'RE TREMBLING WITH PLEASURE!
OOOOH!

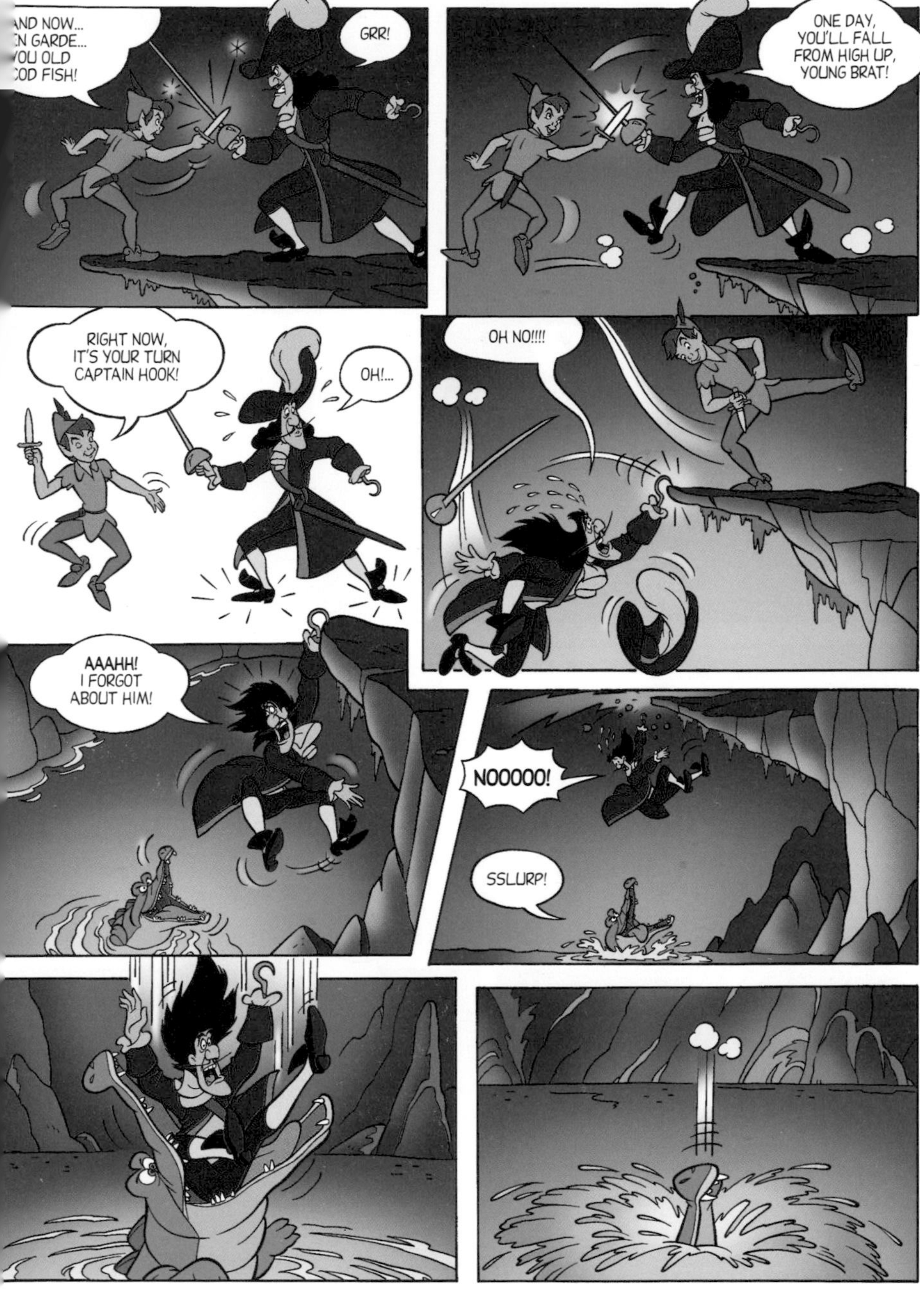
AND NOW...
EN GARDE...
YOU OLD
COD FISH!
GRR!
ONE DAY,
YOU'LL FALL
FROM HIGH UP,
YOUNG BRAT!
RIGHT NOW,
IT'S YOUR TURN
CAPTAIN HOOK!
OH!...
OH NO!!!!
AAAHH!
I FORGOT
ABOUT HIM!
NOOOOO!
SSLURP!

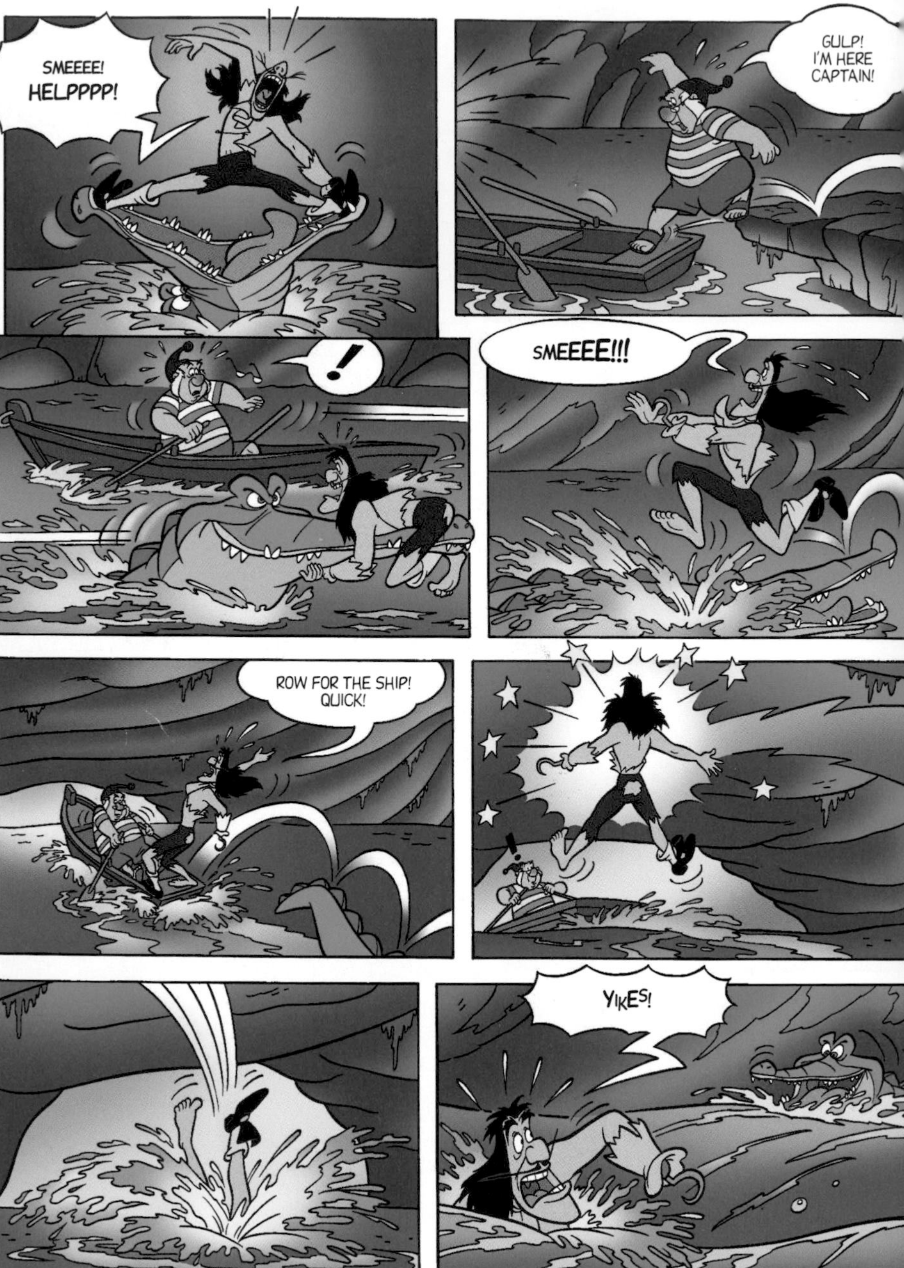
SMEEEE! HELPPPP!
GULP! I'M HERE CAPTAIN!
!
SMEEEE!!!
ROW FOR THE SHIP! QUICK!
!
YIKES!

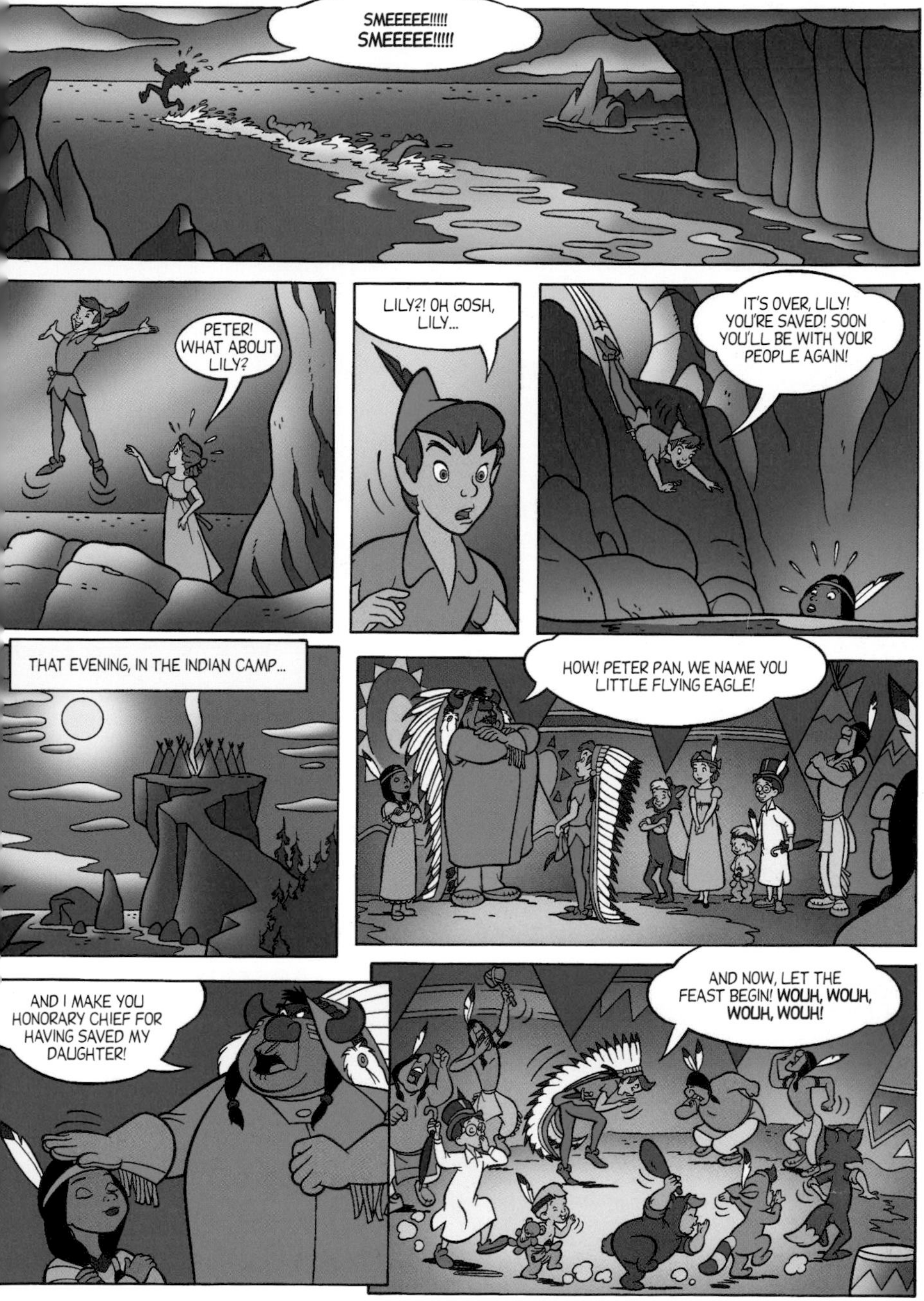

SMEEEEE!!!!! SMEEEEE!!!!!
PETER! WHAT ABOUT LILY?
LILY?! OH GOSH, LILY...
IT'S OVER, LILY! YOU'RE SAVED! SOON YOU'LL BE WITH YOUR PEOPLE AGAIN!
THAT EVENING, IN THE INDIAN CAMP...
HOW! PETER PAN, WE NAME YOU LITTLE FLYING EAGLE!
AND I MAKE YOU HONORARY CHIEF FOR HAVING SAVED MY DAUGHTER!
AND NOW, LET THE FEAST BEGIN! **WOUH, WOUH, WOUH, WOUH!**

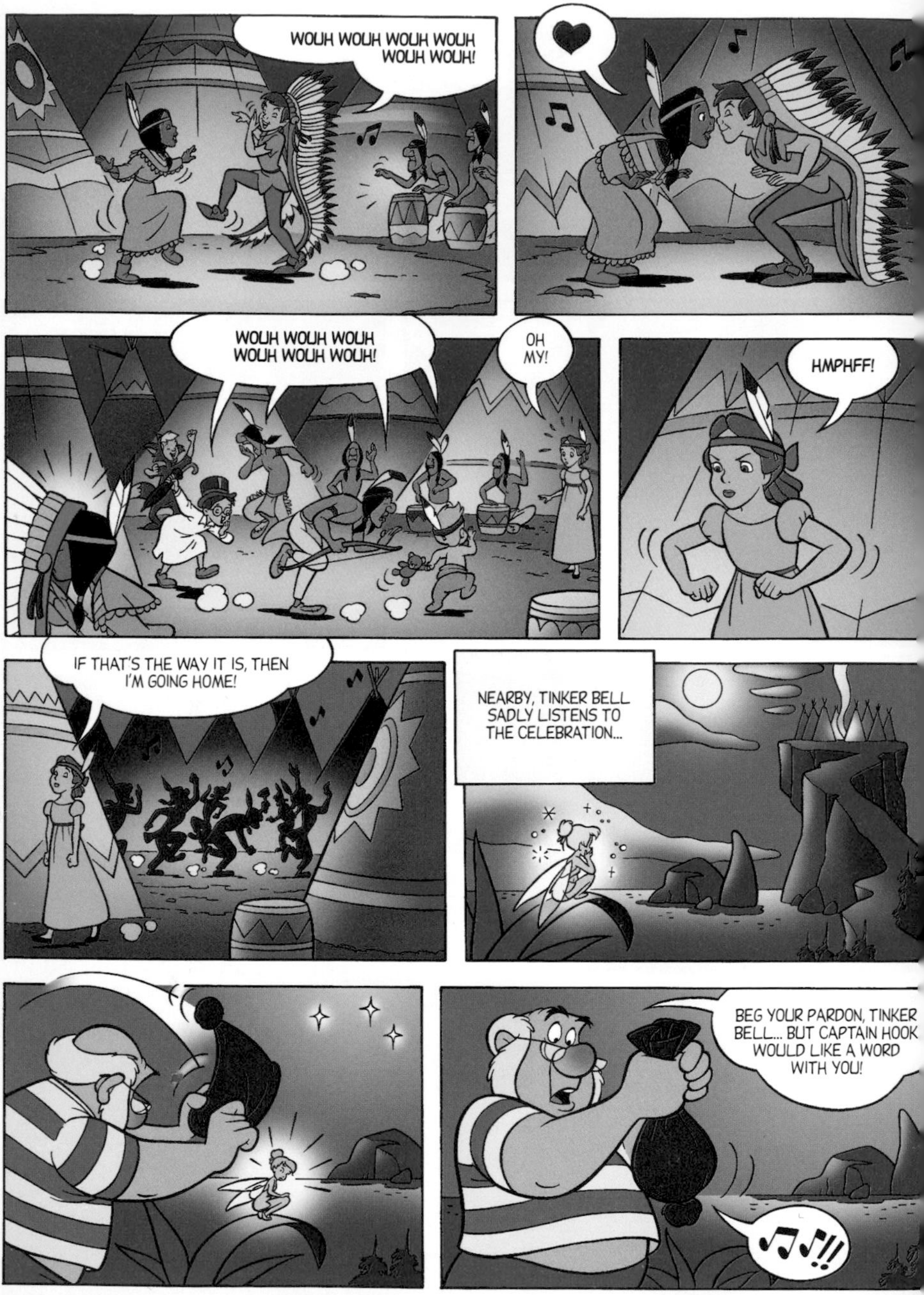
WOUH WOUH WOUH WOUH WOUH WOUH!
WOUH WOUH WOUH WOUH WOUH WOUH!
OH MY!
HMPHFF!
IF THAT'S THE WAY IT IS, THEN I'M GOING HOME!
NEARBY, TINKER BELL SADLY LISTENS TO THE CELEBRATION...
BEG YOUR PARDON, TINKER BELL... BUT CAPTAIN HOOK WOULD LIKE A WORD WITH YOU!

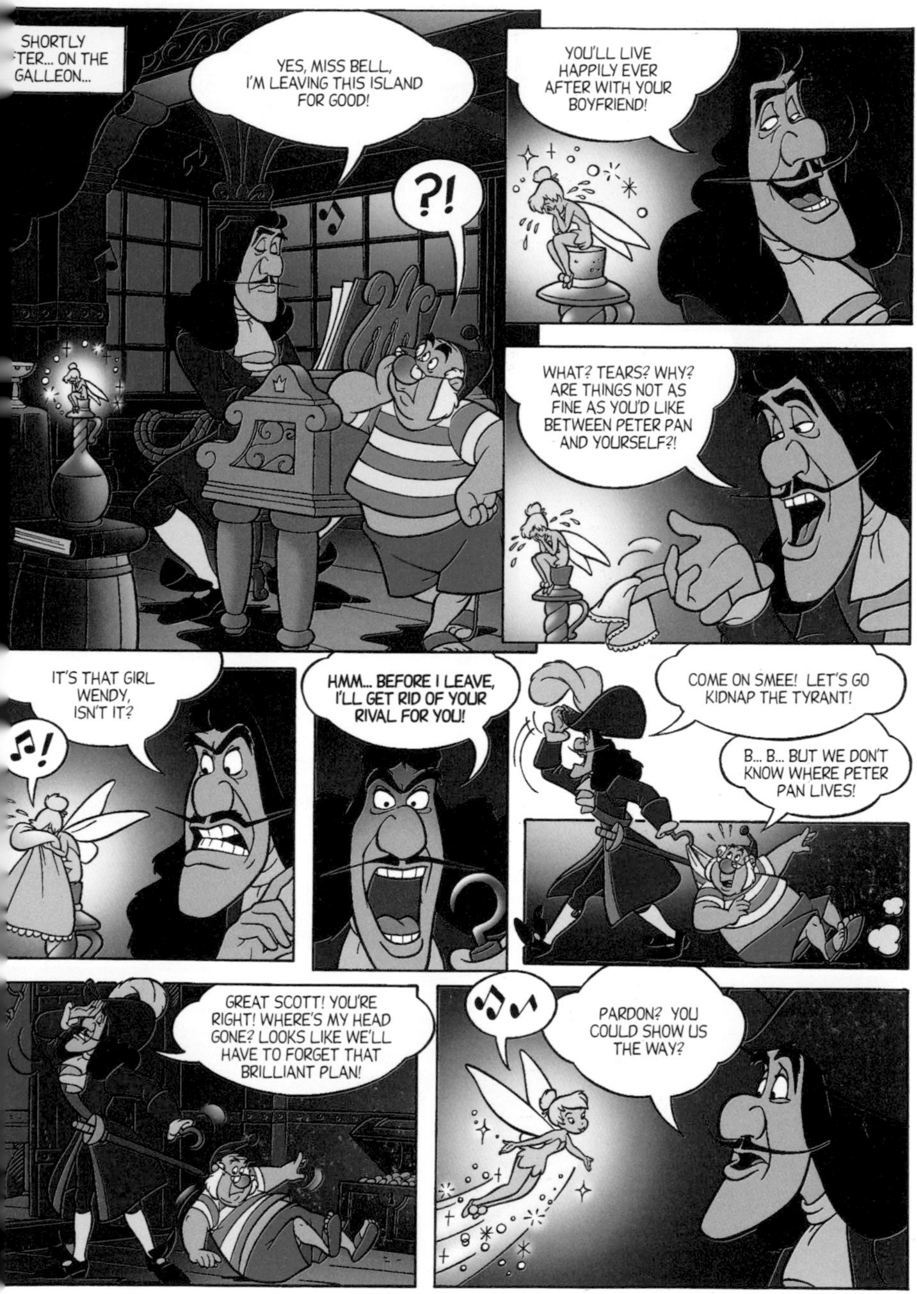
SHORTLY
TER... ON THE
GALLEON...
YES, MISS BELL, I'M LEAVING THIS ISLAND FOR GOOD!
?!
YOU'LL LIVE HAPPILY EVER AFTER WITH YOUR BOYFRIEND!
WHAT? TEARS? WHY? ARE THINGS NOT AS FINE AS YOU'D LIKE BETWEEN PETER PAN AND YOURSELF?!
IT'S THAT GIRL WENDY, ISN'T IT?
!
HMM... BEFORE I LEAVE, I'LL GET RID OF YOUR RIVAL FOR YOU!
COME ON SMEE! LET'S GO KIDNAP THE TYRANT!
B... B... BUT WE DON'T KNOW WHERE PETER PAN LIVES!
GREAT SCOTT! YOU'RE RIGHT! WHERE'S MY HEAD GONE? LOOKS LIKE WE'LL HAVE TO FORGET THAT BRILLIANT PLAN!
PARDON? YOU COULD SHOW US THE WAY?

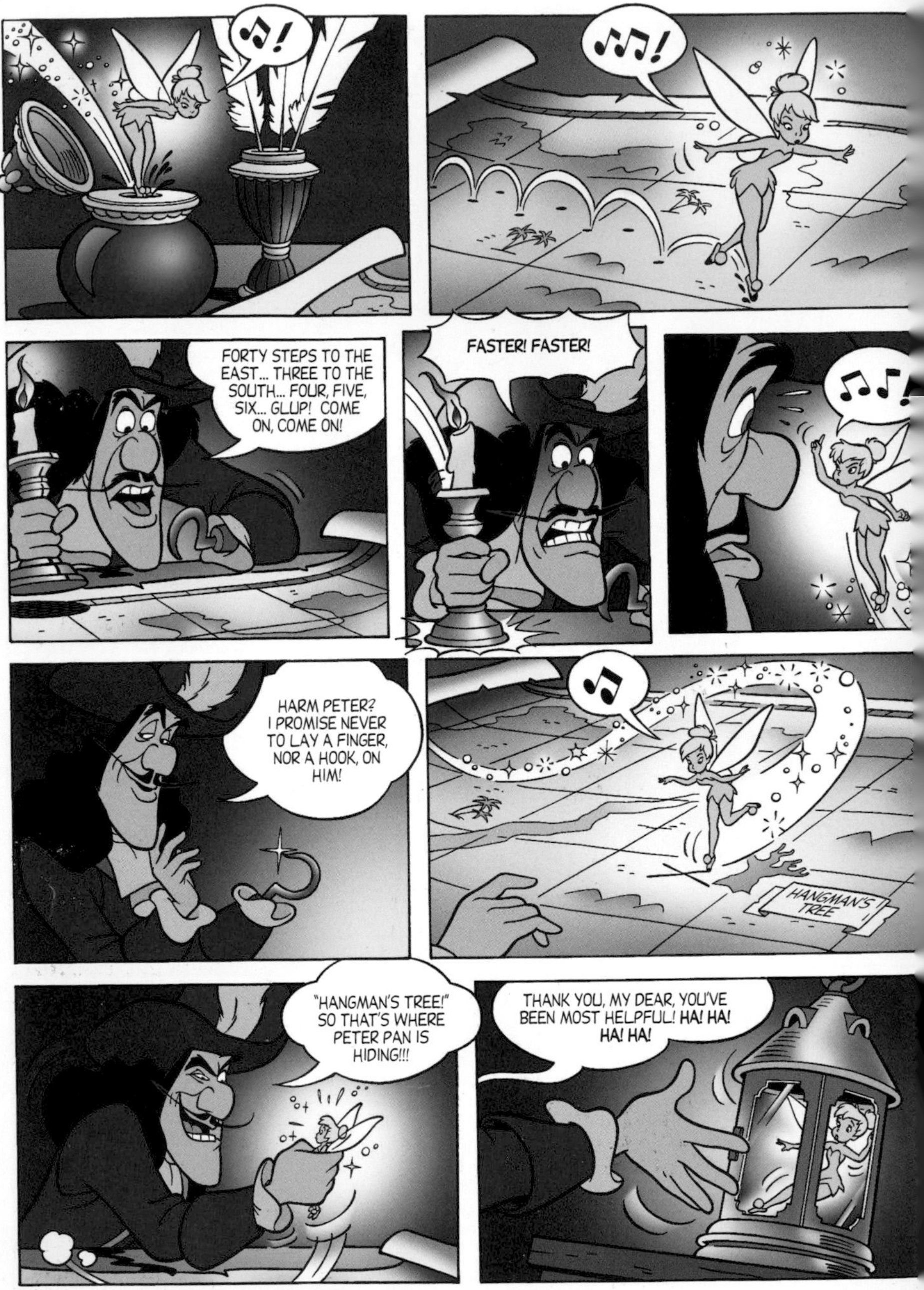
FORTY STEPS TO THE EAST... THREE TO THE SOUTH... FOUR, FIVE, SIX... GLUP! COME ON, COME ON!
FASTER! FASTER!
HARM PETER? I PROMISE NEVER TO LAY A FINGER, NOR A HOOK, ON HIM!
HANGMAN'S TREE
"HANGMAN'S TREE!" SO THAT'S WHERE PETER PAN IS HIDING!!!
THANK YOU, MY DEAR, YOU'VE BEEN MOST HELPFUL! HA! HA! HA! HA!

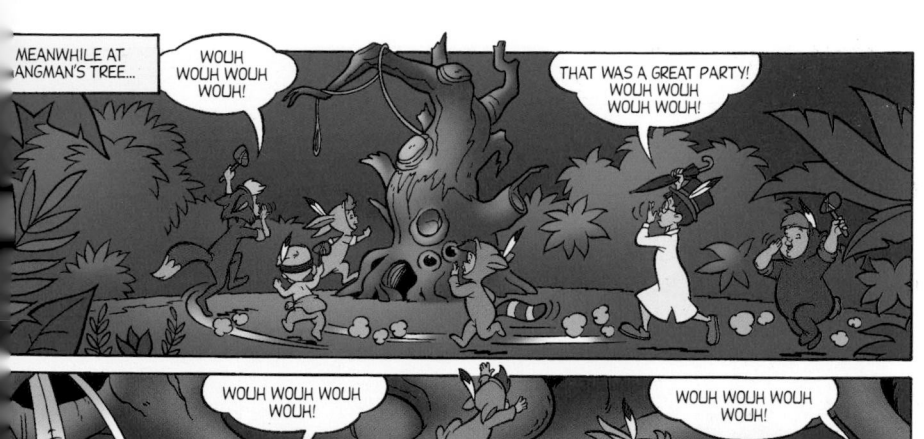

MEANWHILE AT ANGMAN'S TREE...

WOUH WOUH WOUH WOUH!

THAT WAS A GREAT PARTY! WOUH WOUH WOUH WOUH!

WOUH WOUH WOUH WOUH!

WOUH WOUH WOUH WOUH!

HOW! LITTLE FLYING EAGLE GREETS HIS MOTHER!

DID FLYING EAGLE HAVE FUN DANCING WITH TIGER LILY?

!

JOHN! MICHAEL! WE MUST GO HOME NOW!

OTHERWISE, MOTHER WILL BE WORRIED ABOUT US!

BUT, AREN'T *YOU* OUR MOTHER?!

OF COURSE NOT MICHAEL, I'M SPEAKING ABOUT OUR *REAL* MOTHER!

REAL MOTHER?!

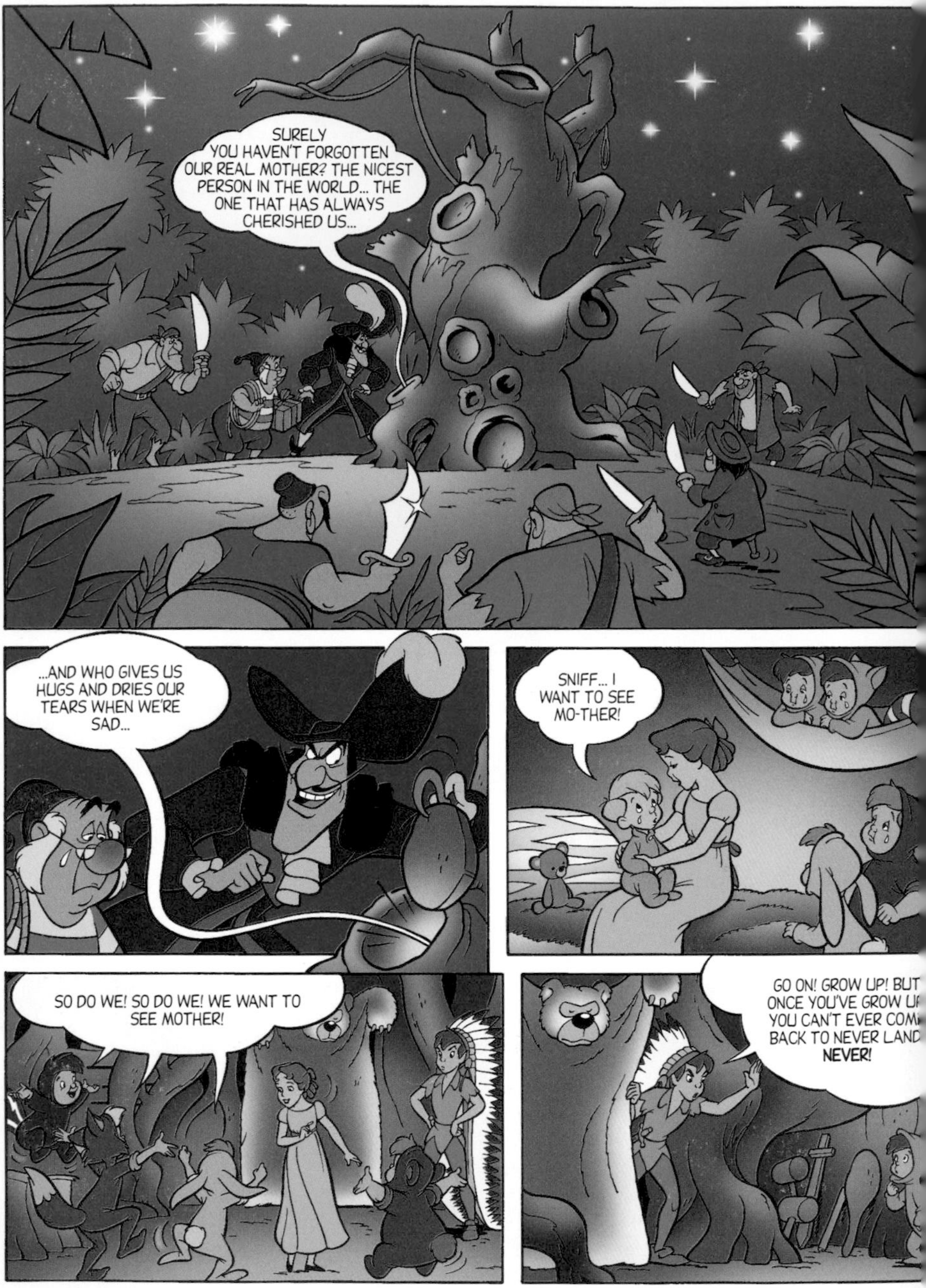
SURELY YOU HAVEN'T FORGOTTEN OUR REAL MOTHER? THE NICEST PERSON IN THE WORLD... THE ONE THAT HAS ALWAYS CHERISHED US...
...AND WHO GIVES US HUGS AND DRIES OUR TEARS WHEN WE'RE SAD...
SNIFF... I WANT TO SEE MO-THER!
SO DO WE! SO DO WE! WE WANT TO SEE MOTHER!
GO ON! GROW UP! BUT ONCE YOU'VE GROW U YOU CAN'T EVER COM BACK TO NEVER LAND **NEVER!**

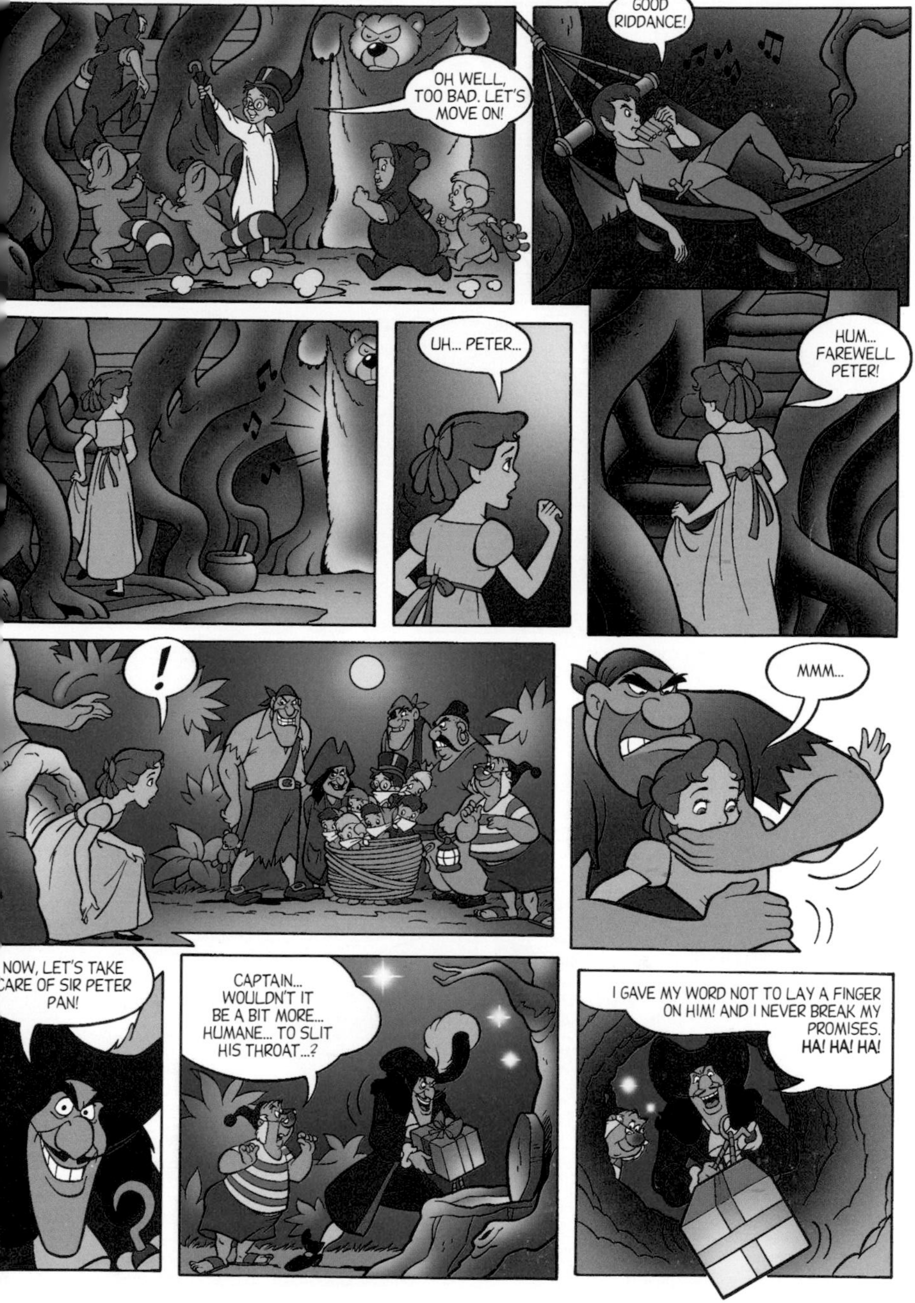
OH WELL, TOO BAD. LET'S MOVE ON!
GOOD RIDDANCE!
UH... PETER...
HUM... FAREWELL PETER!
!
MMM...
NOW, LET'S TAKE CARE OF SIR PETER PAN!
CAPTAIN... WOULDN'T IT BE A BIT MORE... HUMANE... TO SLIT HIS THROAT...?
I GAVE MY WORD NOT TO LAY A FINGER ON HIM! AND I NEVER BREAK MY PROMISES.
HA! HA! HA!

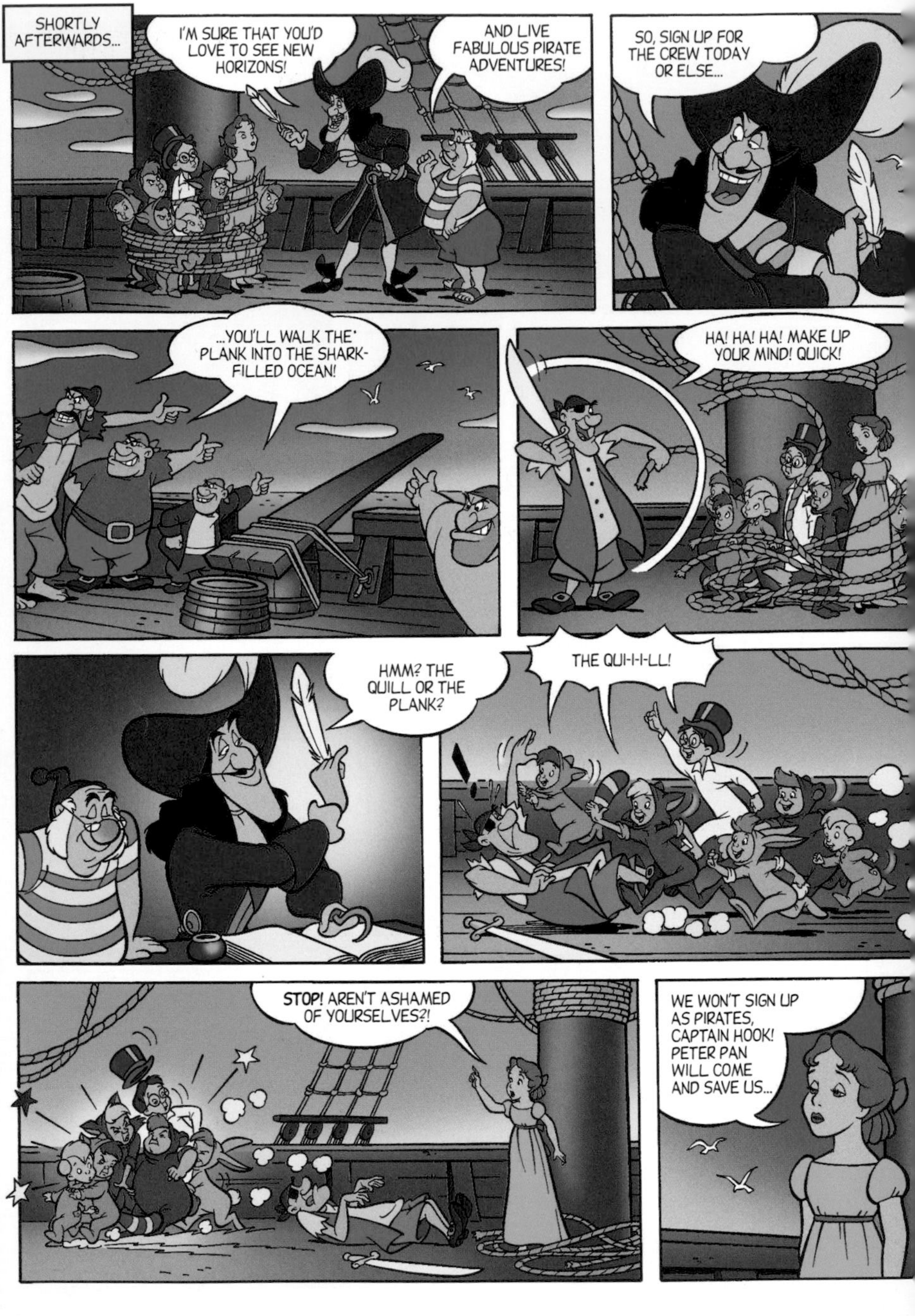
SHORTLY AFTERWARDS...
I'M SURE THAT YOU'D LOVE TO SEE NEW HORIZONS!
AND LIVE FABULOUS PIRATE ADVENTURES!
SO, SIGN UP FOR THE CREW TODAY OR ELSE...
...YOU'LL WALK THE PLANK INTO THE SHARK-FILLED OCEAN!
HA! HA! HA! MAKE UP YOUR MIND! QUICK!
HMM? THE QUILL OR THE PLANK?
THE QUI-I-I-LL!
STOP! AREN'T ASHAMED OF YOURSELVES?!
WE WON'T SIGN UP AS PIRATES, CAPTAIN HOOK! PETER PAN WILL COME AND SAVE US...

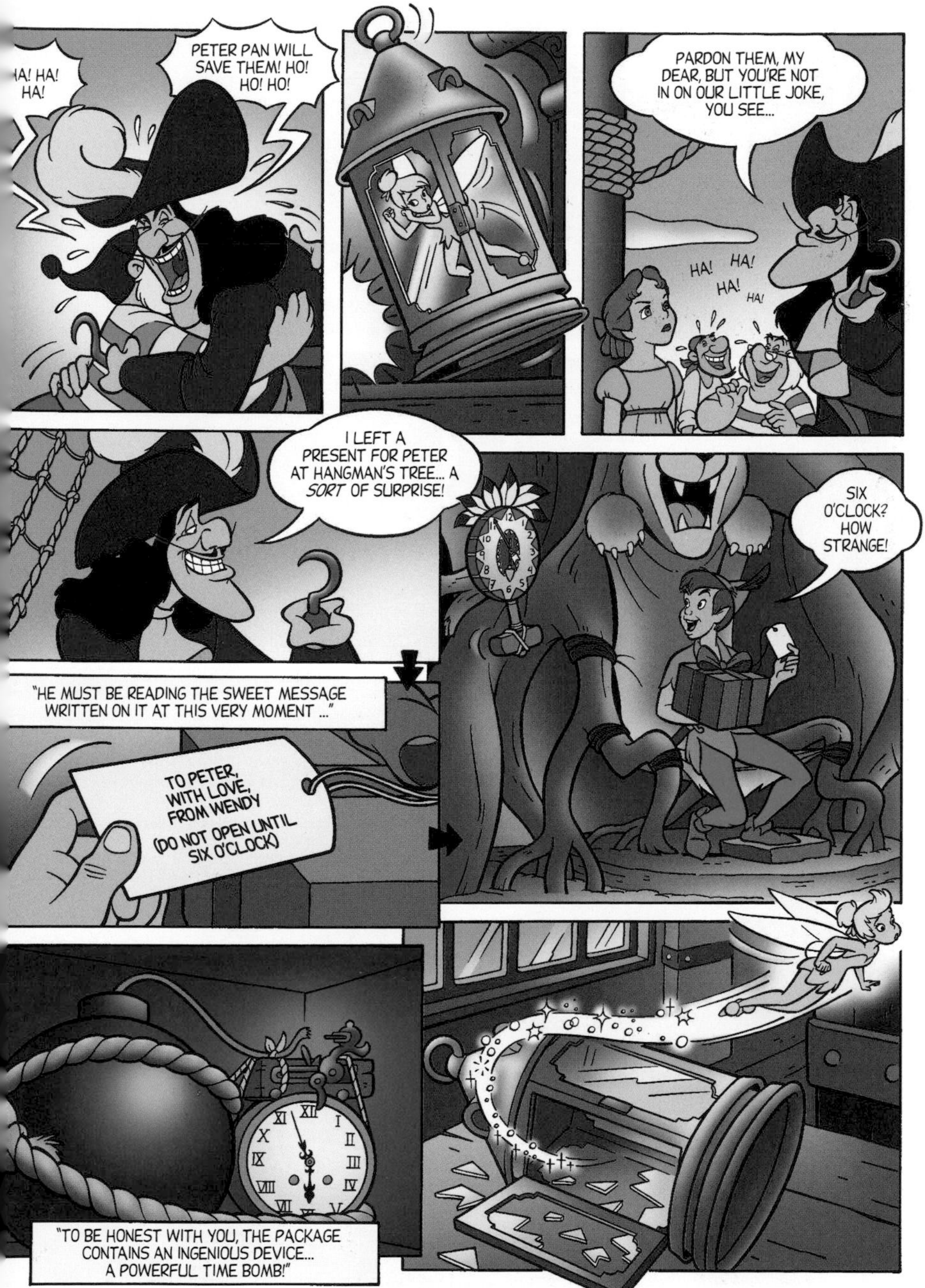
HA! HA! HA!
PETER PAN WILL SAVE THEM! HO! HO! HO!
PARDON THEM, MY DEAR, BUT YOU'RE NOT IN ON OUR LITTLE JOKE, YOU SEE...
HA! HA! HA! HA!
I LEFT A PRESENT FOR PETER AT HANGMAN'S TREE... A *SORT* OF SURPRISE!
"HE MUST BE READING THE SWEET MESSAGE WRITTEN ON IT AT THIS VERY MOMENT ..."
TO PETER, WITH LOVE, FROM WENDY (DO NOT OPEN UNTIL SIX O'CLOCK)
SIX O'CLOCK? HOW STRANGE!
"TO BE HONEST WITH YOU, THE PACKAGE CONTAINS AN INGENIOUS DEVICE... A POWERFUL TIME BOMB!"

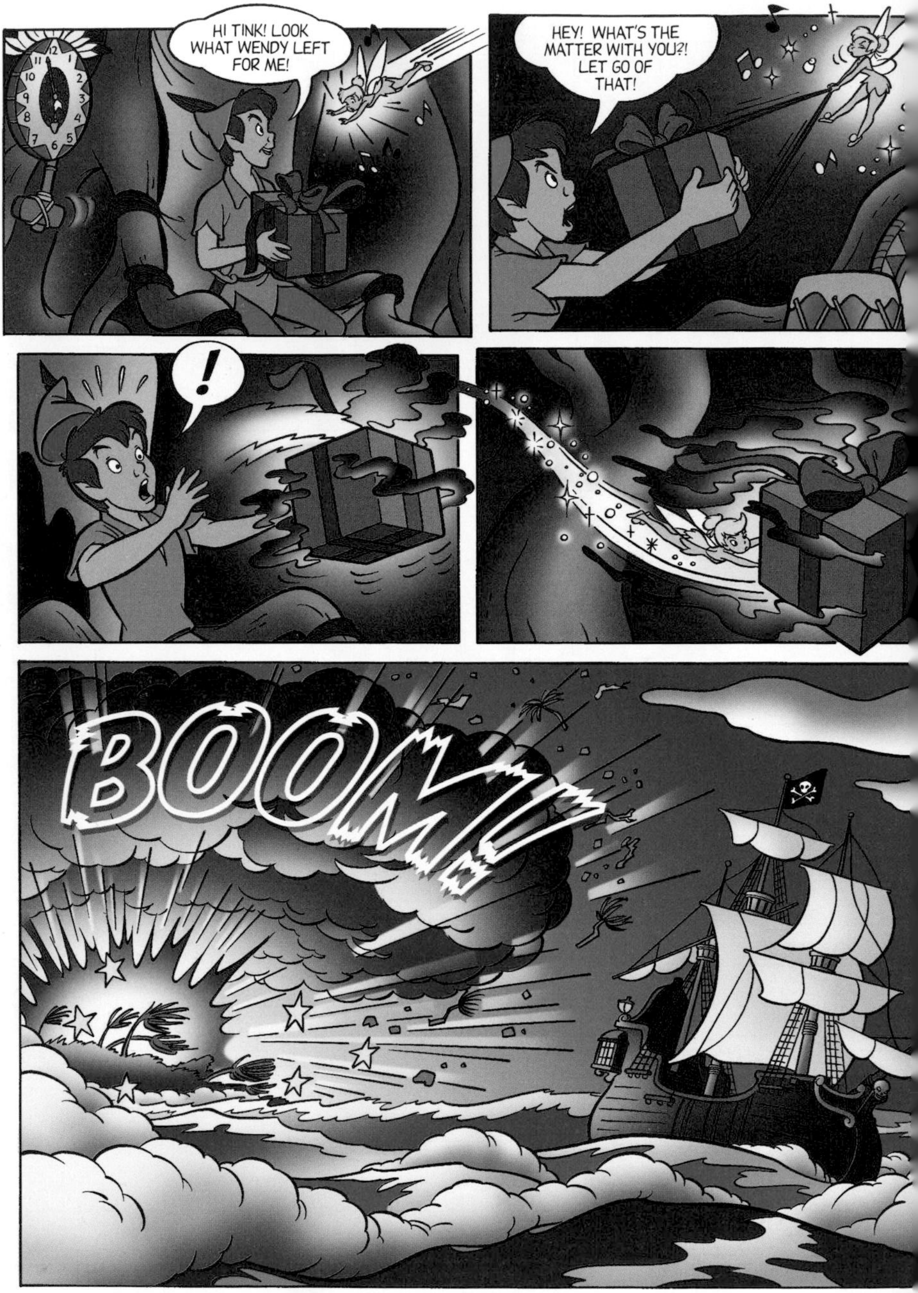

HI TINK! LOOK WHAT WENDY LEFT FOR ME!

HEY! WHAT'S THE MATTER WITH YOU?! LET GO OF THAT!

!

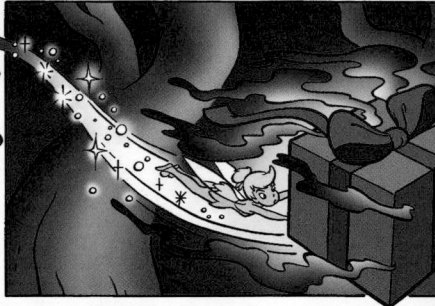

BOOM!

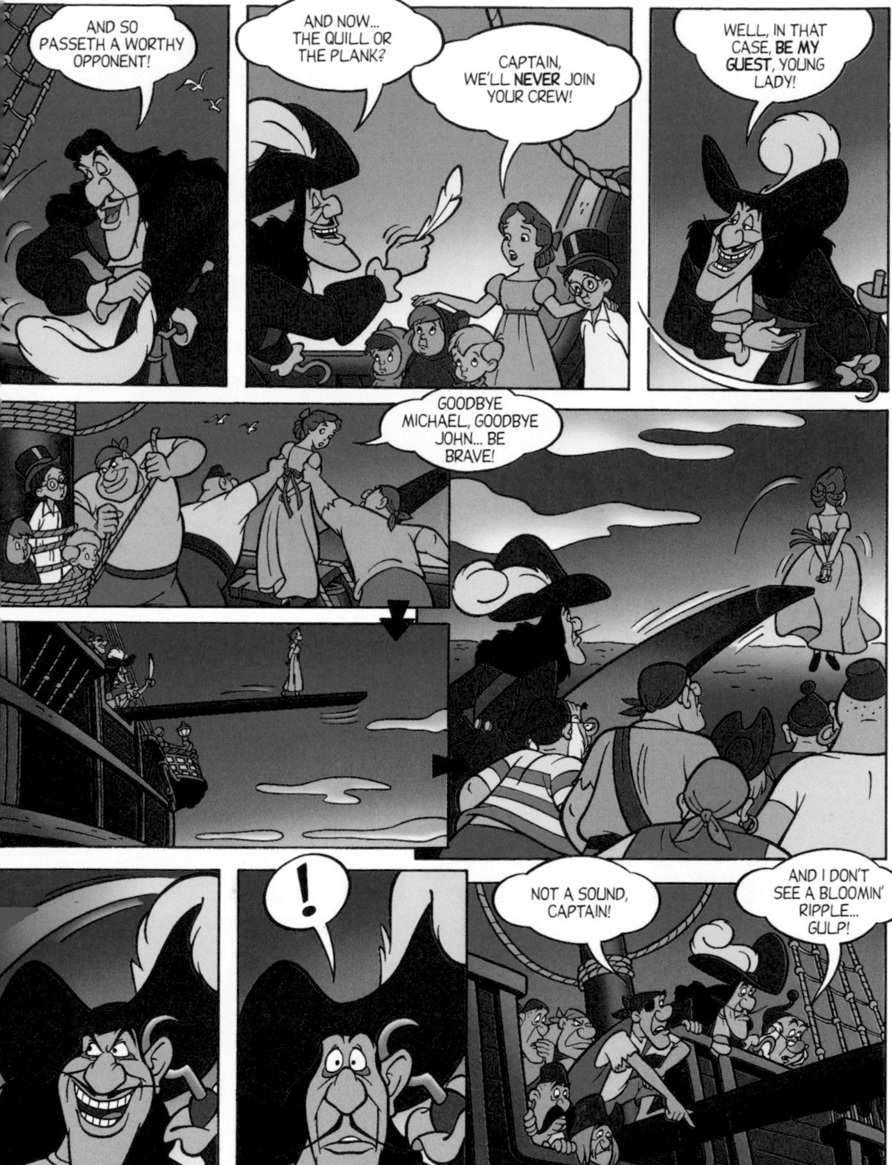
AND SO PASSETH A WORTHY OPPONENT!
AND NOW... THE QUILL OR THE PLANK?
CAPTAIN, WE'LL **NEVER** JOIN YOUR CREW!
WELL, IN THAT CASE, **BE MY GUEST**, YOUNG LADY!
GOODBYE MICHAEL, GOODBYE JOHN... BE BRAVE!
!
NOT A SOUND, CAPTAIN!
AND I DON'T SEE A BLOOMIN' RIPPLE... GULP!

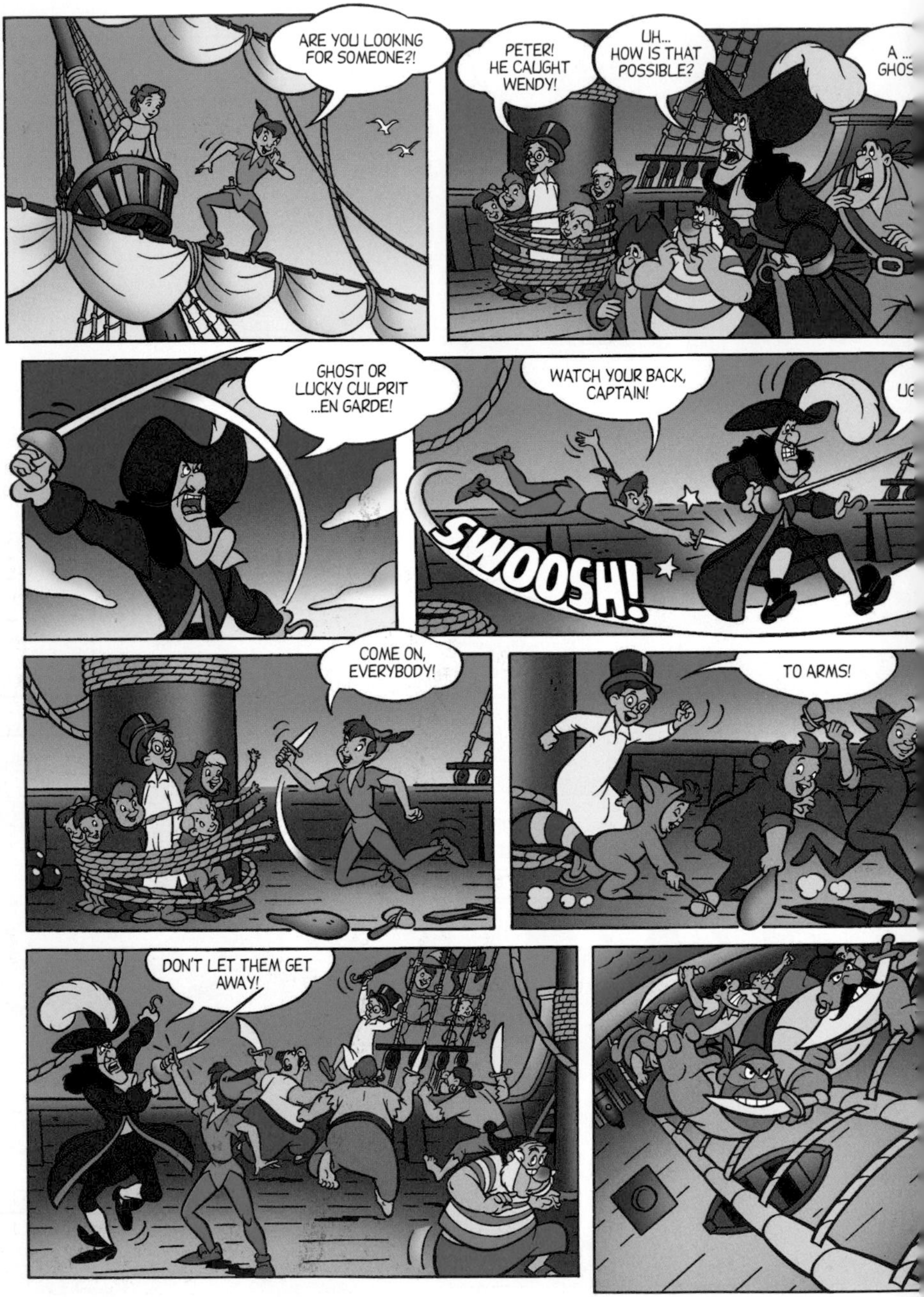
ARE YOU LOOKING FOR SOMEONE?!
PETER! HE CAUGHT WENDY!
UH... HOW IS THAT POSSIBLE?
A ... GHOS
GHOST OR LUCKY CULPRIT ...EN GARDE!
WATCH YOUR BACK, CAPTAIN!
UG
SWOOSH!
COME ON, EVERYBODY!
TO ARMS!
DON'T LET THEM GET AWAY!

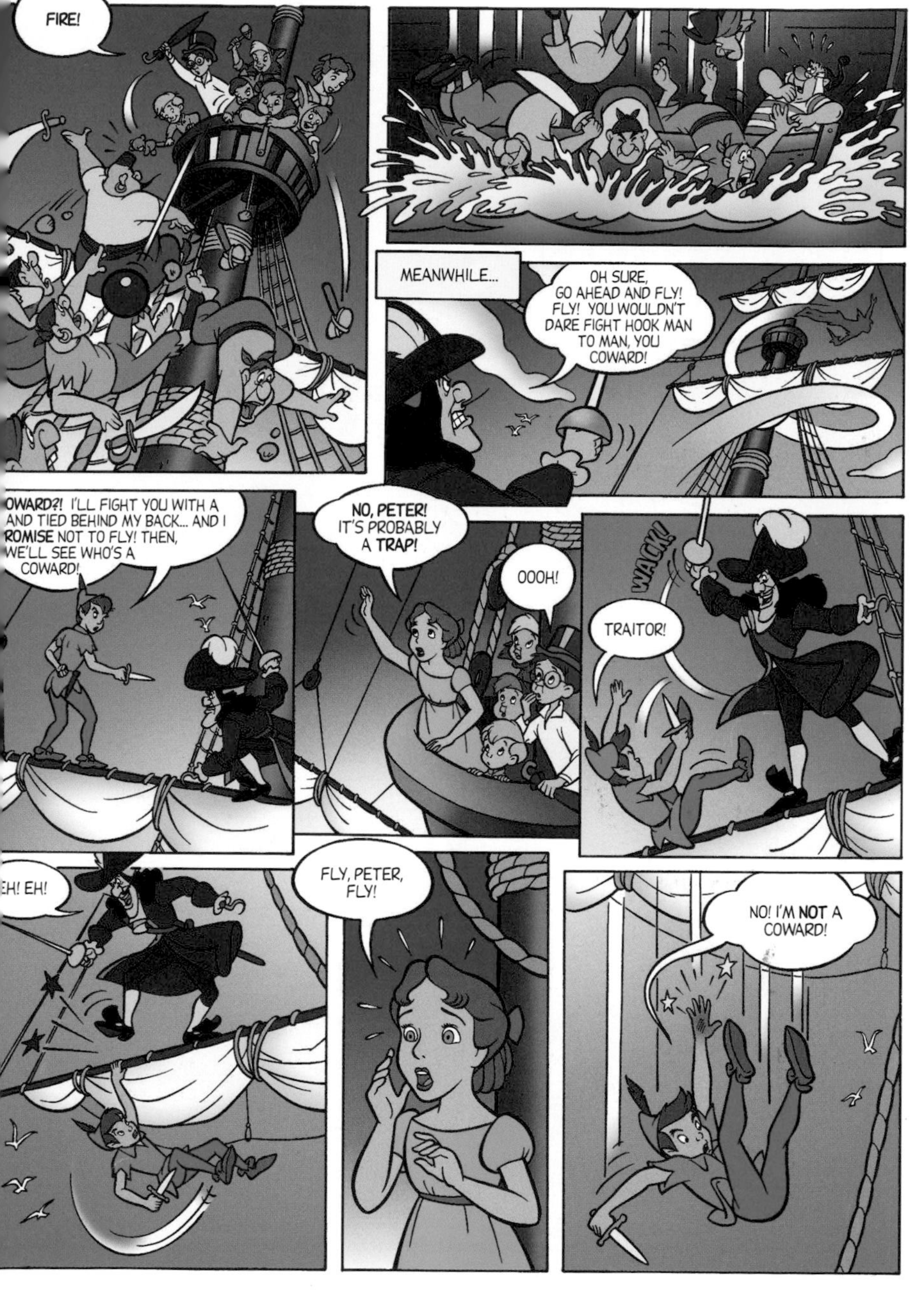
FIRE!
MEANWHILE...
OH SURE, GO AHEAD AND FLY! FLY! YOU WOULDN'T DARE FIGHT HOOK MAN TO MAN, YOU COWARD!
OWARD?! I'LL FIGHT YOU WITH A AND TIED BEHIND MY BACK... AND I ROMISE NOT TO FLY! THEN, WE'LL SEE WHO'S A COWARD!
NO, PETER! IT'S PROBABLY A TRAP!
OOOH!
WACK!
TRAITOR!
EH! EH!
FLY, PETER, FLY!
NO! I'M NOT A COWARD!

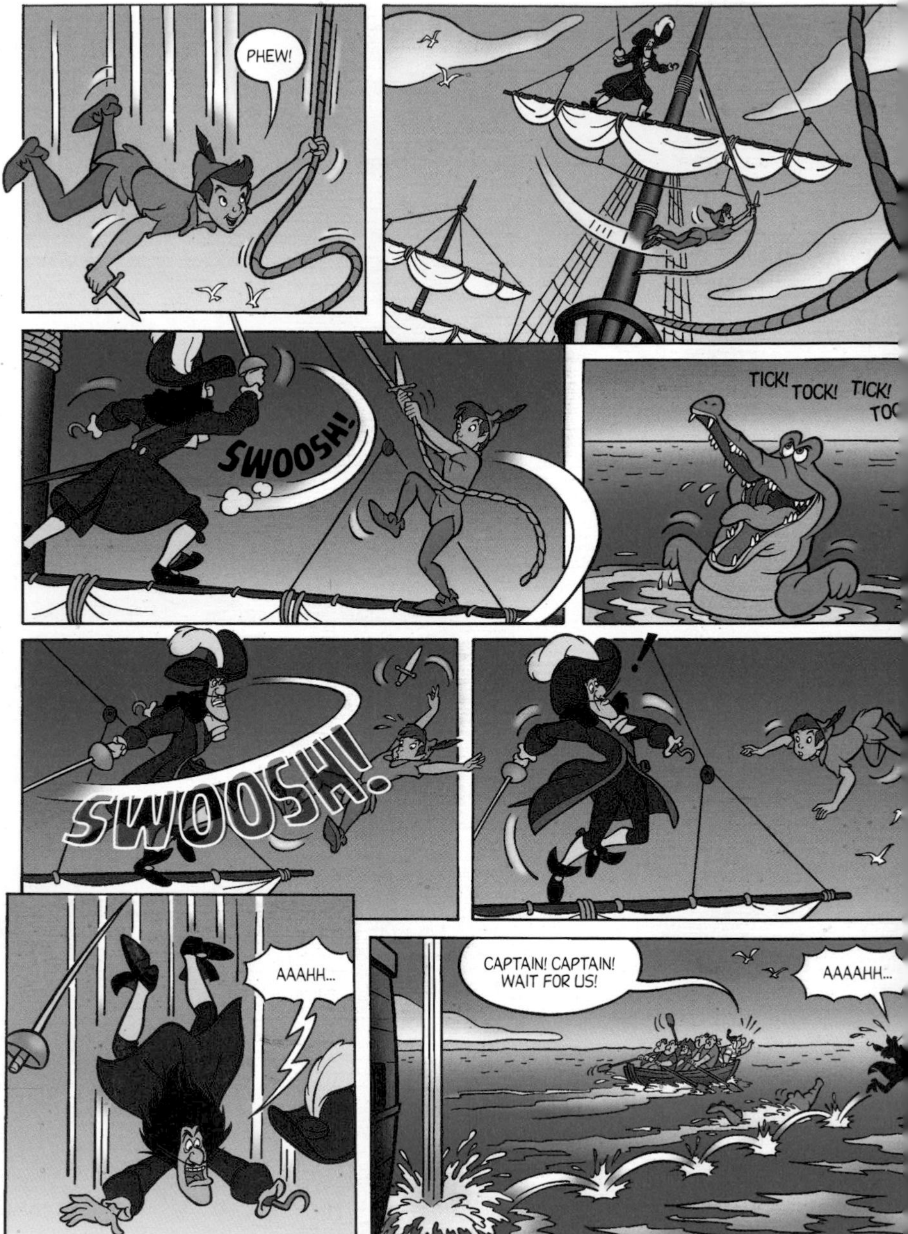
PHEW!
SWOOSH!
TICK! TOCK! TICK!
SWOOSH!
!
AAAHH...
CAPTAIN! CAPTAIN! WAIT FOR US!
AAAAHH...

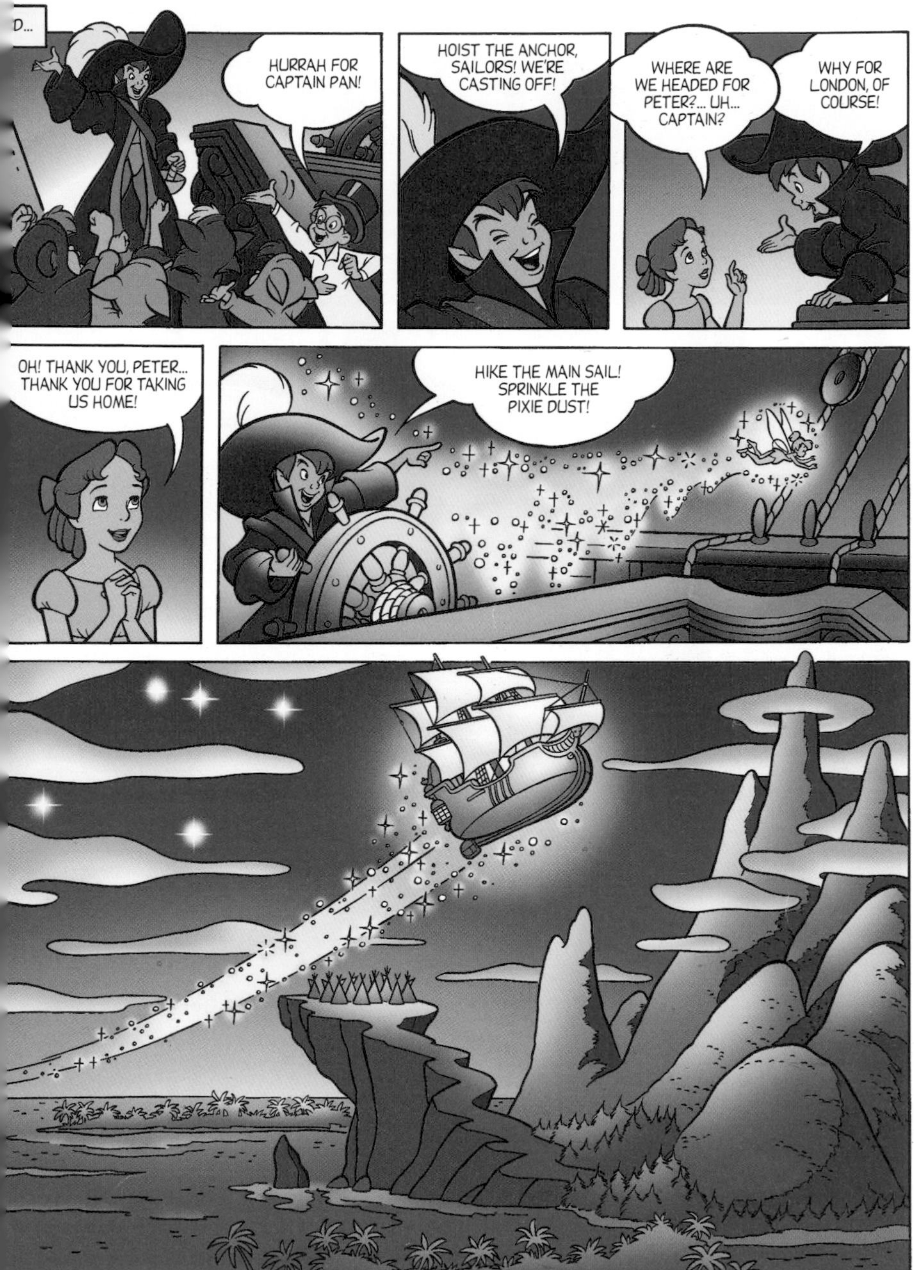
D...
HURRAH FOR CAPTAIN PAN!
HOIST THE ANCHOR, SAILORS! WE'RE CASTING OFF!
WHERE ARE WE HEADED FOR PETER?... UH... CAPTAIN?
WHY FOR LONDON, OF COURSE!
OH! THANK YOU, PETER... THANK YOU FOR TAKING US HOME!
HIKE THE MAIN SAIL! SPRINKLE THE PIXIE DUST!

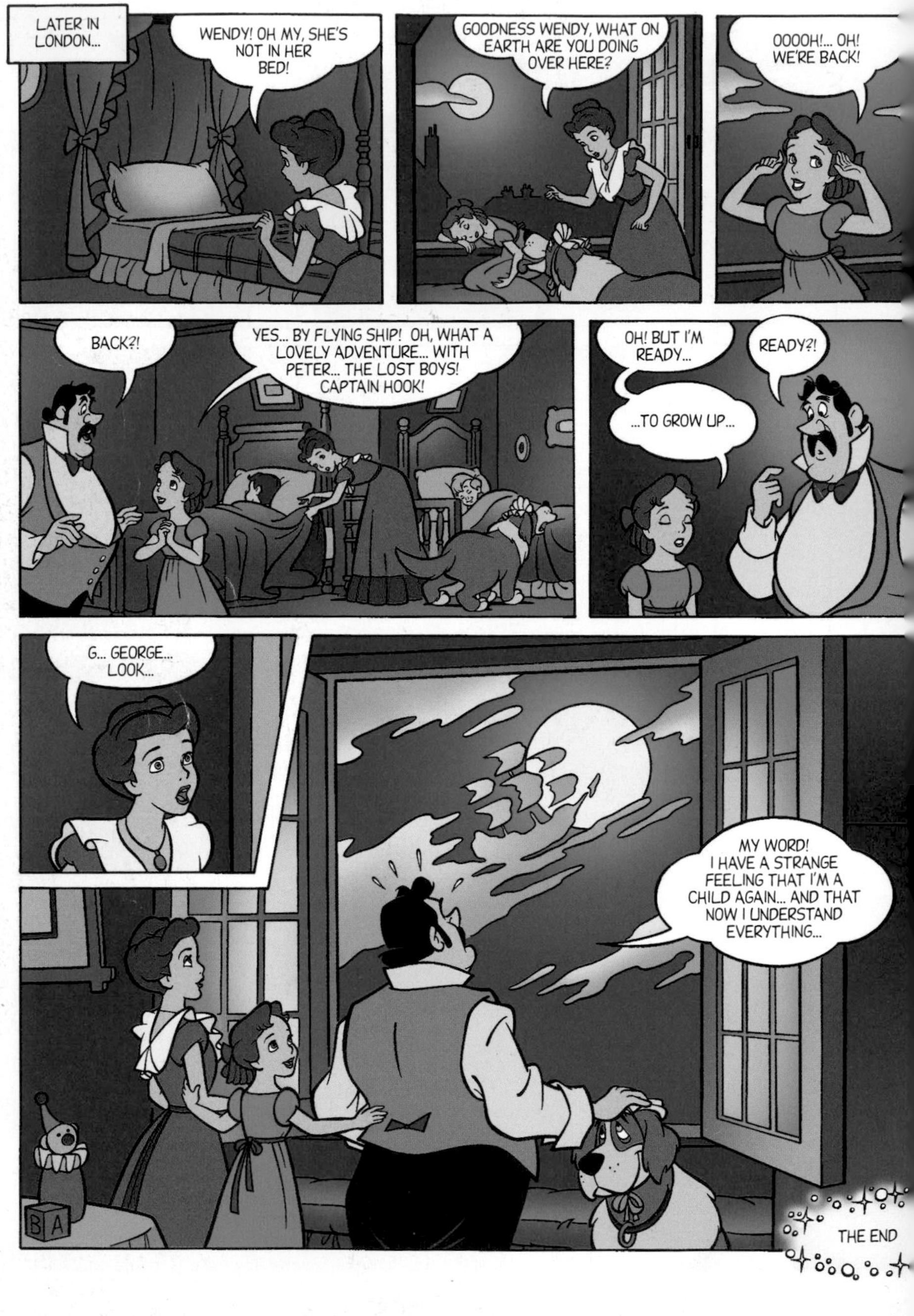
LATER IN LONDON...
WENDY! OH MY, SHE'S NOT IN HER BED!
GOODNESS WENDY, WHAT ON EARTH ARE YOU DOING OVER HERE?
OOOOH!... OH! WE'RE BACK!
BACK?!
YES... BY FLYING SHIP! OH, WHAT A LOVELY ADVENTURE... WITH PETER... THE LOST BOYS! CAPTAIN HOOK!
OH! BUT I'M READY...
...TO GROW UP...
READY?!
G... GEORGE... LOOK...
MY WORD! I HAVE A STRANGE FEELING THAT I'M A CHILD AGAIN... AND THAT NOW I UNDERSTAND EVERYTHING...
B A
THE END

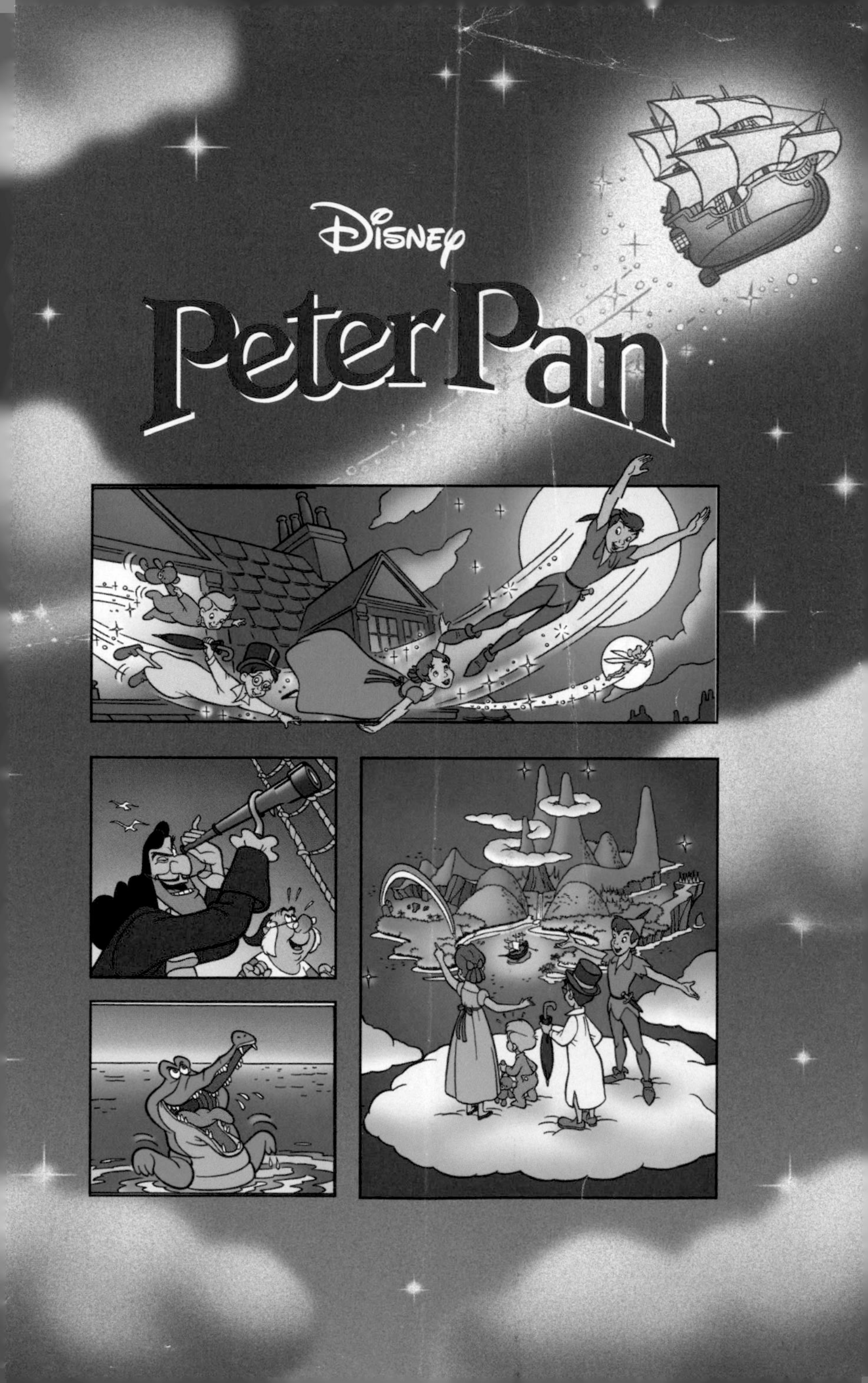
Disney
Peter Pan

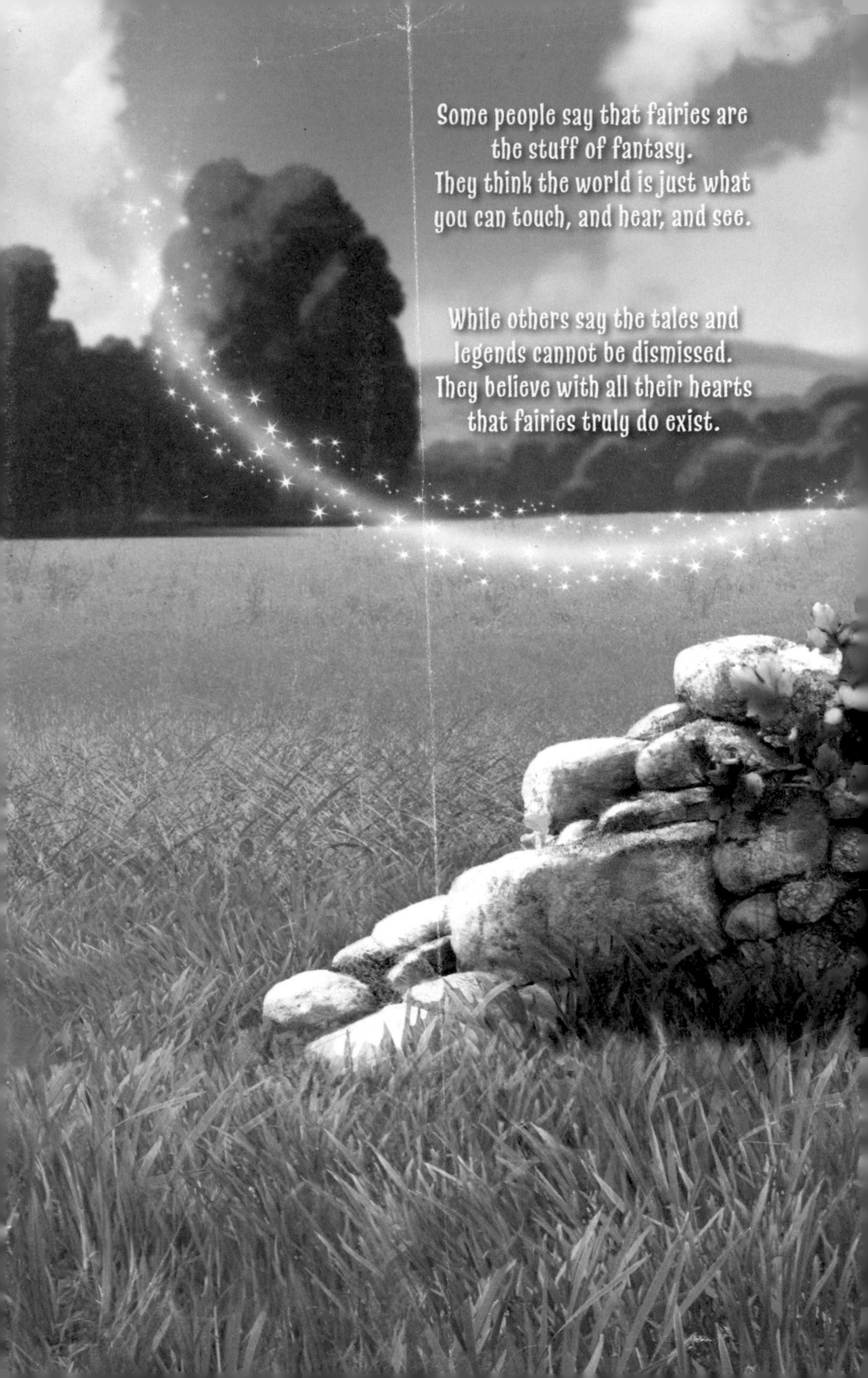

Some people say that fairies are
the stuff of fantasy.
They think the world is just what
you can touch, and hear, and see.

While others say the tales and
legends cannot be dismissed.
They believe with all their hearts
that fairies truly do exist.